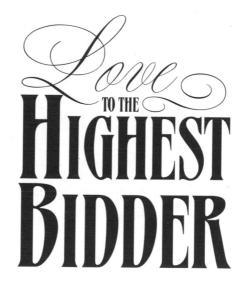

Love
TO THE
HIGHEST BIDDER

BOOKS BY RACHEL ANN NUNES

ARIANA: The Making of a Queen

ARIANA: A Gift Most Precious

ARIANA: A New Beginning

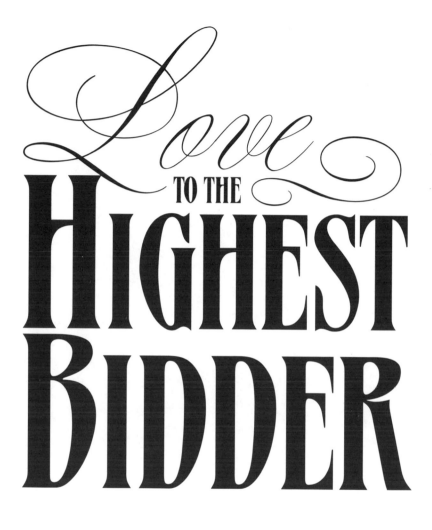

Love
TO THE
HIGHEST BIDDER

a novel

RACHEL ANN NUNES

Covenant Communications, Inc.

Covenant

Published by Covenant Communications, Inc.
American Fork, Utah

Printed in the United States of America
First Printing: August 1998

04 03 02 01 00   10 9 8 7 6 5 4 3

Library of Congress Cataloging-in-Publication Data

Nunes, Rachel Ann, 1966-
    Love to the highest bidder / Rachel Ann Nunes.
       p.   cm.
    ISBN 1-57734-278-X
    I. Title
    PS3564.U468L6   1998
    813'.54--dc21   98-24031
                          CIP

To my daughter, Cassi. May you always be as beautiful on the inside as you are on the outside.

CHAPTER
1

Laranda was excited. Jared could tell from the way her eyes fixed on him as he walked into the back room of her New York art gallery. Though she always looked at him with a pointed glint in those green eyes, as if daring or taunting him, today her gaze was more intense. Jared shrugged, trying to ignore her. For six years he had put up with her overt stares and innuendos because she was not only his boss and sole owner of the gallery, but also his friend. Besides, he loved his work as the gallery's head art buyer and didn't want to endanger his position.

She paced from one end of the packaging table to the other, her strides taut and jerky, movements foreign to her usual sultry grace. Jared watched her warily as he set the box on the table and began removing the small statues for her approval. Her gaze flicked over them admiringly, yet she didn't pick them up and study them as she normally did. From her peculiar behavior, Jared realized that Laranda's agitation wasn't directed toward him or the new art objects he had just purchased at auction. His curiosity was piqued, but he remained silent. It was best to let Laranda tell him of her own accord.

"I need you to go to L.A.," she said finally, when he had finished unpacking the five new statues.

"Today?" Jared didn't bother to keep the surprise from his voice. He often went to Los Angeles on buying trips for the gallery, but rarely on such short notice.

She stared at him, her delicate eyebrows drawing together. Her hands nervously smoothed the tight-fitting green silk dress that was cut short to show off her stunning legs. "You will go, won't you? There's an auction at the Hilton starting on Monday. Today's only

Friday, so if you get there tonight you'll have the weekend to check out the items I want."

"Oh, that auction. But you said you didn't want anything there."

"I do now." Laranda picked up an oversized flyer on the table and shoved it under Jared's nose. A Buddha figure filled the page. "A man in India decided to sell this. And I want it."

Jared examined the figure. Contrary to the contemporary image of a fat, jovial Buddha, this roughly eight-inch-tall statue was lean and stern. It sat on a large, six-inch-square pedestal, hands resting one on top of the other, palms upward, with legs tucked and back held stiff in the classic meditation pose. Large-petal flowers and elaborate swirls decorated this throne where the Buddha had sat with unsmiling lips for sixteen centuries, peering out on the world from heavy-lidded eyes. It was hard, ugly, and expensive—just the sort of thing Laranda adored.

"You've got a buyer?" he asked, scratching at his shoulder under the thin, short-sleeved button-down dress shirt he wore. Last weekend he had gone water skiing with the young men in his ward, and his sunburn itched terribly.

She nodded. "Sure do. And she wants it, badly."

"How much do I have?"

"Four hundred thousand. I doubt you'll need more. Three years ago it sold for two."

Jared whistled. "This buyer does want it bad. Who is it?"

Laranda's eyes narrowed. "That's confidential. I'll tell you after it's over. If you need more money, call me."

Jared studied Laranda's perfect features—the porcelain skin, the blonde hair artfully arranged, the cold green eyes. At forty, she was certainly the most beautiful woman he knew. Physically, he was attracted to her as she was to him, but he wasn't in love with her, and to her exasperation he had never let their relationship develop beyond friendship. At times he almost wished he could, but inside Jared knew their religious differences were too great, and he wouldn't let go of the values he cherished. Values were something Laranda had done away with years ago.

Loneliness filled Jared's life. He didn't know exactly when it had happened. Once he had been the most eligible bachelor in his LDS ward, wanted by all the single girls because of his money and good looks. He had let them chase him, had even led some of them on, though not actually considering marriage seriously; he felt too young to settle down. Then, seemingly all of a sudden, Jared found himself alone at thirty-three. All the pretty Mormon women he had dated had disappeared, becoming the wives of his friends and the mothers of cherub-faced babies.

There was only Laranda, and women like her, who were attracted to him openly—but only for a time, until something better or more interesting came along. Jared didn't want to settle for such a relationship. He wanted a future that included all the blessings of the gospel and someone to love and to cherish forever. Sadly, there was no one around to fill his need.

"Well? You will go, Jared, won't you? I've already made reservations." Laranda's sharp voice penetrated his thoughts. He refocused to see that she was waving a hand with long, red-painted nails in front of his face. "It's not like you have a wife to consult," she added. Her words made Jared's need stand out in his mind like a neon sign.

He shoved the hurt away and smiled at her. "Of course I'll go, Laranda. I enjoy going to L.A. and looking up old friends. And June is a great time to visit the beaches."

She eyed him with an amused smile on her painted lips. "That's right. You went on a . . . what do you call it?"

"A mission."

"That's right, you went on a mission there. See? I'm really doing you a favor." She trailed her manicured nails over the dark-blond hairs on his bare arm, causing a tingling response throughout his body.

He laughed and shook off her hand. "Right. But don't think that gets you out of paying me a bonus when I bring back your precious Buddha. Remember, I do double duty as buyer and guard." He patted the gun at his belt.

"I'll never forget that." Laranda pursed her shapely lips into a pout and sidled up to him so close that he could smell her breath. It was sweet like her perfume. "I never forget you at all." She reached up and kissed him lingeringly on the cheek, coming too close for comfort.

Jared stepped back, rubbing his cheek. Red lipstick stained his fingers. "Since I'm going, is there anything else you want me to bid for?"

Laranda laughed, but her eyes hardened. "I wonder if you even know what I'm offering," she said lightly.

"I'm not stupid, Laranda." Jared matched her tone. "But there are some things that are just too important to play with."

Laranda laughed again, though she was not amused. "I live only to play."

"I know," Jared said sorrowfully. He thought of how he, too, had once toyed with relationships and had ended up alone. "Sometimes the price of play is too high," he muttered.

Laranda didn't hear him. She had moved to the table and was rifling through papers that would list the other items she wanted him to buy for her. The incident between them was already forgotten.

*****

The bright lights in the hotel room hurt Jared's tired eyes. After meeting Laranda at the gallery, he had hurried home to pack. He had also asked his next-door neighbor to pick up his newspaper, rescheduled the arrival of his new sofa, and found someone to teach his lesson to the young men on Sunday. Afterward, he'd barely made his plane to Los Angeles. Once in his room, exhaustion overwhelmed him. He threw his suitcase to the floor, shed his jacket, and sank onto the double bed. With one hand, he loosened the tie at his throat.

Sleep did not take him. He thought about Laranda and her blatant offer, contrasting her to the "good" Mormon girls he had dated. Why hadn't he married one of them? Some stood out clearly in his mind: Cindy with the innocent blue eyes; Wendy with her beautiful curly hair teased to perfection; and Julie with her lithe runner's body. Each had shared his firm testimony of the gospel and had been interested in Jared—for a time. Now they were all happily married, busy with their lives and growing children.

"I need to go down and get a complete list of the auction times," he said aloud to distract himself. Still he didn't move. He knew there would be plenty of time the next morning to get the list before the hotel opened the items for inspection prior to the bidding on Monday. Besides, there could be some last-minute additions or changes that wouldn't be reflected on the flyers tonight.

I'll go tomorrow, he decided. Jared would spend all of Saturday talking with other buyers or studying the merchandise. That was why he was so good at what he did.

"I didn't know what was important," he said, returning inevitably to the reason he was alone. "I wanted to work, get money, have fun. But why? It doesn't mean anything now." He shook his head and sighed. A hand went out to touch the pillow next to his. Of course, no one was there.

Fighting his loneliness, Jared sat up and slid onto his knees next to the bed, at last finding some solace in prayer.

CHAPTER 2

The dark brown curls were everywhere. They were a curse, and had been for twenty-eight of Cassi's twenty-nine years. They puffed out from her scalp and plunged halfway down her back as if they had lives of their own, helplessly tangled and twisted together. The bathroom lights above the double sink reflected from the tresses, bringing out their subtle auburn highlights.

Cassi stared at herself in the large, well-lit mirror and sighed. It would take her at least half an hour to tame those unruly locks; thirty precious minutes. And even then they wouldn't look much better than they did now. "I just want a peek at the auction schedule," she murmured to the olive-skinned girl in the mirror, her frustration evident in the flushed face. "Oh, Mom, why did you have to give me your hair?"

But her mother was far away in Utah with her father, where they lived close to Cassi's only sibling. Her mother couldn't hear her complaints or say, as she usually did, "You're so lucky to have curly hair, Cassi. Your friends spend hundreds of dollars on permanents to look like you do." Cassi sighed and lifted the brush.

A banging on the door took her attention away from the imposing task before her.

"I gotta go!" her best friend, Renae, shouted through the closed door. "Aren't you done yet?"

"Yes, come in." Cassi threw down the brush and hurried to the door. Renae wasn't joking when she said she had to use the bathroom. She was over eight months pregnant and had a baby sitting on her bladder.

Renae burst through the door before Cassi reached it, dancing slightly. "I seem to spend all my time in the bathroom these days."

Cassi shut the door behind her as Renae sighed with exaggerated relief. She shook her head in mock disgust; but in reality, she envied Renae her situation, despite the obvious discomfort.

"I need to get the auction schedule," Cassi called out. "I want to know what items will be auctioned at what time, and when they're letting us in to see them today."

"Don't you know those things already?"

Cassi shook her head, though Renae couldn't see her. "Things are never completely finalized until the morning before the display. Before that, the times and items can change from day to day."

"Why do you have to see them today?" Renae asked, her voice muffled by the bathroom door. "Does it make any difference? You're not going to bid on them until next week."

Cassi sighed. It was hard explaining to someone not in the art business how important the few days before an auction could be. It was a time to size up the competition. It was also a time to make certain deals—*I won't bid for that item if you won't bid for this one*—and to search for additional pieces that looked good and would be resalable. Many times Cassi's sharp eyes had turned a good profit for her San Diego art gallery. Its owner, Linden Johansen, a calm, elderly man, had just promoted Cassi to head buyer, and she took her job very seriously.

She shed her pajamas as these thoughts ran through her head, quickly pulling on the faded jeans and old T-shirt she had worn when she had met Renae at the hotel the night before. She knew that she looked a mess, quite unlike the professional buyer she normally portrayed—all because she had overslept.

Cassi and Renae had been best friends in high school. Now, eleven years later, they were separated by miles and their vastly different situations. Renae had married young and was expecting her fifth child. Cassi had served a mission to England and concentrated on her career.

It wasn't that Cassi hadn't wanted to get married, but the opportunity hadn't yet presented itself. Over the years she'd had many friends who were men, and had often set them up with her girlfriends. Years later, after they were safely married, several of these men had confessed to having liked Cassi. Many had asked to be set up simply as an excuse to be close to her; but when she showed no interest in them, they had moved on. Such confessions always surprised her because she had usually liked the men but felt that they weren't interested in her.

"You seem to have blinders on when it comes to men," Cassi's sister-in-law, Jarelyn, kept telling her. "You can't even see when a man is attracted to you."

Maybe it was true.

So Cassi remained single and slightly aloof, almost afraid to hope or to set herself up for failure.

"I'm so glad you called me," Renae said, coming from the bathroom. "This was a great idea, us being here together."

Cassi smiled, pushing aside her lonely thoughts. When she had known she was going to be in L.A. for the auction, she had called Renae, hoping her old friend would like to get away for a few days. Renae and her husband lived in Covina, just over an hour away.

"I can stay until Monday night," Renae had said. "It'll be my last fling before the baby comes. Trent won't mind staying with the kids for a few days." Last night they had talked over old times until three in the morning, which was why Cassi was running late.

"Goodness, it's already nine o'clock," she said now. She walked to the door. "I'm just going down to get a schedule. I could call and ask them to bring it up, but I don't want to wait. Order some breakfast, would you? I'll be right back to eat and change. Then we'll go down to see the auction items and mingle a bit. Hopefully it won't start until ten. You'll see, it'll be interesting."

Renae picked up a menu from the table. "We're going out this evening, aren't we?"

Cassi nodded. "Yes. They usually close the previewing at four or so. They'll open it again tomorrow, but I won't be going."

"Of course not. We'll be going to church. Do you have any idea where the closest ward is?"

"No. We'll just look in the phone book, and in the morning we'll call for the meeting times. The bishops are usually in their offices by eight."

"At least eight," Renae agreed. "When Trent was in the bishopric, he was usually there by six-thirty." She sighed. "Tomorrow's going to be wonderful. You know, I think I'm looking forward to going to church more than out on the town tonight. I'm actually going to hear the whole meeting!" She giggled. "Poor Trent. I think he's going to have his hands full."

Cassi smiled. "He'll only appreciate you more."

"That's what I'm hoping."

Cassi slipped out of the door and down the hall, patting her hair down. She felt incongruous and hoped that no one from the auction would recognize her. The art world was fairly limited, and people who had been in the business for any length of time knew most of the prominent buyers—a rank Cassi had earned with her recent promotion. It was one thing to be seen as the appropriately dressed businesswoman, and another to be caught garbed like a teenager. "I'll just run down quickly," Cassi reasoned aloud. "I'll be back in my room before anyone notices."

The elevator was occupied, so Cassi used the stairs. The light glinted off the polished floor and affronted her tired eyes. She jogged down the first flight of stairs, slowing to a walk as she heard people approaching. Four flights later she arrived at the main floor and opened the door. There were people in the main hallway, but no one glanced twice at her. Cassi sighed with relief when she didn't see anyone she recognized. She tried to walk inconspicuously to a corridor near the back of the hotel, where she knew the items for the auction were kept and would be displayed later that morning. Her sandaled feet moved soundlessly over the rich gold carpet. The lights here were also bright, but most of it was sunlight radiating through the glass windows and doors.

At last she arrived near the auction corridor. Down the hall, she could see that the door was closed and well protected by two solemn-faced security guards. Cassi quickly located what she had come for. In front of her, where the main corridor intersected with the auction corridor, was a display of pamphlets detailing the auction offerings. Most of these Cassi had already studied carefully. What she had really come for was the simple white flyer on the side of the display which announced the hours for the previewing and the auction time for each item. Three items had been added last night to the schedule, but only one looked promising. As she had expected, the previewing would begin at ten, leaving her six hours to study the offerings and to converse with her fellow buyers.

She looked up from the paper and scanned the pamphlets again until she found the one she was looking for. It was near the bottom, and she bent to retrieve it.

A hideous-looking Buddha stared out at her. "Boy, are you ugly," Cassi whispered. This was the main item she had come to bid for. "Why on earth would anyone want you?" She traced the lines of the Buddha as she remembered her conversation with Linden only the day before.

"I want you to bid for the Buddha," he said. "It's a very interesting piece from the late Kushan period. It is believed to have been made at Mathura, and is a well-preserved piece for the price. If you get it, call me and I'll come down with Justin and Gary to get it." Justin and Gary were the guards who worked for the gallery, and they always picked up the most important items.

"Don't go over three hundred thousand for it, though," Linden had added.

"And if I don't get it for that?" asked Cassi.

Linden frowned and shook his gray head. "Then find out who does get it. This is very important, Cassi. I don't want you to contact the person; just find out who it is and call me. Okay?"

"Sure." But Cassi was puzzled. Linden had never asked her to find out who scooped an item from them, though Cassi's curiosity usually made her find out who the person was and what gallery he represented, if she didn't already recognize him. Besides being a matter of professional pride, it helped her to know who to look out for in the next bidding war.

"Why would someone want you?" Cassi repeated to the silent Buddha. While she recognized that some people were more intent on design than beauty, she still found it hard to overlook the Buddha's sharp, repulsive features. It certainly wasn't something she would display in her own home. She brought the paper closer to study the image, searching for signs of the Kushan period. Linden had said it might have actually come out of Mathura, located in central India, where a distinct Greco-Buddhist art had evolved. Of course, the poor photograph couldn't reveal such marks, even to eyes as practiced as Cassi's.

"You like him?" A male voice asked casually from behind her.

Cassi's head jerked around, and she found herself praying it wasn't someone she knew. To her relief, she saw a young man who didn't seem familiar. He was tall, with medium-blond hair and well-molded facial features. His chin was slightly prominent, giving him an air of confidence. Unlike Cassi, he was dressed for the occasion. He wore an expensive-looking suit, and his short hair was combed meticulously into place. His startling blue eyes stared intently at her.

"Intellectually, yes. Physically, no," she replied hurriedly, feeling horribly self-conscious. This man was obviously one of the buyers, and Cassi hoped he wouldn't remember her later. "Excuse me." She turned abruptly and retreated down the hall, forcing herself to maintain a sedate walk until she was out of his sight.

"Darn it," she mumbled. "Why did I stay? I almost got away without being noticed by anyone."

She grumbled all the way up the stairs and into the room, where Renae lounged at the table. Breakfast was already waiting, and the aroma of the bacon made Cassi's mouth water.

"I should have just sent out for a copy," she said, flinging herself onto one of the chairs.

"What's wrong?"

Cassi told her. "I was so embarrassed. What if he sees me later, and I have to try to deal with him? He'll never think of me professionally after this." To Cassi's chagrin, Renae started laughing.

"Oh, Cassi, when did you get to be such a snob? Who cares what you're wearing? And who cares what that stranger thinks? Is this the same Cassi who went to the Junior Prom dressed as a sexy cave woman? You aren't acting like the girl I used to know!"

Cassi scowled, but slowly her face relaxed into a smile. "You dared me to." She giggled. "Did you remember poor Tom's face when he saw me?" Tom was the only boy who had ever come out and told Cassi he liked her, which was why she had gone out with him. But, alas, her spontaneity at the prom had been too much for him, and he had turned to less impulsive dates.

"Oh, you're right. I guess I'm putting too much importance on this." *It's just that my work is all I have,* she wanted to add, but didn't. Renae, with her adoring husband and nearly five children, could never understand the loneliness Cassi endured daily.

Renae laughed. "Sure. He won't even remember you. And if he does, maybe it will be as a man instead of a buyer." Before Cassi could protest, Renae continued. "Now hadn't you better eat so we can get downstairs? I'll comb through your hair for you." Renae's own dark-blonde locks were thin and straight, and she had never hidden her envy of Cassi's hair.

Cassi smiled. "I haven't had a better offer in weeks." She sighed. "It's good to be with you, Renae. I'm so glad you came."

CHAPTER
3

Jared awoke early Saturday morning, the longings of the night before put firmly behind him. He showered, dressed, and ate before reviewing pamphlets that detailed the items Laranda had requested. At the previewing, he would also search for additional items that would bring profits to the gallery.

By nine o'clock, Jared felt prepared. The previewing would most likely open at ten, and if he went now he would have an hour to talk with the few other buyers who would appear early. He also wanted to look at the auction schedule.

He whistled as he left his room, eager to begin another interesting day. If nothing else in his life was satisfying, his work was; he loved it. The elevator took Jared down to the main floor. The gold carpet and elegant wallpaper gave the hallway an air of opulence. He felt confidence flood through him.

Near the auction hallway, he could see someone bending over the typical array of pamphlets—a slim, shapely girl. Her long, dark-brown hair had auburn highlights which glinted in the sunlight streaming in from a large window at the end of the corridor. Tiny ringlets splayed over her head and down her back, reminding Jared of Wendy, one of the girls he had dated. It was a look he had always admired, until he saw first-hand the hours she wasted achieving it— and until he felt the hair itself, stiff and dry like curly straw.

The girl bending in front of Jared didn't hear his approach on the thick carpet. She was wearing old jeans that strangely accentuated her feminine features. This was certainly no stuffy buyer, but perhaps just a young girl who happened upon an interesting display and decided to investigate. Jared supposed she had spent hours on her hair in the hopes of being noticed by some male who didn't know what it had cost her to attain the look. He was not impressed.

"Why would someone want you?" The girl straightened, and over her shoulder Jared could see that she held the pamphlet featuring the Buddha. He was close enough to her now to smell her hair. Not cloyingly sweet like perfume, but nice and clean. To his surprise, even this close it looked soft, quite unlike Wendy's sculptured locks. He squelched his sudden desire to reach out and touch it.

Maybe it's natural, he mused silently. *Naw, they have just invented better products since Wendy.* Aloud he said, "You like him?" The girl's head swung around. He had intended to explain to her why someone would want such an item, but her expression stopped him. Her dark eyes darted, avoiding meeting his; she looked trapped.

"Intellectually, yes. Physically, no," she replied, lifting a hand to toss her curly locks over her shoulder.

Her answer implied that she knew more than he had expected. He searched her smooth, slightly olive-skinned features and found them also far removed from his preconceived picture of her. She was older, about twenty-five, he guessed; not a girl, but a woman. She wore no makeup and her face, framed with all those tiny ringlets, was not beautiful in the regular, flawless sense of the word, but very appealing. Jared stared.

"Excuse me." The woman turned abruptly and walked away before Jared could think of anything else to say. Who was this woman? An interested bystander? Or one of the buyers who cared little for convention? Jared found himself hoping for the latter. Interest rose in his heart, though he tried to stifle it.

"Two hours," he mumbled to himself. "It took her two hours to get it to look that way."

"What? Jared, is that you?" said a voice behind him. It was said in perfect English, but with a decidedly French accent. "It is you. Whatever are you talking about?"

"Darn carpet," Jared said under his breath before turning to face an owner of a prominent L.A. gallery. Léon-Paul Medici was not only an owner but an astute buyer as well. "Léon, pleased to see you again. So what can I outbid you on this time?"

Jared forced his mind away from the puzzle of the woman and

back to his work. He would get that Buddha for Laranda, if only for the huge bonus he would receive.

*****

Jared didn't go directly to the Buddha when the two auction guards finally opened the viewing. First he went to see the other items on Laranda's list, keeping a sharp ear out for any information he could use. He eliminated three out of the other four art objects Laranda had marked, and one of the two paintings; they either weren't suited for her gallery or wouldn't likely bring a large enough profit. Then he systematically worked his way over the rest of the items. Only three caught his attention; on these he would bid, leaving the rest for the smaller, less discriminating galleries.

"That Buddha's something else," Léon said, appearing at Jared's elbow.

Jared shrugged with practiced nonchalance. "It's not the most expensive item here."

"No, but it's the one you came to bid for."

Jared turned his head and raised his eyebrows questioningly.

"I know you," Léon said, exaggerating his French accent. One dark eye closed in a wink. "You haven't gone to look at it yet."

Jared smiled. "Are you bidding for it?" If Léon was really interested in the Buddha, the price would go to the ceiling. He represented serious competition.

"I was. It is an interesting piece. However, I am more interested in that." Léon nodded toward the painting in front of them. It was an item that hadn't received much publicity, but which would bring a great profit to the gallery that purchased it.

Jared nodded seriously. "It is very good. I think it'll look excellent in your gallery—until you sell it for a hefty profit."

"As the Buddha will in yours." Léon smiled and held out his hand to seal their bargain. Jared felt like whistling again.

Together he and Léon made their way to the Buddha. A group of people were just moving away from the display as they approached. Only two women remained. One was in the last stages of pregnancy, and the other—

Jared caught his breath. With the expectant mother was the

woman he had seen earlier by the pamphlet display. Her hair looked much the same, but now she was wearing makeup, so subtle that Jared noticed only its effects, not its presence. She was dressed in a form-fitting suit coat and skirt. Unlike many of the women buyers, her skirt reached nearly to her knees and was modest.

Léon whistled under his breath. "What I wouldn't give—"

"Who is she?" Jared interrupted.

Léon glanced at him in surprise. "You don't know? But that's right, you're in New York. She's the new head buyer for the Johansen Gallery."

"San Diego?"

"Yes. She's upset quite a few of my little bids. Quite surprising. Innovative. I tried to ask her out, but . . . ," Léon shrugged.

"How old is she?"

Again Léon shrugged. "I don't know. Looks about twenty-five but has to be older than that. She was an assistant buyer at Johansen's for at least five years before her promotion."

They had come within earshot of the women, and Jared could hear Cassi pointing out features on the Buddha which stood on a pedestal in front of them. She obviously knew what she was talking about.

"And this mark here is . . . that's strange, there should be a—" Jared found himself waiting anxiously for her explanation, but Léon interrupted them.

"My dear Cassi, how good to see you." Léon stepped forward and reached for the woman's hand. Her wide-set eyes narrowed, but she shook hands with him. Léon held her hand longer than necessary, sidling closer to her. Jared noticed that she pulled her hand away as quickly as possible. As she did so she glanced up at Jared, but she showed no sign of recognition. Either she was a very good actress, or she didn't remember him.

Léon continued his spiel. "And who is this mother-to-be? Another new buyer for Johansen?"

Cassi smiled. "No, Léon, this is one of my high school friends, Renae Benson. We're just spending some time together."

"She's trying to give me a little culture," Renae said bluntly, her voice rich with earthy amusement.

"And are you enjoying it?" Léon asked as he shook Renae's hand.

"I enjoy *any* time away from my four children," Renae joked.

"Four?" asked Jared. He was surprised that Renae was expecting her fifth child. There weren't a lot of people who wanted many children nowadays. Jared was the third child of six, and he had always enjoyed the bustle of life that had surrounded his parents' house.

"Yes, a boy and three girls. But who are you?"

"Ah, yes, excuse my manners," Léon said. "Cassi Mason, Renae, ah, Benson, wasn't it?—This is my friend, Jared Landine, from New York. He represents the Garrettson Gallery."

Jared stuck out his hand to shake Cassi's. He was determined not to mention that they had already met—at least until she herself remembered. Her grip was firm on his, not like the limp excuse for a handshake that Léon and most of the other buyers gave him. It was a missionary handshake. Yet her hand was also soft and delicate, seemingly fragile in his larger one.

As she had with Léon, Cassi pulled away quickly. Jared didn't stop her, but wondered why she seemed so unfriendly. She turned slightly toward the Buddha, her thick eyebrows knitted in concentration while Jared shook hands with Renae, whose grip was only slightly less firm.

"Are you interested in this thing?" asked Renae. "It sure is ugly. I wouldn't want it for my living room, not if someone gave it to me." Léon laughed.

"I wouldn't either," Jared said with a smile. "But people are ready to pay a pretty price for this 'thing,' as you call it."

"Are you one of those?" Cassi stared at him, her eyes so intent and dark that for a moment Jared was lost in them. Irritation at his reaction flooded through him, and his reply was sharper than he intended.

"Are you?"

Her eyes met his in challenge. "I am."

"So am I."

"There are other items here of value . . ." She was trying to make a deal.

"Are there?" Jared kept his voice hard and tried not to look into her eyes. "In which of them is *your* gallery most interested?" Jared's words let Cassi know that he would compromise on other objects, but certainly not when it came to the Buddha.

She glared at him, her chin raised slightly. "Which do you suggest?" She didn't give up easily.

"Come, come." Léon broke in between them. "We shall see what shall be at the bidding, no?" Jared nodded and glanced over to the puzzled Renae, who had taken the conversation literally, completely oblivious to its subtle undertones.

"Until then," Cassi said. She nodded toward the men. "It was nice to meet you." Her voice was polite, but her eyes shot icy darts at Jared. She tugged on Renae's elbow and they walked off, leaving the men staring after them.

"She's a strong one, that girl," Léon said. "But cold. Cold as a—how do you Americans put it?—a fish. That's it. Cold as a fish. I asked her out, and she didn't give me the time of day. Others have tried as well, but she doesn't even acknowledge them. Either she's totally missing the subtleties of dating, or she's a snob."

Jared himself leaned toward the snob idea, for she was certainly well-versed in the bargaining subtleties. "I can't imagine you ever being subtle in regards to dating, Léon," Jared said, still staring after Cassi. Her curly hair stood out even from across the room, and he noticed that many male eyes were fixed on her figure. What was it they saw in her? While attractive, she was certainly not as beautiful as many of the other women in the room. No, there was something else, something radiating from her. Jared had to admit that she intrigued him. Imagine caring so little about convention that she ran around in jeans before an important auction, not caring who saw her! She didn't act like any woman he'd ever known—certainly not like Laranda. But then Cassi had been so cold. Jared shrugged and sighed, vowing to stay away from the woman. He didn't like the way he seemed to lose himself when she was near.

"I wasn't," Léon said, turning his black head to stare at Cassi.

"What?"

"I wasn't subtle."

Jared rolled his eyes. "Big surprise. Let's go mingle, huh? I've got work to do." Léon nodded and left in the direction of the women. Jared sighed again and turned back to the Buddha. Already another crowd of buyers had gathered. Time to eliminate a few more competitors.

CHAPTER
4

Just before four, Cassi and Renae left the auction display and retraced their steps down the gold carpet to the elevator. The hallway was crowded now as many buyers had come to the previewing. Cassi waited until they were alone in the elevator to speak.

"An arrogant pig," she muttered darkly.

"Who?"

"That man we met."

"You mean the French guy? I thought he was kind of cute. He seems interested in you. Why don't you go out with him?"

"Him? Are you kidding? He wants to go out, all right. Try a two-week love tryst in France, way out in the country where there's nothing to do but enjoy each other, if you get what I mean. He's a pervert!"

Renae nodded. "Not convert material, huh? Too bad. He's cute. But his blond friend was better looking anyway, even without a sexy accent. Jared Landine, wasn't it? I noticed he didn't wear a wedding ring. What about him?"

Cassi gritted her teeth. Why did it seem that all her married friends felt they had to constantly look for a man for her? It wasn't Cassi's fault that men weren't attracted to her and didn't often ask her out. And it certainly made things worse when her friends tried to pawn her off on every man under sixty who had a heartbeat! So what if this guy was practically gorgeous? What did that matter when he acted like—

"An arrogant pig. *He's* the arrogant pig!"

"What!" Renae shook her head. "I'm sorry. I didn't see that. I've a feeling I missed a lot. Now, why is he an arrogant pig?"

"He . . . he . . . ," Cassi floundered. "He wouldn't even try to deal with me. It was like he thought I was an inexperienced buyer and didn't care to discuss it. It was probably because he saw me dressed like a kid today. Oh, why couldn't I have waited for the papers? Why do I have to be so impulsive?"

"Don't you think you're exaggerating just a bit?" Renae ventured. "I didn't think he was rude or anything, just determined. Kind of like you. Did you ever think that maybe he's under orders to get the Buddha, just like you are?"

"Well, I don't care if he is. I don't like the man, and I'm going to smoke him. I'll get that Buddha yet, even if I have to resort to certain tactics."

"Like what?"

"I don't know. I'll think of something." Cassi paused. "Better yet, *you* think of something. You were always good at coming up with ideas for me to carry out. We just need a way to keep him away from the auction."

"Like how, spiking his coffee?"

Cassi bit her lip in concentration. "That would be a good idea . . . except what if I gave him too much, and he died or something?"

"You're serious!" Renae gawked in amazement.

Cassi's face fell. "Not really. But I live a good fantasy life. When it comes right down to it, I want the Buddha but I'm not willing to do anything dishonest. I guess I'll just have to beat him the old-fashioned way."

"How?"

"Bidding."

"Oh."

They looked at each other and sighed.

*****

That evening Cassi and Renae ate at a nice restaurant, where Renae seemed almost at a loss because she didn't have to cut anyone's meat or wipe any small mouths. "You can cut mine, if you want," Cassi offered, making them both laugh.

"I think I'll manage, thanks," Renae said dryly.

After a peaceful dinner, they went to the movies. "I want to see anything except a Disney cartoon," Renae said. "That's all my kids ever like to see."

Cassi laughed. "I wish we lived closer together, then I'd take your kids to the Disney movies. I need some excuse to see them. I usually wait until they come out on video and then see them in my house, like they're X-rated or something."

"But you said you saw one last week. Were your brother and his children visiting from Utah?"

"No, I saw it because I've been working with the Cub Scouts. I took them to the movies for an activity. It was great!"

And it had been. Cassi had only worked with the Scouts for one month, and already she loved the job. The boys were active, excited, and each one had fallen in love with her. They were a great boost for her ego, and had given her something to live for besides her work.

When they arrived back at the hotel, Renae telephoned her husband while Cassi got ready for bed. "Is everything all right?" she asked when Renae hung up.

"Oh, yes. Trent's very capable when I'm not home. It's only when I'm home that he forgets how to do things for the children," Renae replied seriously, bringing a smile to Cassi's lips. "The kids don't seem to even miss me. Little Sandy's been sleeping with Trent and being spoiled to death; she's always been his little angel. I think she'll survive for two more nights."

"She's two now, isn't she?" Cassi asked.

Renae nodded. "And just started potty-training. I hope she's made progress before I get home. We're trying to get her trained before the baby comes. Three weeks doesn't leave much time."

"Well, I just hope Trent knows how to do the laundry," Cassi said. "Or you're going to have a mountain of wet underwear to wash when you get home."

"Oh, he'll wash them, they'll just be pink. Or green. Or something." Renae rolled her eyes.

On they talked until midnight, Renae mostly about her children and Cassi about her work. "You're so lucky to have your family," Cassi said as they finally turned out the lights. She settled on her bed, face up, staring at the black ceiling.

"Yes, I guess I am. But, you know, I envy you your freedom. I sometimes feel so trapped." Renae's voice was faint in the darkness of their room. "My children are so precious, but sometimes I feel like they suck the life right out of me. They constantly want something. At times I don't have anything left inside to give, and I want to scream, 'What about me? What about what *I* want?'" She paused before adding softly, "Do you know that this trip is the first time I've been away from my children since Scotty was born over nine years ago?"

Cassi was quiet. She had never seen this side of Renae's perfect life. She felt the need in her friend's voice and ached to help her. *Please, Father,* she prayed silently. *Help me to help Renae.*

"What is it you want to do?"

There was a silence. Then, "I don't know, really."

"Well, what if you didn't have any children, what would you be doing?"

"Working, probably."

"Doing what? Or better yet, let's say that you didn't have to work. What would you do then?"

"Well . . . I . . . uh . . ."

"You always liked music in high school," Cassi remembered. "Not the band stuff, but the popular music. You made up songs, and you said that one day you were going to learn to play the guitar."

"Oh, yeah. I remember. With ten children my parents were too poor to pay for lessons, so I started to work and was going to pay for them myself. But then I got involved in cheerleading and spent all my money on that. Then I met Trent . . ."

As a child from a family of only two, Cassi had always envied Renae's large family. But she didn't feel now was the time to bring it up. "So would you still like to take guitar?"

"Well, I have had a lot of songs running through my head." Renae's voice was full of desire. "I—I think I'd like to take voice lessons, too."

"There you go, then! Trent's got a good job. Isn't he still working for that import company?"

"Dalton Importing. And he just received a raise."

"See, then there's no reason why you can't swing a few lessons, is there?"

"No, there's not. But to leave my children? I've always been taught that mothers should be at home with their kids. I know that's best. Oh, what's wrong with me for not being satisfied with just being a mother?"

Cassi heard the pain and winced. "But you *would* be at home with your children. Music and voice lessons only take a couple of hours a week, don't they? You could arrange them at night when Trent can watch the children, and then practice during the week at home. You might not get the ironing done, but you would be there for your children if they needed you."

"But isn't that cheating somehow?" There was wonder in Renae's voice.

Cassi didn't laugh, knowing that Renae was serious. "No. In fact, at almost every general conference the General Authorities stress how important education is. By being better educated you can teach your children and be happier doing it. Heavenly Father wants you to be happy, don't you think?"

"I guess so." Renae sniffed. "I just never looked at it that way before. How come you have? You don't even have children yet."

Cassi felt a loss as Renae spoke. She clutched at the blanket on her chest, willing the ache to leave. "Exactly. Not having children means that I've had time to think about it. You would have figured it out eventually yourself, you know."

"Maybe."

"So, are you going to do it?"

"Yes." Renae's voice had now taken on a note of determination. "I'd even baby-sit other people's children if I needed money to pay for the lessons. But luckily, I won't have to; Trent does have a good job. And he can watch the kids two hours a couple of nights a week, and . . . Cassi, what if I'd told you I wanted to be a writer, or a physicist, or . . . or an art buyer like you?"

Cassi laughed into the darkness. "Then instead of music lessons, you'd go to school two nights a week. They've got great night programs at the colleges now. You could earn a degree."

"Maybe I will. Oh, this is so exciting! I never thought I could be a good mother *and* be educated. I can't wait to get started!"

"At least wait for another few days," Cassi said. "You're mine until Monday night, remember?"

"You sound just like my children."

"Good night, Mommy."

Renae giggled. "Good night."

*****

Early Sunday morning, bright light filtered through the partially closed blinds. Cassi yawned and stretched contentedly. She had slept well. Since her job required a great deal of traveling, she could fall asleep anywhere within minutes. It was a learned ability, and Cassi was proud of it.

She arose quietly and made her way to the bathroom to shower. Her sweet-smelling shampoo lathered readily in the warm water, and she relished the clean feeling it gave her.

In the foggy warmth of the bathroom, she dressed in a decidedly delicate dress with aqua-colored flowers, quite unlike her business suit, but just as form-flattering. She sprayed leave-on conditioner in her hair and worked out the last few knots, twisting it expertly into a French roll. She almost always wore her hair this way on Sunday, feeling that it showed her respect for the Lord. It also kept people from asking which permanent she used. "The one I got in my mother's womb," she would always reply on those unfortunate days when she didn't have time to wash and coif her hair. That always startled people enough to curb further questions.

Cassi left the bathroom to find Renae still sleeping. She sat at the table near the beds and thumbed through the phone book to find the nearest church house. It was nearly eight o'clock.

Renae mumbled in her sleep, and Cassi looked over to see her friend's bulging stomach move under the light blanket. Renae's eyes flew open. "What?" She glanced around, puzzled. "Oh, I was dreaming that the kids were jumping on me, trying to wake me up." Her stomach moved again and Renae laughed. "It wasn't a dream. This baby *is* jumping on me."

Cassi left the table and went to sit on the edge of Renae's bed. "I never knew they moved like that. I can see it beneath the blanket!"

"You think that's bad . . ." Renae flipped off the blanket and parted her pajamas to bare her stomach. The baby's movements were even more noticeable. Cassi laughed as one part of the stomach poked out a half-inch above the rest and glided across the surface.

"Is that a foot?" she asked.

Renae shrugged. "I think so. She must be stretching or something. She does this quite a bit."

Cassi's gaze was still fixed on the movements, her eyes feeling strangely moist. Renae suddenly grabbed her hand and put it on top of the baby. Cassi felt the baby kick against the abrupt cold of her hand.

"Oh," was all Cassi could say, her heart full of wonder and longing.

"It'll be your turn one day," Renae said lightly. "You do believe that, don't you?"

"I do," she said softly. She took her hand away from the baby and returned to the table.

"But you're going to have to date more," Renae added, sitting up.

"And how do I do that, if they don't ask me out?"

"Ask them. They do want to go out with you; they're just afraid. Or maybe they ask, and you just don't get the drift. You did that in high school, you know."

Cassi's anger flared, and she had to fight to make her voice sound normal. "So now I'm stupid?"

"No, I didn't say that. You're just . . . innocent and unassuming, I guess. You don't realize when men are admiring you. Take that man from yesterday, the blond-haired one. He admired you, I could tell. He seems like a nice guy."

Cassi look at her friend incredulously. "You mean the arrogant pig? You have *got* to be kidding. With Léon for a friend, he's probably a pervert. I don't care how good-looking you may think he is, I don't like him. And I certainly am not going to ask him out!"

Renae held up her hands. "Okay, okay. It was just a suggestion. He's not a member anyway, so there's no question, right?"

"Right. When I finally do get married, it has to be in the temple. I'm not waiting this long to settle for second-best."

Renae heaved her way out of the bed, stomach first, and turned in the direction of the bathroom. She was already doing her customary dance to alleviate the pressure on her bladder. "But just because that Landine guy knows Léon doesn't mean he's a pervert. I mean, you know Léon, and I don't consider you a pervert." Before Cassi could retort, Renae danced into the bathroom and shut the door.

While Renae bathed, Cassi called the nearest wardhouse to find out the meeting times. It was a family ward that didn't start until ten o'clock, leaving plenty of time for Renae to get ready and for them to have breakfast before leaving the hotel. Cassi went to the small refrigerator in the corner of the room next to the sink to retrieve some of the groceries they had bought after the auction display on Saturday. In order to make their Sabbath special, they planned to eat all of their meals from the groceries, avoiding the hotel restaurant or room service. Cassi set out yogurt and fruit juice. In the cupboards above the sink she found the package of croissants.

"It's not very far. Do you feel like walking?" she asked as Renae joined her at the table.

"Sounds great. I feel rested. And you don't know how wonderful it will be to walk without having to carry Sandy."

*****

At fifteen to ten, Cassi and Renae arrived at the chapel. They were greeted eagerly by the missionaries, who only showed a slight disappointment when they learned that the women were not investigators. The building was well-kept and familiar to both Cassi and Renae, though they had never set foot in it before. Like all LDS church buildings, it had a foyer with couches, long hallways with doors opening into classrooms, and a large chapel where sacrament meetings were held. The building itself seemed to welcome them.

Cassi and Renae were still talking to the missionaries and to the second counselor, Brother Smithy, when the man Léon had introduced them to the day before approached the building. Cassi could see the arrogant pig's handsome features clearly as he sauntered through the glass doors of the church.

"Him!" Cassi blurted out before she could stop herself. The missionaries and Brother Smithy turned in the newcomer's direction.

"Oh, that's Jared Landine," Brother Smithy said.

"You know him?" Cassi had been ready to accuse Jared of following her.

"Yeah. He served his mission in L.A. and was stationed in our area for awhile. In fact, he taught my wife and me. It's because of him we were baptized. I owe him a lot. He telephoned Friday to tell me he was going to be here this weekend; he comes three or four times a year, and we keep up in between. If you'll excuse me for a moment . . ." Brother Smithy darted off in Jared's direction while Cassi simply stared. The men met halfway across the foyer in a friendly bear hug.

"It's so great to see you again!" Brother Smithy said, loud enough for Cassi and Renae to hear. "How's work?"

"Going well," Jared replied. "How are the kids? Is April here today?"

Cassi's eyes were still fixed on him. He looked much as he had the day before, except that he was wearing a different suit. He was undeniably handsome with his blond good looks and unnerving blue eyes. Cassi clenched her jaw. For no reason she could pinpoint, her heart was racing. She wasn't sure she appreciated the feeling.

She glanced at Renae, who was watching her closely, then back at Jared. This time he met her stare with those piercing eyes. Cassi gulped. *The arrogant pig, a member? How can this be?* she thought. All her preconceived notions about the stranger exploded into a burst of nothingness, leaving her feeling strangely naked and unprotected.

CHAPTER 5

The air was crisp and clean, not yet smothered by the heat that would come later in the day. Jared enjoyed his walk to the church near the hotel. He knew these streets well because of his time as a missionary in the area. Yet each time he returned there was some change—an old building gone and a new one in its place, or perhaps a street of houses replaced by condominiums or stores. He took these changes in stride, knowing that things had to change to stay alive. In his heart, though, he would always remember the city as it had once been—the city he had grown to love while serving the Lord.

He reached the building shortly before church began and was glad to see Larry Smithy at the door. A smile came unbidden to his face as he remembered the first time he had seen Larry twelve years ago. Jared and his companion had been tracting doors all day with no success. Both missionaries were discouraged yet determined to teach at least one discussion that day. Hour after hour they'd had no luck. Their stomachs growled with hunger and their bodies were hot from the constant physical exertion, but the biggest blow was the repeated rejection. Door after door slammed in their weary faces, and sometimes curses followed their hasty retreats. Their hearts were heavy with the knowledge that the people who refused them were also rejecting the Savior.

Night was falling quickly when they reached the Smithys' door. It was Jared's turn to give the missionary spiel, and as the senior companion, he prepared to muster excitement and energy into his speech, praying silently and fervently for guidance. A short, strong-looking man opened the door. His expression was severe, and Jared immediately wished they had skipped the house. He took a step back-ward, thinking to simply apologize and leave, but something about the man's gray eyes wouldn't let Jared go. The thought came to him that the lines around those eyes stemmed from pain, more than from age.

"I'm Elder Landine and this is my companion, Elder Liechty. We're missionaries from The Church of Jesus Christ of Latter-day Saints," Jared said firmly, gathering courage as he spoke. "We've come to share a message about the Savior. Do you believe in Jesus Christ?"

The man stared at the missionaries as if they were insane. His jaw clenched tightly, yet when he spoke, his words weren't loud or angry, just bitter and utterly sad. "I don't think so," he said slowly. "There's too much pain in this world. If he lives, why doesn't he help?" The suffering around the man's eyes seemed more noticeable, but somehow Jared knew that he was seeing the man through the Spirit and not with his natural eyes. Jared had been brought here to help this man; he felt it more strongly than he had ever felt anything in his life.

"Larry!" an agonized voice from the back room cried out.

The man's face twisted around to look down the hallway behind him and then back to the missionaries. "My wife needs me," he said without feeling in his voice. "I have to go to her."

Panic welled up within Jared. He couldn't let this man go. The words tumbled out of his mouth before he realized what he was saying. "Jesus Christ does live! And he loves you! Please, sir, let us give your wife a blessing." To Jared's surprise, he felt tears welling up in his eyes. He blinked furiously to keep them from falling.

"A blessing?" asked the man. "What's that?"

"We're elders of the Lord's church, and we've received authority from others who have passed it in succession from the time of Jesus Christ. It is the power to act in the name of God. Please, sir, you have nothing to lose. Let us bless your wife. Please, try to believe that what I say is true!" Jared stared anxiously at the man. One part of him couldn't believe that he, Jared, was acting so boldly. He had always been a good missionary, but he had never felt so driven by the Spirit before; its strength amazed him.

Larry Smithy looked appraisingly at both Jared and his companion. "I think you're sincere," he said finally. "You believe in what you're saying. My wife also believes in Christ. Come in; she will be comforted to receive your blessing, even if it doesn't change the outcome."

The elders followed Larry into the house and down the hall, scarcely believing what was happening to them. They were ushered into a large bedroom where a woman lay under the blankets. Her face was streaked with tears and her beauty marred by despair. Jared felt his heart go out to her. *What's wrong with her?* he thought. *Is she dying? Oh, please, Father, help me know what to say.*

"April, these are missionaries. They want to give you a blessing," Larry said, sitting down on the bed beside her. He took her hand in his and stroked it tenderly.

Hope flared in April's gray eyes. "You can help?" she asked almost pitifully. "The doctor says there is nothing we can do. Just like the last times."

Jared had hoped that she would elaborate more about her condition, but he felt constrained by the Spirit not to question the couple. "We're messengers of Jesus Christ," he said. "We've been given his priesthood, the same priesthood that Jesus and his disciples had. Through your faith and God's will, miracles can happen."

Her eyes began to water, and she struggled to sit up. "I believe that God can work miracles. I do. I do."

Larry's jaw clenched tightly. He seemed unwilling to shatter his wife's belief, but he didn't want her to go on about it. "How is a blessing done?" he asked quickly.

"My companion will anoint her head with holy oil and say a prayer. Then together we will put our hands on her head and bless her."

"How much does it cost?" Larry asked.

Jared's eyes met his. "There is never a price on priesthood blessings. They are from the Lord; it is not our power, but his. The only payment you can give to him is the way you live your life."

Larry appeared surprised at the answer but nodded in agreement. "Go ahead." Then he muttered, so softly that Jared nearly missed the words, "And would that your God hear you."

Elder Liechty anointed April and Jared blessed her. "You're a good woman," he felt impressed to say, "and the Lord is pleased with your life thus far." Then he said something that surprised him. "The Lord will bless you, April. This baby you carry will live to adulthood, as will the others to come. Be a good parent to them, and teach them about the Savior and his great love."

Jared finished the blessing and looked up, feeling his companion and Larry Smithy watching him. Both of the other men knew Jared hadn't known what was wrong with April, yet he had been told by the Lord. There was a new light in Larry's eyes, a fragile hope that had been missing before. The Spirit in the room testified of Jared's words.

They said good-bye to April, whose tears had subsided. Larry walked them to the door quietly. "You will come back," he said. It was more a statement than anything else. The elders set up a time and left, feeling wonder at what they had seen happen that night.

The Smithys eventually accepted baptism, and not only did their baby live—the first after several second-trimester miscarriages—but they went on to have five more children in the twelve years after Jared's mission. Since then Jared had had many special experiences in his life, but none ever equaled the dramatic display of the Spirit that night. He felt it had happened because the Smithys were special and worthy; Jared and his companion had simply been the Lord's tools.

"It's so great to see you again!" Larry said now as the two friends embraced. "How's work?"

As Jared replied, he raised his eyes to search for April and the children, only to stare across the church foyer into the eyes of the woman he had met the previous day: Cassi Mason. The Snob with a capital S. Her brown eyes were opened wide, and she seemed oddly vulnerable—a far cry from the self-assured buyer of the day before. Jared felt himself drawn to her, and he loathed the feeling. He forced himself to examine her dispassionately.

In her flowered, floor-length dress she was overwhelmingly feminine. Her slim figure was about five-foot-five to his six-one. Her face was not overly painted, and she looked as wholesome as any woman he had ever known. He didn't like that assessment, so he searched further to find something wrong. Then he had it: her hair. The reddish-brown locks were done up in some kind of a twist. The full, bouncy ringlets had disappeared. Why would this woman spend so much time making her hair look perfect on other days, but neglect it on Sunday when it really mattered?

Larry followed Jared's gaze. "Oh, yeah. Do you know them? I think they know you. They're visiting our ward, same as you."

Jared shook his head, then nodded, aware of the contradiction, but unable to control himself. "We've met," he said. "At the hotel."

"How wonderful to meet members like that," Larry said. "I'm always so excited to meet members from different places. It certainly brings it home that we're all children of God and brothers and sisters." Larry was positively beaming, and Jared felt slightly irritated. He knew what was coming next; Larry would try to set them up.

"Church is probably about to start," Jared said quickly. "Are April and the children inside? Show me where, and I'll help her with the kids. It's got to be hard for her with you always on the stand." As he talked, Jared moved toward the chapel, passing by Cassi and Renae.

"That reminds me," Larry said, walking with him, "Sister Martin and Sister Jukes won't be here. Sister Martin is bedridden; she's eighty-five, and the doctor isn't sure how long she'll live. And Sister Jukes had surgery on her leg last week. They've both asked after you. Do you think you could go with me to take the sacrament to them this afternoon?"

Jared was painfully aware that Cassi and Renae were following them into the chapel, close enough to hear every word. "Sure, I will. But I already went to see them both last night. They were like second mothers to me when I served here, and I always visit them when I'm in L.A." Jared saw the women behind him exchange looks, Renae's a triumphant I-told-you-so, Cassi's completely unreadable. Jared wanted to shake her.

Instead, he pretended not to see. He made his way to April, who sat near the back of the chapel where she could make a quick getaway with a crying baby if necessary. The oldest child, now twelve, looked up at him shyly. "Hi, Jared," she murmured, unable to help the blush that covered her cheeks.

Jared smiled inwardly to see that the child still hadn't lost her girlish crush on him. "It's very good to see you, Meagan. You've sure grown up in the last six months."

The girl blushed again, pleased that he had noticed. The other children clamored around until Jared shushed them. "Look! The meeting's about to start. How about we listen, and then tonight when

I come over for dinner we'll see who's the most ticklish?" The children giggled but soon quieted, knowing Jared's promises were good; they would have fun tonight!

Jared felt the familiar ache when he was near children. He knew that the presence of his own children was sorely missing in his life. No matter how much he played with his numerous nephews and nieces or volunteered in the church nursery, those substitute children never completely filled the void. Mostly he tried not to think about it.

Ahead of him two rows and to the side, he could see Cassi sitting with her friend, Renae. His eyes continued to search her out as if drawn by some magnet. He forced himself to remember how Léon had said she treated potential suitors, and her apparent hardness when trying to make art deals. *She's got her priorities mixed up,* he thought.

Jared felt better with his rationalization and refocused his mind as the first sacrament prayer was said. As he waited for the bread, he glanced up again to look at Cassi, despite his resolve to forget her. Her head was still bowed discreetly, and Jared could almost swear he saw a tear fall from her eyes onto her lap. *She's thinking about the Savior,* he thought before he could stop himself. He shook the thoughts away and closed his own eyes. Suddenly he didn't see her as a snob or as a businesswoman; he saw her only as she had looked yesterday morning, the first time he had seen her, dressed in faded jeans and an old T-shirt, her long hair curling in every direction, and her face without makeup or guile. Was that the real woman? And if it was, why was he so attracted to her?

Yet thoughts of the Buddha chased away any idea he might have of making friends. He wouldn't let Cassi have it—no matter what. He smiled grimly, completely aware that there was something in him that enjoyed a good fight.

CHAPTER 6

Sweat ran down Cassi's face as she ran in place on the marbled carpet in their hotel suite. At home she usually went jogging each morning, but on trips she exercised in her room or used the hotel gym.

Renae laughed as she watched Cassi's antics. "I don't know if it's worth it," she said. "It seems like a lot of work to be fit."

"Well," puffed Cassi, "it'll get me ready for the battle for the Buddha today."

"Oh, yeah. The Buddha battle with the good-looking, eligible member."

"The arrogant jerk, you mean," corrected Cassi.

Renae's eyebrows raised. "Oh, so he's only a jerk now. That's a step up from the sty."

Cassi glared at Renae but said nothing. She was already confused with regard to Jared, and she didn't want to think about him. Seeing him at church and hearing good things about him had changed her perspective. What her new perspective was she hadn't figured out yet, and she wasn't sure she wanted to.

"From what I heard about him, the guy's worth checking out."

Cassi stopped running in place and stood there puffing. Her face was flushed, but not all of it stemmed from exercising. "Maybe for someone else. Me, he didn't give the time of day. Did you see how fast he went into the chapel when he saw me? My being there cut off all his small talk. He couldn't wait to get away from me. I don't care, either; I'm going to beat him and walk away smiling. I won't ever have to see him again."

"What if he has a bigger budget than you do?"

Cassi frowned. "It's all too possible," she said. "He represents a fairly large gallery in New York, the Garrettson Gallery. They have a very specialized clientele. It's likely that they already have a customer who has commissioned them to get the statue, and for me that spells trouble. I wish I really *could* slip something into his coffee . . ."

"Except that he doesn't drink coffee," said Renae with a big smile on her face. "He's a member, remember?"

Cassi sighed and sat down on the bed next to her friend. "How can I forget, with you always reminding me?"

"So what are you going to do?"

"You tell me." Cassi stood up and went to look at her watch on the nightstand. "Oh, I've got to get ready. The auction starts at ten, and there's a few things I wanted to bid on."

"Not the Buddha?"

Cassi shook her head. "At noon the auctioneers take a break until two. The Buddha will go at threeish."

Renae nodded. "This should be interesting."

"Let's hope it doesn't bore you to death."

They dressed and were heading to the door when a folded sheet of white paper was slipped under their door. Cassi bent to pick it up while Renae opened the door.

"No one's there," she said. "Cassi, what's wrong? Why are you so white?" She grabbed at the note. "Do not bid for it, if you want to live," she read. "Bid for what? Is this some kind of a joke?"

Cassi met Renae's eyes, feeling her knees go weak. The black type on the otherwise unmarked sheet was perfectly clear to her. "The Buddha," she said. "It has to be the Buddha."

"But no one even knows you want the ugly thing. Except—"

"Jared," Cassi finished.

Renae's mouth rounded to an O. "That's ridiculous. Anyone could have sent it." Then she added more doubtfully, "Or if he did, it's a joke."

"Well, this kind of joke I could do very well without." Cassi crumpled the note and threw it into the wastebasket. "I won't be intimidated by anyone, especially not an by an—"

"Arrogant pig. I can see we're back where we started."

"I'm not discussing this with you. Come on. Let's go." As Cassi led the way to the elevator, chills crawled down her back. What if the note wasn't a joke? What if Jared Landine was serious in this threat? Or what if he hadn't sent it at all? She glanced nervously over her shoulder, feeling eyes following her, but no one was there.

At the door to the auction, a man stood guarding the entrance. Only people who were pre-registered could enter, although those registered could bring guests. Most of the items were expensive enough to prevent the average person from wanting to attend, and art dealers made up nearly the entire clientele.

"Card please," the man said. Cassi handed him her registration card.

"Cassi Mason," he read aloud, and his hand slid down the list to find her name. "You're number forty-four." He handed her a long white card with a number printed in bold black letters. Cassi thanked him, and she and Renae walked into the auction room. Rows of gold-cushioned chairs had been set up, and already many were filled. Everyone looked eager and excited for the competition, and a buzz of voices echoed through the room. Cassi couldn't help noticing that Jared Landine was nowhere in sight.

"We have a number?" asked Renae. "How does it work?"

"Well, when we want to bid on an item, we simply raise the number. This makes the auction people's jobs easier because they know exactly who is bidding for what, even if they don't remember us from prior auctions. And they don't have to worry about payment, because they have a list of what galleries we represent and they know our history. Only the independents are regarded with any reserve."

"Are all auctions like this?" asked Renae.

Cassi shook her head, feeling her curls dance around her face annoyingly. "No. There are as many different ways to conduct auctions as there are people who want to buy. It just depends on the company doing it. For instance, some auctions have sealed bids instead of open bidding like this one. In sealed bids, you never know if you get the item until they open all the bids. The highest bid wins, and they notify you later."

"But that takes all of the excitement out of it!"

Cassi grinned. "I agree. But they can be profitable."

More people had come in and were quickly seating themselves; the auction was about to start. Cassi glanced around but still saw no sign of Jared. Her mouth tightened angrily as she realized what she was doing. Why did she care? She deliberately focused her attention on the auctioneer, who was standing in front of a small podium. To both sides of him were long tables filled with the first batch of items to be sold. To the far side, the guards responsible for keeping the art safe until given to its new owners stood alertly against the wall.

"Now, who would like to bid for this item?" began the auctioneer, pointing to a small painting. He went on to describe its qualities, then asked for a starting bid of ten thousand dollars.

Renae gasped. "And I was thinking of trying to get it for my living room!"

Cassi smiled but didn't answer. The painting sold quickly, and her attention was on the next item up for bid, a small statue of a mother and baby that tore at her heart. It had been one of the last-minute items added to the auction, and she knew without a doubt that it would sell very well, especially since it was made of exceptionally fine quality porcelain. It was worth far more than the starting bid of four thousand, but it was an obscure piece, and only those who had taken the time to look beyond its simplicity would have seen its real value.

Cassi raised her card.

"I have four thousand for *Mother and Baby*. Let's make it four thousand five hundred. Who will make it four five for the mother dancing with her infant? I have four five. Anyone for five thousand . . ." A few others bid on the piece, some simply because Cassi had done so, and the price went slowly up. Cassi won the bid at six thousand. She felt it was worth at least twice that price and smiled in satisfaction.

Renae bumped her shoulder. "He's here," she whispered, jerking her chin to the right. Cassi looked and saw Jared Landine coming in the door. The guard at the door didn't look pleased at the latecomer's interruption, but Jared simply smiled and slipped into an empty seat. His eyes scanned the crowd, and Cassi quickly turned her head before he could see her watching him. Inexplicably, her pulse quickened.

Cassi bid for only one more item that session, a painting, and was beaten out by Léon, who shrugged and gave her a friendly wave. With *Mother and Baby* hers, Cassi felt no ill will. After the last item sold, people stood to stretch their legs. Renae's face suddenly paled.

"What's wrong?" Cassi asked quickly.

"I feel really tired. And I keep having these false contractions. They're enough to drive me insane sometimes."

"Is there anything you can do for them?"

Renae shook her head. "Not medicine-wise. But lying down always seems to help."

"Let's go, then."

They were nearly out the door when Léon stopped them. With him was the last man on earth Cassi wanted to see: Jared Landine. "What was so interesting about the *Mother and Baby?*" Léon asked.

Cassi shrugged. "I like babies, I guess."

Léon laughed. "But only because it will bring your gallery a profit, no?"

"You got the *Mother and Baby?*" Jared asked. A peculiar expression passed over his face.

Cassi saw the look as a questioning of her knowledge and abilities. She stiffened. "Yes. Wouldn't you have bid for it if you had been here?" She almost bit her lip as she realized that her statement made him aware that she had noticed his earlier absence. Well, what did she care? If Mr. Landine couldn't see the beauty and quality of the *Mother and Baby*, it only proved how moronic he really was.

Jared gazed at her, his face serious. "I would have. It's a singularly beautiful piece."

Cassi willed her face not to show her triumph.

"Why weren't you here?" asked Renae curiously.

Jared's mouth tightened and his expression grew severe. "Something came up," he said.

Cassi watched him closely. There was more to his story than he was willing to tell. Could it have something to do with the note? But what did it matter to her? There was no way she would back down from bidding on the Buddha. She glanced at Renae's white face. "Renae's not feeling too well. If you'll excuse us?"

"Sure," Léon moved to the side. Jared nodded but said nothing.

Before Cassi could leave, a voice called out to her. "Miss Mason! May I talk with you?" A buyer from another gallery walked over quickly. He had brown hair and light blue eyes, seemingly dull after the brightness of Jared's.

"You're Mr. Boader, aren't you?" she asked.

He nodded. "Sam Boader." He looked nervously at the group but plunged bravely on. "I'd like to talk with you about your purchase. Do you think we could get together sometime? Maybe have lunch?"

He was obviously interested in her *Mother and Baby* statue. "I'd be glad to talk with you about the statue," she said, "but we don't have to have lunch or anything. We can just talk about it after the auction this afternoon. There isn't much to tell, really. I'd stay now, except that my friend isn't feeling well."

To her surprise, Sam's face fell. Why? Hadn't she agreed to do what he wanted? Her eyebrows gathered together, trying to decipher what had gone wrong. She looked at Renae, Léon, and Jared in turn, searching for a clue. Léon's face seemed amused; Jared only stared expressionlessly. Renae, however, saved the situation.

"We could talk about it over dinner," she said to Sam. "After the auction. That way we can take our time. It really is a beautiful piece."

Sam smiled at Renae gratefully, while Jared frowned and his eyebrows furrowed. Cassi simply nodded, relieved that whatever problem Sam Boader had with her answer had now disappeared.

"We'll see you then, after the auction," Sam said.

Again Cassi nodded and turned with Renae to the door. This time they made it to the elevator without being stopped. Renae was breathing heavily while Cassi stood looking on helplessly. "Maybe the baby's coming," she suggested as they arrived at their room.

"Three weeks early? I doubt it. All my other children were overdue." Renae lay down on her bed.

Cassi went to the refrigerator to see what was left of their food. "There's not much here," she said after a cursory search. They had a few cartons of yogurt and some bread left, nothing more. "Shall I go down and buy something, or order room service?"

"Room service," Renae said. Cassi was happy to notice that already her voice sounded much better. "This is my last day to be spoiled," Renae added. "After dinner it's home to the gang, and my days of luxury will be over."

Cassi laughed. "But speaking of dinner, why did you ask Sam Boader to eat with us tonight? We could have talked beforehand about the statue. Now we'll have to share our last night together with a near stranger."

"I don't believe you," Renae said, shaking her head back and forth. "You haven't changed since high school. That man doesn't give a hoot about your statue. He wants to go out with you."

"With me? That's not true. If he had, he would have asked."

"He *did* ask, silly." Renae sighed in exasperation. "Everyone knew it except you." She laughed. "You just see who pays for dinner tonight. It won't be us, I can guarantee that."

"But that's wrong!"

"Why? Because a man admires you enough to want to take you out? There's nothing wrong with that, Cassi. He wants to get to know you. And he seems like a nice guy, doesn't he? Wouldn't you go out with him if he asked you?"

"Yes, but this is different. You asked him."

Renae sighed. "No, Cassi. I just helped him ask you. You weren't taking any hints. Now, can we just forget this until tonight? We'll have fun at dinner regardless of Sam Boader, I think."

"Okay, okay. It's forgotten. Besides, I've got to figure out a way to get the Buddha from you-know-who."

"Oh, now he's you-know-who. That's another step up from arrogant jerk. I do believe you're getting soft in your old age."

Cassi ignored Renae and called room service. "Send me up two grilled chicken dinners and some arsenic. No, I didn't say arsenic. What, do you think I want to poison someone? I want milk. No, no coffee, thanks." When Cassi hung up, Renae was laughing.

"You never change," she said.

"And neither do you," Cassi countered. "We both get older, but we never change."

"I hope you never do change. You could always make me laugh."

CHAPTER 7

It was all Jared could do to hide his annoyance when Sam Boader of the Stanton and Son Gallery came up to Cassi and used the thin pretense of the *Mother and Baby* statue to ask her out. After she refused, Léon made a motion to Jared as if to say, "See, I told you she was a snob." But from the way Cassi had reacted, Jared wasn't so sure Léon's assumption was correct.

When she and Renae had started again toward the entrance, Jared suddenly wished he could reach out his hand to stop her. But why should he do that? Besides, Renae's face was pale and she looked tired. She obviously needed to rest.

Boader grinned at the men, victorious. "You shouldn't have been late," he said to Jared. "You missed some great pieces."

Jared told himself to be calm. "There's always a next time." He regretted that the *Mother and Baby*—the one statue he had come prepared to bid for that morning—had been sold before his arrival. The statue portrayed a mother dancing with a baby cuddled close to her chest, a piece that was singularly simple in its elegance. He was amazed to learn Cassi had bought it, that she had recognized the quality of the piece. *Maybe I can buy it from her,* he thought. He wanted it for his private collection, not for Laranda's gallery. His elegant boss had never been capable of appreciating the value in such simple pieces; its beauty would have been wasted on her.

"So, where were you?" Léon asked. Boader waited with an expectant grin on his boyishly good-looking face.

Jared felt his lips tighten as the memory of his dreadful morning came rushing back. Long before the bidding at the auction had opened that morning, the phone had rung shrilly in the stillness of his room. He had jerked into consciousness from a deep sleep and reached for the receiver with an unsteady hand, an apprehensive feeling growing within him. No one called this early unless it was bad news.

"Hello?"

"Jared, this is Larry. Sister Martin's been rushed to the hospital. She's dying. She asked for you. Can you come?"

"Of course, I'll meet you at the hospital." Jared hung up the phone and dressed quickly in jeans and a blue oxford shirt. Not bothering to put on socks, he slipped his feet into the leather loafers by the bed. He ran a hand through his hair while the other reached for his car keys. In moments he was out the door, still rubbing the sleep from his eyes.

When he arrived at the hospital, he found Larry and April with Sister Martin. The bishop from the ward was also there, a man Jared only knew from his visits to L.A.

"How is she?" Jared asked.

Larry shook his head and said nothing.

At Jared's voice, Sister Martin opened her eyes. "I'm dying," she said softly. There was pain in the heavily lined face, but the soft brown eyes were strangely animated. "I'm going to be with Lane and Karen." Lane was Sister Martin's husband, and Karen, the baby she had lost at two years old.

Jared didn't deny Sister Martin's statement. From her appearance, he, too, felt she was dying. "Would you give me a blessing, Jared, so I won't be afraid when it comes?" she asked. "Please?"

Tears came to Jared's eyes. "Of course I will. It'll be an honor."

After Larry anointed Sister Martin, Jared blessed her. As he had expected, his blessing said nothing of physical healing, but emphasized the spiritual aspects of her life and imminent reunion with her husband and daughter. Part of him wanted to bless the dear woman to get well, but it wasn't meant to be.

As Jared finished the blessing, two people he recognized from photographs in Sister Martin's house came rushing into the room and up to the bed.

"Mother," said a woman in her sixties, "I'm here. And Anthony, too. Miriam and Rebecca are on their way." The woman sobbed but quickly gained control of herself. "Please hold on, Mom."

"Gary won't make it from Utah," Sister Martin said weakly. "Did you call him?"

"Yes, Mother."

Jared backed away and said nothing as Sister Martin's children gathered. Many of the grandchildren and great-grandchildren also arrived to give a farewell kiss to their grandmother. They were sad, yet the knowledge that Sister Martin would finally be free of pain and reunited with her husband sustained them.

Near the end, Sister Martin opened her eyes and called, "Jared, where are you? I have something to say."

Jared approached the bedside hesitantly, not wanting to push the family out of the way. Most of the grandchildren and great-grandchildren were in the hall or waiting room, but all of Sister Martin's children except Gary were with her. The bishop and the Smithys had left the room to allow Sister Martin private time with her family. Jared had been nearly out the door himself when she called for him. "I'm here," he said.

"See all these children around me?" she asked.

"Yes."

"That's why having children is so wonderful. Through the hard times and the good times, you're not alone." Her voice grew imperious. "Jared, you haven't been doing what you should. Get going. The Lord has someone prepared for you. Open your heart and let her in." Sister Martin's voice was growing weaker now, and she gasped for air.

"I'll do it. I promise," he said hoarsely.

Sister Martin said nothing further, obviously satisfied with his vow. She shut her eyes to rest as Jared backed away from the bed and left the room. He waited with Larry and April, exchanging stories of Sister Martin, until nearly ten o'clock when she passed away. Then he bid the family farewell and left the hospital, promising to attend the funeral in two days' time.

Now he closed his eyes briefly and sighed. "I was busy," he said to both Léon and Sam Boader, clearly indicating that his private life was not up for discussion. He felt the sorrow of Sister Martin's death wash over him. It was too fresh to be talked about casually.

"It's your life," Léon mumbled.

Sam gazed down the hall where Cassi, with her arm about Renae, was quickly retreating from view. "What should I bring her tonight?" he asked. "Chocolates? Flowers?"

"Try both," suggested Léon. "All women love flowers, and with an expectant friend, chocolates might make some points. My fourth wife loved to eat chocolates while she was pregnant."

Sam grinned. "Fourth, huh? Maybe I will try both." With a nod of his head, he turned back into the room, leaving Jared and Léon alone.

The crush of art dealers had swallowed Cassi and Renae, but Léon gestured in the direction they had disappeared. "Did you see how she turned him down flat?" he asked. "Cold, I tell you. She's cold. If it hadn't been for her friend, Sam would have been blasted out of the water." He chuckled. "Lucky devil."

Jared let his anger loose. "Are you blind?" he asked. "She didn't even realize he was asking her out. She thinks he wants the statue! Didn't you see that?" His anger surprised him, and he made an effort to curb it. His reaction was completely out of proportion, stemming from his own frustration in the matter. He recognized all too clearly that he, Jared, wanted to be in Sam Boader's shoes that evening, and the fact didn't sit too well with his ego.

"Didn't she really, or was it an act?" Léon said lightly.

Jared wanted to tell Léon that Cassi was nothing like him. Maybe Léon, with his French flair, could carry off such a deception, but not her. Or could she? Jared remembered Laranda. She was a woman and completely capable of deception. What made Jared think that Cassi wasn't? Maybe it *had* been an act, simply because she hadn't wanted to go out with Boader. But then why the relief when Renae arranged to have dinner with him? Jared shook his head and sighed. There couldn't be any answers unless he knew her better, and that was out of the question—at least while the hideous Buddha stood between them.

Abruptly, Sister Martin's last words to him at the hospital whispered in his mind. "The Lord has someone prepared for you. Open your heart and let her in." Jared shrugged the painful memory away.

"You see? It's not so easy as all that," Léon commented, accepting Jared's silence as agreement. "But you do have an advantage over Boader, you know."

"What?"

"She noticed that you weren't here this morning. She said as much when she asked if you would have bid for the *Mother and Baby* if you'd been here."

So she had! For the first time since Boader had interrupted them, Jared smiled.

Léon slapped him on the back. "I guess I'd better go make arrangements to pick up my painting," he said.

"Yes, you did get your painting, didn't you?" Jared returned. "An excellent piece." As promised, he had refrained from that particular bidding war. It had not escaped him that Cassi Mason had bid several times for it before stopping when she recognized Léon's determination. "A gentleman's word is always kept," he added.

This subtle hint was not lost on Léon. He bowed slightly. "I am also a gentleman, as you will see when you bid for the Buddha."

At least with Léon's promise the morning had not been a complete waste. Jared had also made a few fake bids that served only to scare some of the other buyers and to evoke feelings of sympathy when he would purposely lose out. When he bid on the Buddha later in the afternoon, he wanted as little competition as possible. The more items he appeared to let people win now, the more those same people would refrain from bidding for the Buddha later. It was a strange system, but it worked more often than not.

The Buddha would soon be his, regardless of Cassi Mason.

When he arrived in his room, he found the note under the door. He had no idea how long it had been there. It was typed in bold black print on a sheet of untraceable white paper: *Do not bid for it, if you want to live.* Despite the warmth of his suit coat, Jared shivered.

CHAPTER
8

When it was time to go to the auction again, Renae still felt tired. Cassi knew the false labor had eased, but she didn't think her friend was ready to sit for two more hours in a straight-backed chair.

"You go ahead without me," Renae said.

"Are you sure you're all right?"

"Yes. I just get tired sometimes near the end. It's not easy to carry around this extra weight. Besides, I think I have a plan to get you your Buddha."

"What?"

"Well, I'll make an emergency call to Jared Landine right at three o'clock. The hotel will have to go get him and, pronto, he's eliminated from the competition."

"What if the Buddha isn't auctioned while he's gone?"

"I'll go down and make sure it is; I'll be rested by then. The guard won't let me in, but I bet he'll tell me what's being auctioned. Just before it goes, I'll call the hotel from a pay phone and they'll go get him. Simple."

It did sound simple. Too simple. And also morally wrong. Or was it? What about that horrid note? The saying went that all was fair in love and war. And wasn't this a war? Cassi's conscience wasn't so sure.

"Don't you think you ought to rest?" She hated the way her voice sounded hopeful.

"I've been resting. I'll be okay. But you'd better go, or you'll be late." Renae made shooing motions from where she sat propped up in her bed.

"Okay. But I don't know about this scheme. It seems dishonest."

"Just go. Leave everything to me, would you? Go! You're going to be late."

Cassi glanced at her watch and flew out the door, leaving Renae behind. *I want the Buddha,* she reasoned. Besides, Landine was insufferable; this *was* war.

The seats were nearly full when she arrived at the auction. Sam Boader waved to her and she slipped into the empty seat beside him near the inner aisle. With Renae's insight, Cassi watched him carefully for signs of infatuation. She didn't see anything overt, but he did seem to pay more attention to her than necessary. Maybe he did like her. The thought was novel, and not unpleasant; he was good-looking and seemed nice.

"You know," he said to her, his voice clearly puzzled, "this morning a note was slipped under my door. It told me not to bid on *it,* if I wanted to live."

Cassi stiffened. "It what?"

"That's just it. I don't know. But it bothered me."

Cassi forced a laugh. "It's some poor fool's idea of a joke," she said.

"You're probably right."

But Cassi noticed he didn't bid on anything. Was he afraid? Should she be afraid? Or maybe it wasn't Jared at all who had sent the note, but Sam. Had he brought it up to test her?

This is ridiculous, she thought. *Next, I'll be suspecting Renae.*

The auctioneer brought out a new item and Cassi listened intently. Despite her attention, her thoughts wandered to Jared. She couldn't see him in front or to the sides of her, and she didn't want to turn around in case he noticed her interest. He had to be in the room; he certainly wouldn't miss bidding on his precious Buddha.

Another interesting painting came up for auction, and Léon again outbid her. The next item was an intricate sculpture of a tree and a lion. She bid for it, against stiff competition from somewhere behind her. She allowed herself a glance over her shoulder to see that it was Jared who was upsetting her bid. Eventually she won out, paying slightly over what she should have, though the item would still bring her gallery a reasonable profit. She sighed contentedly. With the two items purchased, she had already more than compensated for her trip.

Finally, it was the Buddha's turn to be auctioned, with a starting bid of two hundred thousand dollars. Cassi allowed others to begin the bidding to see who was interested. It soon became apparent that Jared and another man she didn't recognize were her stiffest competition.

Her thoughts flitted to Renae, and Cassi wondered if her friend had been serious about calling the hotel to get Jared out of the auction. Part of her hoped Renae would do just that, while the other part wanted to win in fair competition. But what if he had more money than she did?

The bid was now at two hundred and fifty thousand dollars. If Renae was going to act, she should do it soon. Cassi glanced behind her and saw that Jared had a thin phone to his ear. She jerked her face forward again and raised her number to bid two fifty-two on the Buddha. Had a hotel worker come in and given Jared notice of an emergency phone call? Was Renae even now on the phone with him? Cassi hadn't seen anyone come in with a message, but she had been intent on the bidding. It was entirely possible that Renae's plan had backfired, simply because they had overlooked the possibility of his owning a cellular phone.

Behind her, Jared bid again and Cassi raised her card to top him. The other bidder also raised his card. Next to her, Cassi could feel Sam watching to see if she would bid again.

"Excuse me," a voice at her side said softly. She looked up to see a hotel worker. "There's this message for you. It's urgent." Cassi took the message from him quickly. It read:

> *Renae Benson has gone into labor.*
> *She's bleeding and we've called an ambu-*
> *lance. It will be here shortly to get her.*
> *Please come. She's asking for you.*

Cassi felt horror sweep through her. Renae in labor? Bleeding? She looked first at Sam beside her and then risked a glance at Jared, feeling suddenly faint.

Then an idea came to her. Could this be a joke? Jared had been on the phone. Had he arranged this to get her out of the competition? Maybe Renae had called him, and this was his way of getting revenge. Or maybe he had come up with it all by himself.

These thoughts raced quickly through Cassi's head as she weighed the options. Her heart pounded, and she completely forgot about the Buddha. *Renae is my friend,* she thought, coming to a decision. *If there is even a remote chance that she needs me, I have to be there for her.*

Cassi stood.

"But—" Sam began.

Cassi shoved the note into his hand for explanation, then ran out the door. Her abrupt movements caused a slight stir in the audience, but she was beyond caring. Her only thought was for Renae.

CHAPTER
9

The Monday afternoon auction went quickly. Jared bid for a sculpture, only to quit bidding when the price lowered the potential profits below Laranda's high requirements. For himself, he would have kept bidding because of the beauty of the piece. He felt a strange contentment when Cassi won the bid. The sculpture would not bring as much profit to her gallery, but would most likely result in a satisfied buyer and repeat business. It was the way Jared would run a gallery, if he had one.

The Buddha came up for bid, and, as expected, Cassi was strong competition. Jared pulled out his cellular phone and called Laranda in New York.

"There's stiff competition," he said into the phone, keeping his voice as low as possible so as not to disturb the other buyers.

"Get it." Laranda's voice sounded strangely tense. "I don't care what it takes, I have to have that Buddha. I've got a buyer waiting!"

"Okay. Don't I always come through? I just wanted to be sure how serious you are." As he spoke, Jared raised his card to up the bid on the Buddha.

"I know, Jared," Laranda said. "You always do what you can with what I give you. This is just very important to me."

"You'll tell me later?"

"Yes. And I'll give you a bonus you won't ever forget," she added huskily. Jared couldn't miss the innuendos, but chose to ignore them.

"G'bye, Laranda." Jared clicked his phone shut.

The bid for the Buddha was now at two hundred and fifty-two thousand dollars. As Jared raised his card again to top the bid, he saw a uniformed hotel worker come in the door and up to where Cassi was sitting and hand her a note. Her back stiffened, and almost immediately her gaze swung around to meet Jared's. Her face was stark white against the dark of her hair and eyes, seeming small and lost in the array of wild curls.

She stood abruptly, pausing only to shove something into the hand of the man seated next to her. As the man turned his head, Jared saw that it was Sam Boader. Before Jared could decide how he felt about that, Cassi was running out the door, hair streaming behind her. In her deep mauve dress, she captured almost every eye in the room.

What's wrong? Jared thought. *Why is she leaving the auction at this critical moment?* Jared's first urge was to follow her, but he wondered if he had the right.

Another buyer bid on the Buddha, and the auctioneer was calling for a higher bid. Jared raised his card without thinking. His mind was on Cassi. He could almost see her white face staring at him. All at once, he remembered the innocence of her voice and the makeup-less face on the morning they had met. *Since when do I have to be given the right to care about someone's problems?* he muttered to himself. *I'm human, she's human. That's all that matters.*

"Four hundred thousand," Jared said aloud, raising the bid nearly forty thousand dollars. People gasped slightly at the outrageous jump, but the auctioneer only smiled.

"I have four hundred thousand. Do I have four hundred thousand and one? Anyone for four hundred and one? Four hundred thousand going once, twice, and *sold* to number eighty-nine."

Jared was out of his seat in an instant and next to Sam. "Where's Cassi?" he whispered, ignoring the stares he was given.

Sam handed him the piece of paper and Jared read it quickly, his heart constricting at the contents. He recalled only too vividly when something similar had happened to one of his sisters. The placenta had come loose at the onset of labor, and the baby was saved only by an emergency C-section. The doctor had gravely informed them that if Trisha had arrived at the hospital only minutes later, the baby would have died.

Jared was out the door and in the hotel lobby before he realized he was moving. He only knew there was a possibility Renae could lose her baby, and maybe somehow he could help.

CHAPTER 10

Cassi looked anxiously around as she neared the main lobby. The elevator dinged, and she whirled to see Renae supported by two women hotel employees. She was disheveled and in obvious pain.

"Cassi!" Renae said when she looked up. "I'm so sorry. But the baby . . . I'm bleeding!"

Cassi didn't know what that meant, but she did know that a woman generally wasn't supposed to bleed until *after* a birth. She put her arms around Renae.

"I didn't want to get you out of the auction," her friend sobbed. "I just didn't know what else to do."

"I don't care about the auction," Cassi practically yelled at her. "Your baby's all that matters."

"The ambulance is here," one of the hotel workers said. Even as she spoke, two men and a stretcher moved quickly toward them. In minutes they had Renae on the stretcher and in the ambulance.

"Why is she bleeding?" Cassi asked, wishing her heart would quit beating so frantically.

"It's probably because the placenta is pulling away from the uterus," one of the medical personnel explained. "That means we have to get the baby out before it comes off altogether, or he won't be able to breathe."

"She," Cassi corrected. "It's a girl. But what if she doesn't come?"

"Then the doctor will take the baby C-section," the man said. "But don't worry too much," he added. "The heartbeat's still strong, and that means we have time."

They raced through the streets of L.A. to the hospital. Cassi's mind was now far removed from the auction and all its comparatively unimportant matters. At the hospital, she immediately called Trent while the doctor on call examined Renae. "I'll find someone to stay with the kids, and I'll be right there," he said when Cassi had explained the situation.

"Just bring them. I can take care of them. Renae needs you *now!*" Cassi's tears were near the surface. She felt terrible that Renae not only had to have her baby's life threatened, but had to face the situation with a strange doctor and no husband.

Cassi filled out the papers she was handed, then went to sit with Renae as the doctor explained the problem. He was rather short, bald, and calm, and Cassi liked him immediately.

"The placenta has come partly loose," he said to Renae. "That's why you have the bleeding. But your baby is in no immediate danger. We can keep an eye on you and see if we can't get the baby here naturally. If his heart rate drops, we'll have to take him caesarean, though I'm hoping that won't be necessary. You're already dilated to a four."

"Her," puffed Renae as another contraction took over. "My doctor said it was a girl."

"Well, he may be wrong," the doctor said with a smile. "Our ultrasound indicates that it's a boy. I hope that isn't a disappointment."

At that Cassi had to smile. "She has one boy and three girls. I don't think she'll be too unhappy to have another boy."

Renae nodded, but was too busy breathing through the contraction to answer aloud. When it was over, she began to sob softly. "I want Trent."

"He's on his way," Cassi said.

"Would you like something for the pain?" the doctor asked.

Renae shook her head. "My doctor once said that it could slow labor down. I don't want to risk that."

The doctor nodded. "That is true, but I'm keeping an eye on your baby. Let me know if you change your mind."

Renae's jaw clenched in determination. "I won't."

The doctor left them in the care of several nurses who seemed to know what they were doing. Renae's obvious pain made Cassi nervous; birth was something she had never been close to before. "Is there anything I can do?" she asked.

Renae didn't answer. Her pretty face was twisted in a grimace, and deep lines were etched around her mouth. She panted and writhed on the bed while tears streamed down her face and beads of sweat dotted her forehead.

When the contraction was over, she looked up at Cassi. "I'm so afraid! I don't want to lose my baby. I need Trent. I can't do this without him!" She gave a long, shuddering sigh, and Cassi patted her shoulder awkwardly.

"Oh, Renae, I want to help you. I'm here for you."

Renae nodded. "I know. But I can't stop this feeling of dread. I think I'm going to lose my baby." She said the last sentence under her breath so the nurses wouldn't hear and jump to reassure her. "Please, go see if Trent is here yet. I need a blessing."

"Okay," Cassi agreed and escaped gratefully from the room, though she knew that her effort was futile. Trent wouldn't arrive for another hour.

As she looked around the halls outside the delivery area, Cassi felt faint. She could never remember feeling so helpless. "Please, dear Father," she prayed aloud. "Please help Renae." She thought of her friend lying in fearful agony and knew that she had to return to her bedside, bringing nothing to help her. Tears rolled slowly down Cassi's cheeks. Despite the doctor's apparent confidence, she worried for the unborn baby.

She turned to go back down the hall, but out of the corner of her eye she saw a familiar figure approaching at a fast walk.

"Jared," she whispered, though he was too far off to hear her. She couldn't stop the relief flooding her body. Regardless of her personal feelings, Jared was an active priesthood holder and available, whereas Trent was not.

He came toward her quickly. "Is she all right?"

Cassi shook her head, not understanding why or how he was at the hospital, just aware that her prayer had been answered. "The placenta's coming loose. The doctor says she may have to have a C-section. He seems to have everything under control, but Renae is frightened. She keeps crying and calling for her husband." Cassi's voice broke on the last word. She looked up at Jared through her tears. "Please, could you give her a blessing?"

"I would be glad to," he said. "But wait just a minute." He turned his head around as if searching for something or someone. Cassi wondered briefly at the delay, but she soon had an answer as she saw Brother Larry Smithy hurrying toward them.

"Two times in one day, huh?" he said to Jared as he approached.

"Thanks for coming," Jared said.

Cassi didn't have time to consider the implications of what they were saying, but she filed the comments away for future study. What mattered was that they were there to help Renae when she needed it.

Within minutes they were covered in white and administering to Renae. Afterward, Cassi felt calm suffuse her being and noticed that Renae's tears had ceased. She was handling both her fear and the contractions much better.

"Thank you so much," Renae said.

"We are glad to be of help," Jared replied. "We'll be in the waiting room if you need us. We'll send your husband in as soon as he arrives. That way Cassi can stay with you."

Cassi remembered Renae's children. "He's bringing the other kids. He didn't stop to find someone to watch them. I said I'd take care of them."

Jared smiled. "We'll watch them until you come out. Larry has six kids of his own, and I have nineteen nieces and nephews. We'll manage."

Cassi looked at him gratefully. "But don't you have other business here?"

"No." Jared's intense blue eyes seem to bore into hers. "I saw you leave the auction and found out what happened from Boader. That's why I came; I thought maybe I could help. I called Larry on the way over."

Cassi bit her bottom lip. She felt terrible for having called Jared names behind his back and for suspecting him of foul play. It wasn't every man who would do what he had done for her and Renae.

"But the Buddha," she said.

"I jumped the bid to four hundred thousand. No one wanted to match it."

Four hundred thousand! That was one hundred thousand more than Cassi had been authorized to pay. Had she stayed, she would have lost anyway. "I'm glad you got it," she said sincerely. "I'm just sorry you didn't get it for less."

Jared shook his head. "What's money in the face of a new life?" he said softly. He turned and followed Larry out the door. Cassi stared after him long after the door had obscured him from view. How could she have been so wrong about him? She shook the thoughts away and returned to Renae's bedside.

"I told you he was all right," Renae said through her panting. Cassi marveled at how calm her friend looked now as compared to before the blessing. Logically she knew that the amount of pain hadn't changed, but Renae's ability to deal with it apparently had. The flow of blood from the placenta had also miraculously decreased.

An hour ticked by quickly. The nurses checked Renae several times and told her that she would soon be able to push.

"Hurry, Trent," Renae said under her breath as another contraction began. "Our baby can't wait for you."

As if he had somehow heard her, Trent burst into the room. "Renae!" His brown head was beside hers in an instant. "I'm here, honey." He held her hand through the contraction, directing Renae to breathe. Afterward he rubbed her shoulders gently. He knew exactly how to help, whereas Cassi hadn't.

Cassi sighed in relief. Trent looked up at her with the suggestion of a smile. "Rough day, Cassi?"

"Does it show?"

He nodded. "It's good to see you again. I'm glad you were here with her. Thanks."

Cassi shrugged. "I'm glad *you're* here." She hesitated. "I guess I'll go out and see the kids."

"No, don't go, Cassi," Renae called from the bed. "I mean, you're welcome to stay if you want."

Cassi did want to stay, but she hadn't been sure she was needed. She felt as though she now had a stake in the baby's life, and she wanted to see him safely into the world.

"But the kids," she said to give the parents a way out, just in case she was intruding.

"They're with your friends out there in the waiting room," Trent said. "They seem pretty capable. Besides, Scotty's nine. He's a good baby-sitter."

Cassi smiled. "Then I'd like to stay."

"It won't be much longer," said one of the nurses. "I'm going to page the doctor now."

Renae began to push. Her face went red with the effort, and at times she cried out with the pain. Soon Cassi could see the top of the head, covered in a mass of dark hair. She watched, praying silently. Finally, the baby's head emerged and the doctor quickly cleaned his face and suctioned his mouth. With the next contraction, the baby's whole body slipped free. Renae had her second baby boy!

Cassi stared with large eyes, almost unable to believe the miracle of life she had witnessed. Familiar longings welled up within her. Those too seemed like miracles in the light of the great pain Renae had suffered. What was it about a tiny, helpless baby that made a woman willing to withstand such agony? Cassi thought she could just barely understand the reasons; her arms ached to hold the baby that wasn't even hers.

Since the baby was early, the doctor immediately took him for tests. At Renae's insistence, Trent went with the baby to make sure he was all right. Cassi stayed with Renae as the placenta was delivered and the bed cleaned. Within a half an hour, Trent and the baby were back.

"Seven pounds!" Trent said as he came in the door. "Three weeks early and still seven pounds! And healthy as a horse." He lifted the baby into Renae's outstretched arms. Both parents had tears of joy in their eyes.

"My last baby was nearly eleven pounds," Renae told Cassi.

Shortly, in bounded four towheaded children, eagerly crowding around the bed to search out their new brother.

"Mom, he's wrinkled!" said four-year-old Janet.

"You'd be, too, if you'd been nine months in water," seven-year-old Andrea replied in a know-it-all voice.

"Can I hold him?" Scotty asked, followed by a chorus of me-too's from his sisters. Even two-year-old Sandy held out her arms for a chance. Trent supervised the two-minute holdings until each child had a turn. They brought to Cassi's mind the perfect image of the family she herself wanted. She backed away from the bed, determined to leave them to their happy moment.

Then, to Cassi's surprise, Trent plopped the baby into her arms.

"What!" she said, feeling awkward and privileged at the same time. "I don't know how to hold a newborn."

Renae laughed. "Don't worry, they're tougher than they look. Just support his head and you'll be okay."

Cassi cradled the baby, smelling his newness and feeling his warmth. His very existence was still a miracle to her. "He's so perfect," she said. She held the baby for as long as she dared, before reluctantly giving him back to Renae.

"So what are we going to name him?" Trent asked. "We hadn't thought of any boy names."

"Jared," Renae said without hesitation. "If Jared hadn't come to give me a blessing, I don't know that things would have turned out so well."

"Jared it is then," Trent agreed. "And what was the other fellow's name?"

"Larry," Cassi said.

"How about Jared Larry Benson?" Trent proposed. Renae nodded in agreement, and the kids cheered.

The doctor came in again, looking pleased with all the celebrating. "Everything checks out great," he said to Renae. "You lost more blood than usual, but I think we can release you in the morning. Of course, you'll want to report any odd signs to your doctor and take the baby in for a checkup there."

"Thanks," Trent and Renae chimed together. The doctor left, promising to send a nurse for the birth certificate information.

"Well, kids, I think it's time for you to all go back with Cassi to her hotel. I'm going to stay here with Mom and baby Jared. We'll come pick you up in the morning."

The kids had seen Cassi a few times each year since their births and felt comfortable with her, even if they didn't know her well. The idea of the hotel added measurably to their excitement.

"Can we watch TV?" asked Andrea as they left the birthing room.

"Of course. They have cable and everything."

"Can we order some food?" asked Scotty, who carried little Sandy in his arms.

"Sure. Or we can go for some hamburgers on the way home."

"Yeah!" the children said together.

"And some candy?" added Janet.

"Why not?"

"Can we play on the elevator and race in the halls?" Andrea asked.

Cassi knew she was being tested. "Sure," she replied. "As long as I get a turn to push the buttons and a head start in the race. I'll be carrying Sandy, you know." The children giggled.

They were still laughing when they reached the waiting room, where Cassi was surprised to see Jared and Larry lounging on the couches. At least she had an opportunity to thank them. "He's beautiful and healthy," she said. "Seven pounds and twenty inches. They're naming him Jared Larry Benson." Both men smiled and slapped each other on the back in congratulations.

"I thought you'd be gone by now," Cassi added. "But I'm glad you're not, so I can tell you thanks. I don't know what we would have done without you."

Jared shrugged, seemingly embarrassed at her words. "We couldn't go without giving you this," he said, handing her a diaper bag. He pointed to Sandy in Scotty's arms. "Sandy here is potty training, and you may need a change or two of clothing. Her father said there were diapers for nighttime."

"Great," Cassi grimaced slightly. She had forgotten that Sandy was only two and hadn't mastered bathroom techniques. That made her wonder, how did you potty train a child? She had zero experience in that field. "Thanks again." She took the bag and motioned to the children. "Come on, gang." She started down the corridor with the children and men right behind her.

"Uh, can I give you a ride?" Jared asked. "You did come in the ambulance, didn't you?"

Cassi stopped in mid-stride. "Oh, I'd forgotten. If it's not too much trouble . . . uh, I could get a taxi." She was upset at herself for not remembering about her rental car. All of a sudden, she found herself dependent upon a person she had despised only a few hours earlier. "But I did promise them hamburgers and candy . . ."

"There's an In and Out Burgers just down the street," Larry said helpfully. "The food isn't expensive and my kids love it. They're too young for indigestion."

"So are we, right?" Jared asked the kids, winking at Cassi. She felt happiness seep into her being. Maybe she was just borrowing Renae's life for an evening, but she would enjoy it while it lasted.

They bid Larry goodbye at the hospital doors and piled into Jared's four-door rental car. The two smallest had to share a seat belt, but soon they were happily eating hamburgers at the fast-food restaurant Larry had recommended. Everyone also had a shake and a dessert. Cassi was surprised at how voracious the children were; by the time they left the restaurant, she was nearly forty dollars poorer and the children so full they could barely walk.

The next stop was the store, where Scotty insisted on pushing the grocery cart. Cassi carried Sandy in one arm and with the other filled the basket with chips and candy, muttering, "I hope Renae doesn't kill me."

Jared laughed. "Hey, it's a celebration. It isn't every day that you have a new baby brother."

"Especially one named Jared," Cassi added. Their eyes locked, and suddenly Cassi couldn't breathe. She looked away, burying her face in Sandy's blonde hair, fighting the emotions that threatened to overwhelm her. Why should she feel so much for this man? What if he didn't feel the same? The insecurity she always felt around the opposite sex overtook her, and her smile vanished.

"Let's get some yogurt and fruit for breakfast," she said to no one in particular, shifting the toddler in her arms. Sandy's eyes drooped as she laid her head against Cassi's shoulder.

Cassi risked a glance at Jared and saw that he was still watching her, his expression veiled. What was he thinking? There was no time to dwell on the matter. She felt a warm flood wash down her dress, soaking into the thin rayon material almost instantly. Sandy's eyes jerked open.

"Pee pee. Oh, noooo. Baby wet!"

Sure enough, both Sandy and Cassi were soaked.

CHAPTER 11

Cassi looked down at her dress, shaking her head in disbelief. Sandy looked up, waiting for her reaction; obviously her parents didn't appreciate it when she had an accident. People in the supermarket paused momentarily as they passed, trying to hide their smiles. Only the mothers nodded sympathetically.

The moments ticked by, and no one said a word. A small grin played around Jared's mouth, but he didn't know Cassi well enough to let it show completely. Like the others, he waited to see how she would react.

"Ah-oh." Sandy twisted and pointed down at Cassi's dress.

Cassi threw back her head and laughed. "Oh, Sandy. It's okay. You were asleep. You could hardly stop yourself. But boy do we stink!"

"Cassi stinky," Sandy said, a smile creeping over her small face.

"You should have taken her to the bathroom at the restaurant," Scotty offered. "She drank a whole soda. Dad says it goes right through her like water."

"I have to go to the bathroom, too," Janet said.

Cassi shoved her wallet into Jared's hands and reached down to grab hold of Janet. "I'll meet you in the car."

After she left, Jared laughed, loud and long.

"What's so funny?" Scotty asked.

"She took it pretty well for her first time. The first time one of my nephews did that to me, I blew my top. Of course, I was only about seventeen then. I soon got used to it. Let's see," he looked up in the air, counting something Scotty couldn't see, "I think I've been peed on eight times now, and I don't even have children!"

"Yuck!" Andrea said.

"Yeah. And the last time I didn't even flinch!" Jared added. Scotty and Andrea nodded, properly impressed.

"Come on now, let's go get Cassi some yogurt and some fruit." The children followed after Jared obediently.

They were putting the groceries into the trunk of the car when Cassi and the girls came out of the store carrying small stacks of paper toweling. As they passed a black sedan near the store's entrance, Janet tried to peer inside the darkened windows, but Cassi pulled her along. Jared stared at the car. Hadn't he seen it at the hamburger joint?

"Well, we're here," Cassi said. If nothing else, she and Sandy were wetter than before from the attempt at washing.

"What are those for?" Jared asked, pointing at the towels.

Cassi looked at him, chagrined. "To put on the seat so Sandy doesn't get it wet. After we were in the bathroom, I realized I should have come out here for her change of clothes, but . . ." She shrugged as her voice trailed off.

"It's not cold, and in my experience, most kids don't really care about being wet unless they're cold."

"That's what I was hoping." Cassi looked down at her dress and then back to Jared. "I'll give us both a bath when we get to the hotel."

As their eyes met, Jared felt a tingle run through his body. With a brief memory flash, he remembered how long the drive to the hospital had seemed after receiving the note about Renae, and how relieved Cassi had looked when he arrived. Her face had been whiter than the hospital smock she wore over her suit dress, and her hair disheveled—just the way he liked it. The Cassi he was getting to know fascinated him. When she had teased him in the store about babies named Jared and he had looked into her eyes, there had been a connection between them. Then she had looked away with some veiled emotion in those eyes, just as she did now. Why? Was this a game? Jared wanted to pull her around and make her look at him, but he didn't dare.

"Come on," he said brusquely. He hated not being able to control his feelings, and being unsure that he even wanted to control them made the situation even more strained.

He opened the door and watched Cassi strap Sandy into the seat belt. The other kids piled in and fastened their own belts. Jared waited to shut Cassi's door before going around the car to his own seat. They were silent nearly all the way back to the hotel. The children were sleepy, and both adults were intent on their private thoughts.

I've been independent so long, Jared thought. *Maybe I'm afraid of caring about someone.* Jared didn't like to admit fear. Then suddenly he had it! Could the look Cassi had given him in the store reflect her own fear of caring for him? He glanced sideways at her. It was at least remotely possible.

Feeling his gaze, she turned toward him. "Larry mentioned that you'd been at the hospital twice today. May I ask why?"

Jared swallowed the sudden lump that came to his throat at the question. "Sister Martin, a good friend of mine, died this morning."

"I'm sorry. That's why you were late to the auction."

"And why you got the *Mother and Baby.*"

Cassi smiled. "I might have gotten it anyway."

"Maybe." She appeared so content that Jared didn't want to bring up the possibility of buying it from her—yet.

Jared drove back to the hotel in a roundabout fashion, and not only because he enjoyed Cassi's company. At each turn, he checked his rearview mirror to see if the black sedan from the store still followed. It did. Anxiety rose in his chest, and he forced himself to drive casually. Could this sedan have anything to do with the warning note he had received? Was the *it* the note mentioned the Buddha?

"Is something wrong?" Cassi asked.

"No," he said.

Jared was relieved to see that the black sedan didn't follow them into the hotel parking garage. He warily searched the area before opening the doors for Cassi and the children. Janet had fallen asleep, but awakened as he opened the door. He picked her up.

"What about the food?" Scotty asked. "There's too many bags for me to carry alone."

"Leave it all," Jared said. "I'll come back for it." His real reason was that he wanted to search for the black sedan.

Once inside the hotel, Andrea's eyes grew wide. "It's so big!"

"Escavator," Janet said sleepily from Jared's arms. "I wanna ride the escavator."

"You mean escalator," Scotty said. "But there isn't one."

"But there's an elevator," Cassi said. She was loaded with the diaper bag and little Sandy, who was now wide awake.

"Goodie!" Janet clapped her hands.

That led to ten minutes of riding the elevator, with each child pressing his favorite number on the panel. Cassi was amazed to find that each child claimed at least four favorite numbers. "Whee!" Janet and Sandy squealed each time the elevator plunged to the bottom. They seemed never to tire of the game. When people got on the elevator with them, the children were remarkably well-behaved.

"Which floor do you want?" Scotty would ask. Then the child whose turn it was would push the appropriate button.

"Such cute children you have," an older lady said to them. "What a lovely family."

Jared only nodded, but to his surprise Cassi glanced at him wickedly and turned to the woman. "Thank you," she said sweetly. "We'd like at least two more. We *love* children." Jared nearly laughed aloud, and he quickly shook his head at Andrea, who had opened her mouth to correct the lady's assumption.

The woman nodded. "That's good. There are not many people who're unselfish enough to have many children. But they're such a blessing, especially when you're my age. Why, only the other day three of my children . . ." The lady rattled on while Cassi nodded in agreement. When the lady left and the door safely shut again, they burst out laughing.

"Are you always this impulsive?" Jared asked. He had enjoyed the charade more than he cared to admit.

Cassi's smile vanished. "I'm afraid so," she said regretfully. Her eyes looked far away, as if remembering something from long ago—something painful. Jared wanted to take her into his arms and comfort her.

"It was fun," he said, breaking the sudden tension. "Who's turn is it next?"

"Mine," Cassi said, reaching around the children to push the button to her floor. "It's time to get ready for bed. And I may be almost dry, but I don't smell too good."

"Stinky Cassi," Sandy agreed.

"Awww," the other children said together, their faces falling. "We don't want to go to bed!"

"But this'll be the best part!" Jared said. "You settle in while I go get the goodies from the car."

"Then we can watch TV, can't we, Cassi? You said so at the hospital." Andrea looked up at Cassi with pleading eyes.

"Of course. A promise is a promise."

Jared tried to catch Cassi's eye, but she refused to look at him. He knew something he'd said had saddened her, but he couldn't think of what. He filed the thought away. Perhaps someday he would ask her.

The fact that Jared was thinking of Cassi in future terms made him blink in amazement. What was he thinking? He had only two more days in L.A. and then it would be back to New York with the Buddha. Cassi would be out of his life forever.

Thinking of the Buddha made him remember Laranda and her anxiousness to have it. He still didn't understand her strange fascination for the ugly statue. It wasn't the cost; he had spent millions of dollars on various objects before, and she had never seemed to care. No, there was something odd about the Buddha, something Jared would make it a point to find out whether she confided in him or not. Meanwhile, he wondered what Laranda would say when he told her he wasn't flying home tomorrow as planned, but staying for Sister Martin's funeral. It wasn't likely that she would be happy, but she would at least understand. As soon as he got the children settled, he would call her.

The elevator opened and the children filed out. The long, deserted hallway stretched before them invitingly. "Wait, wait, wait," Cassi ordered. "Remember our deal at the hospital? I get a head start." The children laughed. They had completely forgotten about Andrea's desire to run in the halls.

"Our room is number 502, the second to the last on the left," she said, pointing until everyone understood which door. "Whoever wins gets to have first choice of where to sleep." She turned to Jared rather stiffly. "Would you like to be the referee?"

"No way," he said, shaking his head. "I'm going to win this race!" He saw Cassi's dark eyes widen in surprise.

"You are?" Her hesitant smile made him laugh.

"Me too! Carry me, Jared! I want to win!" Janet shouted, bouncing up and down beside him. Jared picked her up.

"Okay then, Scotty," Cassi said. "You give the count. No fair going early." She slipped off her high heels and put them in Sandy's diaper bag. Then she picked up both the little girl and the bag and walked down the hall a short way. "Okay, I'm ready."

"On your mark, get set, *go!*" said Scotty. In a flash, he and Andrea were running down the hall. Cassi in her bare feet was ahead of them, with Jared and Janet slightly behind.

"Go, Jared, go!" urged Janet, kicking his sides in her excitement. Jared ran faster, pulling ahead of the children and Cassi. He noticed that Cassi kept looking back at Scotty and Andrea, whose little faces were red with exertion as they ran. Scotty pulled ahead of Cassi, and Jared slowed slightly until he was neck and neck with the boy. At the very end, Jared slowed even more to let Scotty pull slightly ahead.

"I won! I won!" shouted the boy. Jared stopped, only to feel Andrea barrel into him, knocking him sideways and in front of Cassi, who tripped over him. They all fell to the floor in a mass of tangled arms and legs. Jared saw Cassi struggling to keep Sandy from hitting the floor and her dress from creeping up any further than it already had. He averted his eyes, but not before he had noticed that her legs could easily rival Laranda's.

A cough drew their attention, and they looked up to see an older couple staring down at them. "My word!" said the woman with a disapproving frown on her face. "Humph!" She turned and stalked down the hall. The old man shrugged and winked at them. "Pay her no mind. We did crazier things than that when we were young. Enjoy yourselves." He chuckled to himself and followed his wife's stiff back down the hall.

Jared jumped to his feet and reached to help Cassi stand. "That was great," he said.

She smiled at him. "It was." She found her keys and opened the door.

"But I won!" Scotty said.

"Next time I'm gonna win," Andrea retorted.

"Hey, go see what cartoons are on," Cassi said to distract them. "We have the Disney channel." The children whooped and ran to the television set.

"I'll be right back with the groceries," Jared said, setting Janet inside the door.

"Thanks. Hopefully we'll be all clean before you get back." She wrinkled her nose and looked down at her disheveled dress. "I hope dry cleaning gets out—"

"Oh, it does," he interjected. "Believe me, I know. Just ask Scotty and Andrea." He gave her another smile and went down the hall.

Before going to the car, he stopped in his room one floor below to change his clothes. He gently tossed the cellular phone he usually carried on the nightstand by the bed before removing his suit. "I've got to call Laranda," he said aloud, then promptly forgot. As he dressed in jeans and a casual button-down shirt, he noticed that it was nearly nine o'clock. How the time had flown when he was with Cassi! He began to whistle, remembering the race and how he had landed close enough to Cassi to smell her subtle perfume. She was as appealing up close as far away.

He was nearly out the door before he remembered to get a T-shirt for Scotty. He knew the children didn't have pajamas with them, and Scotty surely wouldn't want to use anything of Cassi's or his mother's. Still whistling, he picked out one of his favorite shirts, the color of midnight blue.

His heart felt light as he retrieved the snacks from the car. To his relief, there was no trace of the mysterious black sedan. *It was all in my imagination,* he thought as he made his way back to Cassi's room. When he arrived, she and Sandy were still in the bathroom. The other children were spread out on the floor in front of the TV in a mound of blankets and pillows from the beds.

"Here. Sleep in this, if you want." Jared threw the shirt at Scotty.

"Thanks," Scotty said. He pointed to his sisters, who were already wearing obviously feminine T-shirts, one a bright yellow, the other the color of peaches. "Cassi's white one was dirty." He bent his head to study the fighter jet on Jared's shirt. "Wow, this is cool."

Jared smiled. "Keep it. It's from New York. I'll get another one."

"Gee, thanks! I love it." His smile nearly covered his whole face.

Jared turned from the boy and set the groceries on the table. The kids crowded around to choose their favorite snacks. Over their heads he could see two double beds, and he wondered idly which one was Cassi's. As he helped the children, the bathroom door clicked open and Cassi herself emerged with a towel-covered Sandy in her arms. She was clad in faded jeans and a copper-colored T-shirt that set off the highlights in her hair. Little tendrils of hair around her face were wet, but still curly. Jared wondered if those were the curls she had added gel to in his absence. He mused that maybe they had been going straight, and she had hurried to correct them before he could notice. He found the idea wasn't as bothersome as it had once been.

Cassi set the baby down and reached for the diaper bag. "Come here, Sandy. Let's put a diaper on so you can go to bed." Cassi motioned, but the little girl ran to Jared and hid behind him. He picked her up.

Jared laughed. "You said the dreaded 'B' word," he said.

Cassi groaned.

Sandy's towel fell, and Jared could see her round bottom as she clutched his leg. To Jared, there was nothing so adorable as a bare baby bottom.

"Come on, Sandy. I've had just about enough accidents for today." Cassi's voice was tired. Jared noticed that she wasn't wearing makeup. She looked younger now than she had before.

"Here, I'll do it," he offered, holding up a hand to catch the disposable diaper as she threw it to him.

"Might as well. I've never done it before," she muttered.

Jared didn't consider himself an expert, but he had changed a few diapers. His sisters took great delight in teaching him exactly where the tabs should go. Diapering was an art in itself, but it was easily mastered if you knew a few tricks.

"Do you want some chips?" he asked Sandy. She nodded, and he took her to the table to choose her spoils. She picked a candy bar and a handful of Doritos.

"Now you just lie down right here," Jared said, laying her on the soft carpet, "and I'll put your diaper on. Then we won't sleep. We'll watch TV." Sandy lay calmly on the carpet chewing her chips as Jared diapered her.

"You're great with kids," Cassi said, sinking onto the couch behind him.

"Well, I've got four sisters who love to teach me what they know," he said.

"You have only sisters?"

"No, I've got one brother. He's the youngest. He just got married last year. His wife had a baby last week. What about you?"

"One older brother, no sisters. My parents are converts. They didn't believe in large families. They were both born in California, but now they live in Utah near Robert—that's my brother—who has five kids."

"What about you? Are you a convert?"

"Yes, when I was sixteen. My parents didn't join, though, until after my mission."

Jared's interest was piqued. While more and more women were serving missions, it was still rare enough to be intriguing. "Where'd you go?"

"England. That's where I became interested in art. I met a member there who's one of the foremost authorities on Indian art."

"Grant Truebekon?"

"That's right."

"Wow! I didn't know he was a member."

"Most people don't; he's rather private. But he taught me a lot. After my mission, I went and studied with him."

Jared snapped his fingers. "That's why you knew so much about the Buddha."

"Yes. I'm not as good as Grant is, but I know my stuff." Cassi's eyebrows wrinkled. "And you know, that Buddha didn't seem quite right to me. I've studied larger-than-life photos of similar Buddhas from the same era, and there was a mark on the base that didn't . . ." She shrugged. "I guess the auction organizers know what they're doing. I mean, it comes with certified papers."

Jared nodded. "It seems that it came up for sale just before the auction deadline. Someone in India had it. When Laranda, the owner of the gallery I work for, found out it was up for auction, she just about went crazy. I guess she has a buyer who's willing to pay big for it."

"Then it's not odd for her to act that way. Money does strange things to people." Cassi fished into Sandy's diaper bag and retrieved a small undershirt. She handed it to Jared.

Jared took the shirt and looked down at Sandy. She was still lying peacefully on the floor, but her head was twisted so she could watch the TV. He helped her to her feet. "That can't be comfortable," he said, pulling the shirt over her head.

"Gumfobull," Sandy repeated through a mouthful of chips. She climbed onto Jared's lap and snuggled next to him trustingly.

They watched TV in silence for a while, enjoying the expressions on the children's faces more than the Disney film itself. Jared noticed that Cassi glanced at him occasionally, as if wanting to say something but not knowing if she should.

Finally she took a deep breath. "You know, Linden Johansen, my employer, was pretty adamant about me getting the Buddha. He acted strange." She bit her lip as if unwilling to say anything further. Then she yawned pointedly. "I'm really tired."

Her comment was addressed to no one in particular, but Jared felt that she wanted him to leave. Reluctantly, he glanced down at Sandy, who was asleep in his arms, clutching her unopened candy bar. He didn't want to leave, but he wanted to respect Cassi's wishes. Besides, he needed to call Laranda, who would already be furious at his delay. Yet at that moment, he found he didn't care about Laranda's anger; what bothered him more was the sudden veil which seemed to come down over Cassi's face.

"Yes, it's getting late for them," he said, motioning to the children on the floor. All were asleep except for Scotty, who was quickly losing a valiant fight against his heavy eyelids. "Shall I help you carry them to the beds?"

Cassi shook her head. "I don't think so. One thing I learned with my Cub Scouts is that sleeping on the floor doesn't damage children the way it does adults." She chuckled, and for an instant the veil was gone.

"You work with the Cubs?" Jared asked. He carefully laid Sandy on the couch and stood up.

"Yes."

She didn't offer anything further, and Jared was beginning to feel desperate. He really liked Cassi, despite their differences. She seemed special somehow, unlike any woman he had ever known.

He turned and walked to the door. "Uh . . . I'm going to be in town until Wednesday for Sister Martin's funeral. What about you?" Jared was hinting that he would like to see her again, but Cassi seemed oblivious to the inference.

"I'm leaving tomorrow after Renae and Trent come for the children. I have work waiting for me in San Diego."

"Yeah. Well, it was nice meeting you." He opened the door.

"Uh, Jared?"

"Yes?"

"Thanks for what you did at the hospital."

"I'm glad I could help."

Cassi shut the door and Jared stood in the hall, feeling slightly lost and shut out from the warmth of companionship. He shrugged off the feeling and walked down the hall to the elevator, thinking of how he would explain his overdue call to Laranda. His watch told him it was way past even Laranda's bedtime, and he knew she wouldn't be in the best of tempers.

As he left the elevator on his floor, a strange feeling overcame him and an abrupt fear rippled through his body. *Leave,* something whispered in his soul. He was near his door now, and unsure of what to do.

"Leave," the voice said more clearly.

Jared hesitated. Finally he backed down the hall, watching his room. As he did so, the door opened and two strong-looking men in suits came out. One had a hooked nose beneath his glittering black eyes, but other than that, they had no distinguishing features. Their eyes widened as they saw Jared, and in an instant they were on him.

Jared fought desperately. He was physically fit because of his daily workouts in a New York gym, though terribly unprepared to fight two large and experienced men. His head reeled with pain and felt like it had just exploded as they hit him again and again. Still he fought on. Every now and then, his fist connected with one of his opponents and he felt a satisfying crunch, but those moments were rare. After what seemed an eternity, the pummeling stopped.

"The Buddha," grunted the man with a hooked nose.

"I don't have it," Jared said as he lay slumped on the carpet. He felt blood from his nose and mouth trickle down his lips and chin. A river of red also flowed over his face from a throbbing cut above his left eye.

The man held Jared while his companion slowly drew back his fist. Jared closed his eyes, waiting for the burst of pain. Before it came, the elevator bell rang and the door slid open. The men dropped Jared and sprinted to the door leading to the stairs. He moaned with relief. A couple left the elevator and ran to him, both speaking at once so that Jared couldn't tell who said what. "What happened? We saw those men running. Did they do this to you? I'm calling hotel security."

The wife ran to their room while the man waited nervously with Jared, eyeing the door to the stairs. Jared's body hurt all over, and he sighed deeply.

"Is there anyone you want me to call?" the man asked, handing him a tissue.

Jared shook his head and wiped at his face, but the man's remark reminded him of Laranda. He lurched to his feet and reached into his pants pocket for his hotel key. "They came from my room," he said absently. He walked to the door and opened it, with the stranger still beside him.

Nothing in the room had been disturbed. Even Jared's cellular phone lay untouched on the nightstand where he had left it before retrieving the treats for Renae's children. He picked it up and pressed the pre-programmed number for Laranda's home, then sank to the couch, motioning for the man to sit with him.

"No. I'll wait near the door for my wife and the security people."

"Thanks."

After two rings, the phone picked up. "Hello, Jared, is that you?"

"Yes, Laranda, it's me."

"What's wrong? You sound faint. Are you sick? Why aren't you here? I thought you were leaving tonight. You did get the Buddha, didn't you?"

"Of course I got it. And the reason I didn't come is because a friend of mine went to the hospital. I've been there all evening."

"So you're coming home tomorrow?"

"Uh, there's been a little change." Jared sighed wearily. "Another friend of mine died this morning, and her funeral is Wednesday. I need to be there."

"So come home tomorrow and fly back again. I'll pay."

"Laranda, that's not all. I was attacked tonight, just a few minutes ago. Someone wanted the Buddha. They must have thought I had picked it up already. And I would have if I hadn't been at the hospital."

"So where's the Buddha?" Laranda's voice was tense.

"Relax. I said I didn't pick it up. The auction security will hold it for me until tomorrow morning, then I'll put it in the hotel safe."

"Are you okay?" Laranda's question came so belatedly that Jared knew his welfare was only of secondary concern to her.

"No, actually not. I've been beaten pretty badly, or maybe I would fly home tomorrow just to give you your Buddha. As it is, I don't think I'll make it."

"Yes, you should rest," Laranda said. "I'm really sorry this happened." Her voice did sound sorry, and Jared silently forgave her earlier preoccupation with the Buddha; after all, her percentage of four hundred thousand dollars would bring them both a lot of money. "But hurry home," she added. "I need that Buddha before any more of your friends drop dead and keep you there even longer. What kind of friends do you have, anyway?"

Jared stifled a sigh. "Oh, that reminds me. I met a woman here who knows a lot about Indian art. She thought there was something odd about the Buddha. It could be there's something fishy about this deal."

"Surely not. We bought it from a reputable firm, and—"

"Even so, while I'm here maybe I should check it out."

"No, don't. It's better to wait until you come back here, where our lawyer can be present. Besides, it just so happens that my buyer is an expert on the subject. She'll soon tell us if there's a problem."

Jared shrugged, though Laranda couldn't see him. "Whatever you want. It's your Buddha." He looked up to see two men from hotel security and the night manager hovering by the door. "Well, I've got to go. I'll see you Wednesday afternoon."

He hung up the phone and began to answer questions. The men appeared shocked as he told his story, including the part about the black sedan following him from the store. The manager wanted to call the police, but Jared shook his head. While he was talking, his thoughts had roamed to the men who had attacked him. They had been professionals; nothing in his room was disturbed, though Jared felt in his gut that it had been methodically searched just as surely as he had been attacked. Now he was worried about Cassi. She had been with him most of the evening, and it was entirely possible that the hook-nosed man and his companion had been the ones following them in the black sedan. They might suspect that the Buddha was with her, and that meant she and the children were in danger. Jared's heart constricted at the thought.

"Of course we won't charge you for your stay here, and we'll move you to another room," the hotel manager droned on anxiously.

"That'll be fine," Jared said. "But I need something from the hotel safe."

"Now?"

"Now." Jared's voice was determined. His attackers might come back for Cassi or for him, but he would be prepared.

CHAPTER 12

The room seemed strangely empty after Jared left. While Cassi had said good-bye to him at the door, Scotty had finally given himself up to sleep, and she was alone. After switching off the TV, she went to the phone to call Linden. As she dialed, she recalled how he had told her to find out who bought the Buddha, but not to contact the person. His tone had inferred danger of some sort. Cassi had remembered his warning when Jared had been sitting on the couch with her. A chill had run up her spine, and she had wanted him out as quickly as possible so that she could call Linden. Now she wondered: could Jared be part of something sinister? Even dangerous? Seeing him with the sleeping Sandy and remembering his help at the hospital, she didn't want to believe it. But there was definitely something strange about the Buddha and how people were reacting to it.

"Hello?"

"Hi, Linden. It's me, Cassi." Cradling the phone between her shoulder and ear, Cassi pulled the fruit and yogurt from the grocery bag and put it into the refrigerator. She felt a touch of tenderness as she realized that Jared had remembered the yogurt while she had been in the store's bathroom with Sandy and Janet.

"Goodness, where have you been? I've left messages at the hotel."

"I'm sorry. I just got in, and I didn't ask for my messages. Renae had her baby three weeks early, and there were complications. I've been at the hospital with her." Cassi found her wallet at the bottom of the grocery bag. She opened it and saw that Jared had not used her money to buy the groceries. *How could a considerate man like him be involved in something wrong?* she thought.

"Is she okay?"

"Yes, both she and the baby are doing fine."

"That's a relief." He paused before adding, "Well, how did the auction go?"

"I didn't get the Buddha. I had to run out in the middle of the auction because of Renae, but I wouldn't have gotten it anyway. It sold for four hundred thousand."

"Who bought it?"

"A buyer for the Garrettson Gallery in New York."

"Ah, Garrettson's. That explains a little bit."

"Explains what? Linden, what's going on? There's something strange about the Buddha, isn't there? It didn't seem quite right, yet it was certified by the auction authorities. Still, something on the base was out of place. You don't want to know what gallery bought it just to try to get it from them later, do you? Tell me! What's going on?"

"Okay, listen. Something is going on, but I want you out of it. Come home now."

"But Jared seems so nice. He was with me at the hospital. He's a member of my church, you see. I'm almost sure he wouldn't be into anything illegal."

"Jared?"

"The buyer for Garrettson's."

"Cassi, stay away from him!" Linden practically yelled. "Don't go anywhere near him! I don't care what religion he claims to be. Many wrongs have been committed in the name of God. Just come back, and I'll take care of the mess with the Buddha."

Fear clutched Cassi's heart. "But why?"

"Will you listen? It's dangerous. Please, Cassi, I'll explain later."

"Okay. I'm leaving tomorrow. But I do know Jared isn't leaving until Wednesday."

"Oh? What'll he do with the Buddha?"

"Well, we have to pick up our purchases from the auction by tomorrow morning, so he'll probably put it in the hotel safe. And that reminds me. I did buy two pieces that will bring a good profit, but I really have fallen in love with one of them."

Linden chuckled. "A woman after my own heart. You're going to end up with more art objects than money."

"Just like you? That'll be okay. Well, can I have it at cost?"

"Of course. But, Cassi, remember what I said. Stay away from that man!"

Cassi hung up the phone, trying to reconcile Linden's fear of Jared with the man she had begun to know. Was he involved somehow with the Buddha, or was he an innocent caught in between like herself?

She dressed in a long white nightgown made of silk-like nylon material and turned off the lights. Instead of going to bed, she lay down on the couch next to little Sandy, who smelled like the soap Cassi had used to wash her small body. She snuggled closer and sighed contentedly. The bed's comfort held nothing over cuddling with this precious toddler—at least as long as she had a diaper on.

Half an hour passed, yet it seemed only minutes until someone was banging on her door. Cassi jerked awake, feeling her earlier fear return. She felt her way to the door in the dark as quickly as her sleep-filled mind allowed. "Who is it?" she called. One hand reached out to flood the small entryway with light.

"It's Jared. Cassi, are you okay?" he said urgently. "I need to talk to you."

"I'm fine, but I'm not dressed. I was just sleeping. Come back tomorrow."

"I can't. I need to make sure you're okay."

"Of course I'm okay."

"Then open the door and let me see."

Cassi remembered Linden's warnings, and her heart began to thud heavily. "No, Jared. I'm not dressed."

"Well, put on some clothes, for heaven's sake! I'll wait." His voice sounded frustrated. "But I'm not leaving until you open the door. Even if I have to kick it down or get hotel security here to open it." He was silent a minute then, "Please, Cassi. I was attacked when I went to my room—by two men with guns. They said something about the Buddha. I was worried they might come here because we were together this evening. Is that why you're not opening the door? Are they there now? I swear if you don't open the door, I'm calling the police!"

His voice sounded so worried that Cassi felt her own fear subside. She unlocked the door, leaving the upper chain still hooked. Jared was outside waiting anxiously, and Cassi gasped when she saw his bruised and battered face. He was wearing the same outfit, except that now a Levi jacket topped his shirt. His eyes were even more startling than before against the dark blue color of the jacket. Cassi closed the door again and unlocked the chain, opening it wide, hoping that her impulsiveness wasn't getting her into trouble.

"Come in," she said.

"Thanks." His eyes traveled over her nightgown, and Cassi felt her face burn. It wasn't that her nightgown was immodest, but its very nature was suggestive. His eyes also roamed over her hair, and she wondered if he noticed how disheveled it was. Jared turned his gaze to the sleeping children, then he searched the apartment with Cassi staring after him. He wasn't satisfied until every possible hiding place had been inspected, including under the beds, the closet, and the bathroom.

"I'll wait outside until morning," he said, avoiding looking at her directly. Cassi got the distinct feeling that he was embarrassed to see her dressed in her nightgown.

"But what if they come back and jump you again?"

He opened his jacket to reveal a revolver in a holster under his arm. Cassi's eyes grew luminous. Jared shrugged. "I've got a license for it, though I usually don't conceal it. I'm armed so I can take care of the art items I buy."

"I usually just send them with a security company," Cassi said. "They guarantee delivery."

"Well, I've never had any problem until now," Jared said. "And it always brought extra profits." He shook his head and sighed. Turning, he walked stiffly to the door.

"Uh, Jared, you could stay here and sleep on the couch." Cassi could hardly believe her own words.

He shook his head. "I want to be awake if they come back."

"Well, we can push the couch in front of the door, and they'll wake you up if they try to get in."

Jared shook his head again, but Cassi was already picking up baby Sandy and carrying her to a bed. "Don't be ridiculous, Jared. If they do come back and find you guarding my door, they're going to assume I've got the Buddha. Then I'll really be in danger."

He sighed and nodded wearily. "Okay, thanks." He helped her push the couch in front of the door and immediately he sank onto it, grimacing as he moved. Cassi could see that he was in pain.

"Does it hurt?" she asked unnecessarily.

"Yes," he said with a groan.

"I have a first-aid kit. You know, from the seventy-two hour kit we're always supposed to have on hand." Cassi went to the dresser, opened the bottom drawer, and pulled out a small backpack. She brought it to the couch, where Jared's lanky form spread out submissively. "Thank goodness I have some butterfly bandages," she said.

Gently, she washed and bandaged his face. Some of the wounds looked pretty deep, particularly the inch-long horizontal cut above his eye, but the special bandages should close the wound efficiently. His lip was also swollen and the left eye was going black, but there was nothing she could do for either, or for the bruises she knew must be covering the rest of his body.

"I guess the note really was a warning," she said lightly.

Jared grabbed her arm and held it in a viselike grip. "What note?"

Cassi hurriedly explained. "Sam Boader got one, too," she added.

"I wonder if those men sent them," Jared said.

Cassi wasn't about to admit that she had suspected him. "It doesn't matter now," she said. "You're safe. That's the main thing. Just hold still; I'm almost finished."

As she re-packed her supplies, Cassi saw Jared's eyes droop. She smiled faintly, no longer feeling any fear. Whatever Jared was, he wasn't a danger to her or the children.

She stood up and went to the lights, but only dimmed them. If something did happen during the night, the lights could come in handy. Before getting into her bed with Sandy, she went around to the children, making sure that each was covered with a thin blanket.

"Cassi?" Jared's voice said hesitantly.

"Yes?"

"You look really beautiful. I just wanted you to know."

Cassi was flabbergasted at the unexpected compliment. She didn't know what to say. "Thanks," she said finally. A comfortable silence filled the room as sleep overcame them.

CHAPTER 13

The next morning, Jared awoke to the sound of giggling. For a brief moment he didn't remember where he was, but the laughter of children reminded him of home. A smile stretched his sore lips, the pain rousing him completely as the laughter had failed to do. He sat up, feeling his head pounding and remembering vividly the events of the night before.

Scotty, Andrea, and Janet were on the floor in front of the TV, laughing at the cartoon animals that filled the screen. Janet saw him and came toward the couch.

"See, Jared? See that rabbit? He's sooo funny."

Jared watched for a moment. "He sure is, honey."

Janet stared at him with the curiosity of a child. "What happened to your face?"

"I ran into some men in the hall," Jared said vaguely, not wanting to lie, but also not wanting to tell her about the fight.

"You should watch where you're going." Her eyes wandered back to the TV.

"That I should," Jared agreed solemnly. He remembered only too well how the Spirit had warned him to leave, and how his failure to obey had gotten him into trouble. He was grateful that at least he had slowed enough to come across the men in the hall instead of in his room, where they could have beaten him without interruption.

"How come you and Cassi don't sleep together?" Janet asked suddenly. Once again her innocent face was turned toward him. "Are you in a fight?"

Jared shook his head. "No, Janet. Cassi and I aren't married. You don't sleep together until you get married."

"Oh, yeah. But when you get married and have a baby, can I come sleep over at your house, like today? This is real fun."

"I . . . uh . . . well, yes." Jared took the easy way out. The relationship developing between him and Cassi was hard enough for him to understand; he wasn't about to try to explain it to a four-year-old.

"Jared, I'm hungry and Cassi's still sleeping."

"Okay, you go and watch TV while I use the bathroom. Then I'll get you something."

Jared settled Janet at the TV with her siblings and went to the bathroom. His body felt even more sore than the night before, but at least nothing was broken. He saw Sandy's clothing hanging over the shower rod, now clean and dry, and Cassi's dress was folded on the counter. He touched the mauve cloth briefly before turning his attention to his face in the mirror, wincing at its appearance. At least Cassi had done a good job with bandaging the deepest wounds. As he washed his hands, his eyes searched almost idly for the secret gel that made Cassi's ringlets. He found nothing. With wet fingers he rubbed his undamaged eye, and immediately felt more awake and ready to face the unexplained problem concerning the Buddha. Only one thing was lacking.

Jared knelt stiffly on the hard linoleum floor and prayed for guidance. He also thanked the Lord for the warning he had been given the night before, and promised to obey more readily the next time. In closing he said, "And please, Father, bless us that my predicament doesn't cause trouble for Cassi. Please protect her and the children."

Jared left the bathroom feeling better than he had felt in a long time. He nearly whistled as he made his way to the refrigerator. From there he could see across the room where Cassi and Sandy were sleeping together on one of the double beds. For some reason, the *Mother and Baby* statue that Cassi had purchased flashed through his mind. The covers were kicked partially on the floor, and Jared could see the white nightgown that had so intrigued him. Lying there, Cassi looked like an angel; and like the previous night, he felt rather devilish as he watched her. Amazingly, her hair looked the same as it had when she had gone to bed.

A feeling of tenderness swept through him, its intensity taking him by surprise. Could this be the woman Sister Martin had talked about when she had said the Lord had someone prepared for him? Was he now supposed to open his heart and let her in? Jared didn't know if he was able.

Cassi stretched and Jared quickly averted his eyes, busying himself with the food he found in the refrigerator. Only when he felt her stand up and walk around did he dare look over at her. She had put on a robe, completely hiding the delicate lace that bordered her nightgown. Jared felt disappointed but knew that it was proper.

"Good morning. Care for something to eat?" he asked.

She smiled. "Yes, I think I do. I was going to shower first, but all of a sudden I'm really hungry."

"Me too!" said a chorus of voices. The children suddenly appeared around the table where he had spread the food.

Jared whistled. "Amazing, the gravitational pull of food!" The kids giggled and Cassi shook her head.

"You're funny," she said, "but boy do you look like something the cat dragged in!"

The children laughed even harder, and Jared chuckled ruefully. "Yeah, don't I? And I feel like it, too." As if on cue, both Cassi and Jared stopped smiling. His eyes met hers, and in them he could see the remembrance of what had happened to make him look the way he did. Suddenly, neither of them felt like laughing.

The children gobbled up their breakfast as fast as they could and sprawled in front of the TV again. Jared shook his head in amazement. "Was that only four point six seconds?" he asked Cassi. "I swear they never even chewed!"

"It's yogurt, you don't have to chew," Scotty said, tearing his gaze away from the cartoons long enough to defend himself.

"He's certainly got a point," she said seriously, but she winked at Jared. Then she turned back to the children. "You guys had better change into your clothes. Your parents will be here to get you soon. You get to take your new brother home today."

"Goodie!"

Cassi's smile returned. "That reminds me, I have to pack Renae's things. But first I'll take a shower. Last night I had time for spot cleaning, but today I need to wash my hair." Jared watched as Cassi hesitated, looking over to where little Sandy was still sleeping. "She's so precious," she murmured.

"Wet underwear and all?" Jared asked.

She focused her dark eyes on his. "That dress needed dry-cleaning anyway."

Jared laughed, genuinely amused. "For someone without much experience with kids, you're doing pretty well."

"I'm a quick learner." She was about to say more when a knock sounded at the door.

"It must be Daddy," Scotty said. He and the girls ran to the door, still blocked by the couch.

Jared bounded after them, one hand already on his hidden gun. "Wait!" he ordered. Cassi pulled the children back and hovered behind him, her eyes large and scared. The children's stares showed their confusion, aware of the adults' concern but not understanding the cause.

"Who is it?" Cassi called.

There was a slight pause. "Uh, I'm looking for Cassi Mason. Is this her room?"

"It's Trent," Cassi said to Jared. She raised her voice. "Just a minute, Trent."

Jared motioned for the children to help him move the couch. Janet complicated things by sitting on it. "I want a ride," she said. "Whee!"

Cassi was already opening the door a crack to see if Trent was alone. Jared noticed her caution and silently applauded her for it. She saw his expression. "I read the spy books," she whispered, bringing a grin to his face. She always seemed to affect him that way.

"Is everything okay?" Trent asked as his children enveloped him with hugs and kisses. His sharp eyes took in Jared's face and Cassi's robe. "Cassi?" his eyebrows raised questioningly.

A slight blush covered Cassi's face. "There was a problem. Not with the children, though. Someone wanted something from Jared, and they jumped him. He was worried they might have seen him with me and the children, so he came to make sure we were safe." Jared noticed that she didn't mention he had slept in the room with her, and he didn't feel inclined to add that juicy bit of information. There was no way he would compromise her further.

"Did you call the police?" Trent asked.

Jared shook his head. "Just hotel security. But they found nothing.

The men who did this were professionals. They wanted something I bought at the auction."

"Do you think they'll be back?"

"Yes, but I'll be prepared this time." Jared knew his words sounded brave, contrasting sharply with the growing apprehension in his heart.

Trent turned to Cassi. "Would you like us to wait for you and take you to the airport? Renae and the baby are in the car, but they could come up and wait for you to get ready."

"Oh, no. I'll be fine. Please don't worry about me. And I'll call when I get home, just to tell you that I'm safe. Come in a minute while I get Renae's things."

Jared and Trent played with the children while Cassi packed. Little Sandy woke up and ran at once to her daddy's arms, smiling shyly at Jared. By the time Trent had taken her to the bathroom and dressed her, Cassi was finished.

"Tell Renae we'll get together again, but not when she's pregnant," she said. "I don't know if I can handle the excitement." Trent and Jared laughed. Cassi bent down and hugged each of the children. "When you come visit me in San Diego, we'll have even more fun," she promised. "I'll take you wherever you want to go."

"When you and Jared have a baby, I want to tend it," said Janet. "I'm going to have a lot of practice, you know."

Jared clamped his lips together to stop the laughter at Cassi's startled expression. Trent looked embarrassed. "I'm sure you will, Janet," he said. "Your new brother is going to love having you tend him. Come on now, Mom's waiting." He waved a hand in farewell, and the children skipped after him down the hall.

Cassi sighed. "It's going to be quiet without them," she said. Jared nodded and followed her back into the room.

"Well, now what?" she asked.

"That depends."

"On what?"

"Well, I want to clean up and then get the Buddha. There's something strange about it, and I want to know what it is."

Cassi's eyes locked onto his. "But wouldn't the owner of your gallery deal with that?"

He nodded. "Yes, and she did ask me to wait. But since I'm going to be in town until tomorrow, I might as well satisfy my own curiosity."

"Yes, it would be nice to know." She paused, knitting her thick eyebrows in concentration. "May I look at the Buddha?"

Jared had hoped that talking about the Buddha would spark her interest, but now that it had, he worried about putting her at risk. "Yes, but it might be dangerous," he said.

She nodded, her face serious. "But at least we'd know why you had to sleep on my couch with a gun."

A heavy silence filled the room before she continued. "Tell me, how are we going to find out about the Buddha? Just from looking at it, I can't confirm our suspicions."

Jared smiled. "You're not the only one who met someone in the art world on your mission. I also met a guy who is an expert at dating paint and materials."

"And he can do it without harming the Buddha, right? It wouldn't do to scrape off some paint if it were authentic."

"Yes. Carl, that's my friend, is highly respected in his field. He has certain lights that he shines onto the surface of whatever object he's trying to date. Depending on what the composition is, a certain spectrum of light will be emitted. He can detect it with special equipment—you can't see it with your unaided eyes. He also uses sound waves and other such technical mumbo-jumbo to determine density."

"It sounds fascinating. May I come along?"

"What about your plane back to San Diego?"

"It isn't until this afternoon. I could pack and take back my rental car. Then you could take me to the airport." She bit her lip. "I mean . . . that is . . ."

"Of course I will," Jared said quickly. "I'd appreciate the company. But afterwards, it's straight to the airport. I'd feel bad if anything happened to you."

Cassi nodded. Then a smile came to her lips and she began to chuckle.

"What is it?" Jared asked.

"Well, when I called Linden, he told me to stay away from you and the Buddha. He knows something about it but won't tell me. He only warned me against the person who ended up with the Buddha, just as he did before I even knew you."

Jared felt her words explained the wall that had come between them the previous night before he had been attacked. She had been afraid of him because of the Buddha! Even so, she had let him in when she had seen his bruised face. That had to mean something.

Jared looked into Cassi's eyes, those deep brown pools that seemed to pull him in, and said with all the sincerity he felt in his heart, "Cassi, I swear to you, I don't know what's going on with this Buddha. Please believe me. And while I feel that this thing with the Buddha is dangerous, I would never do anything to hurt you!" Jared finished his spiel and waited for Cassi's reply. He had exposed his feelings; now, once and for all, he would see if Léon had been correct about her coldness to men. He held his breath.

"I do believe you," she said softly. "I do."

CHAPTER 14

Cassi showered hurriedly while Jared waited outside. She washed her hair and blow-dried it as best she could. The curls were so thick that the hair underneath was still wet, but it was all she had patience for. As she pulled on a light green, semi-casual dress with a crinkled broomstick skirt, she thought about Jared and what had brought them together. Her fear of his hurting her physically had vanished along with her idea of him as an arrogant pig. While she had nearly hated him before, she now felt admiration, and yes, even something vaguely romantic for him.

"You really take the cake," she whispered aloud to herself as she dabbed on a bit of makeup. "One minute you hate the very sight of him, and the next you're begging to go with him." She gave her hair a last pat and said to the mirror, "Not that this is anything other than just a professional relationship, of course. It's not like he's asked you out or anything." Sighing, she opened the door.

"What?" Jared was lying on the couch with a look of surprise on his face. He glanced at his watch and back to Cassi. "Fifteen minutes?"

"I'm sorry I took so long. I hurried."

"No, it's not that. I had expected longer." He shook his head. "Wow, that must be some gel!"

"What?"

Jared stood up. "Never mind. You look really great."

"Thanks," Cassi said, a trifle uncertainly.

"I mean it. But who was that you were talking to?"

"Eavesdropper!"

Jared smiled. "Don't worry, I do that too—talk to myself, that is."

Cassi bit her lip. "Did you hear what I said?"

"Every word." But Jared's expression told her that he hadn't. She sighed with relief and walked to the door where her single suitcase and dress bag were waiting. Jared picked up the suitcase and opened the door for her.

"Well," she said, scooping the dress bag up in her arms and tossing her purse onto her shoulder, "I hear that the most intelligent people talk to themselves."

"Like us?"

"Exactly."

****

An hour later found Cassi and Jared in his rental car. She had waited in Jared's room while he had showered, reluctantly holding the gun he had insisted she keep while he was in the bathroom. Then they had eaten a hurried breakfast before picking up their purchases from the auction. The Buddha now sat in the trunk, packed in a special box. Next to it was the *Mother and Baby* statue, also in its case. Cassi had sent the lion sculpture by special messenger to Linden, but had been reluctant to send her own purchase. Finally, she decided to risk taking it home on the plane with her. Cassi noticed how Jared's eyes had fixed on her statue when they had picked it up, and a creeping doubt of him stole into her heart. She struggled to push the thought aside.

Jared's hand touched hers briefly. "It won't be long now," he said. Over his dress pants and shirt, he wore a tan jacket. With such beautiful weather, she questioned the need for it—until she remembered the gun. Of course he would bring it. She had to admit it made her feel a little safer.

They drove to Venice where Jared's friend, Carl, lived in one of the most expensive apartment buildings near the beach. The sky was cloudless, and already promised a hot day. Though she couldn't yet see the beach, Cassi could smell the ocean and hear the squawking of the seagulls. She felt a sudden longing to remove her sandals and feel the sand squishing through her toes. Even as a child she had adored the beach, especially at night when the sun set over the ocean, sending sprays of color reflecting off the water. She almost wished she didn't have a plane to catch. To watch the sunset with Jared would be . . . Cassi brought herself up short. What was she thinking? He hadn't really shown an interest in her personally; he was simply worried about her getting hurt because of him, just as he would worry about anyone else. Or was it something more? Cassi felt confused. *Oh, why can't relationships be as clear as art deals?* she asked herself.

"Penny for your thoughts," Jared said.

"What?" Cassi glanced up at him in surprise. Jared had parked the car and come around to open her door.

"You look so serious with your eyebrows all scrunched together like that. Is something wrong?"

"Oh, no," Cassi said hurriedly. "I was just thinking about all that's happened."

Jared nodded. "Hopefully, Carl can shed some light on what's going on." He went around to the back of the car, opened the trunk, and drew out the Buddha's box. Cassi picked up her case with the *Mother and Baby*, not wanting to leave it in the car.

"I thought you always sent the items to Linden by courier," Jared said as they began the walk to Carl's place.

"I do," said Cassi. "But this isn't Linden's, it's mine."

Jared laughed. "Good choice."

They walked a little further before Jared said, "I'll buy it from you."

"What?"

"The *Mother and Baby*. At a profit for you, of course."

Cassi was offended. "Is that why you let me come with you, so that you could make an offer for it?"

"No, not at all. I just admire it. If you're attached to it, forget it. I understand."

Cassi was silent. She felt angry, principally at herself for starting to think that just maybe this good-looking man liked her for herself.

"I'm sorry," Jared said. "I didn't know it would upset you like this. Please, will you forget it?" His voice was sincere, and Cassi met his eyes to see if she could read the truth. A current ran through her body, much like she imagined electricity would if she touched a hot wire.

"It's okay," she said. "I'm just overreacting. I tend to do that sometimes."

As they climbed the front steps to the apartment building in silence, Cassi noticed a wheelchair ramp built in front of the structure. The building was old but immaculate and in excellent repair, giving it an interesting air of elegance from the past.

"He lives there," Jared said, motioning to the bottom left apartment just inside the heavy front doors.

"I hope he's home."

"He'd better be. I called him while you were showering."

"Oh. You said you met him on your mission. Did you baptize him?"

Jared's face fell. "No. Not yet, anyway. I'm still working on him. He's pretty bitter about something that happened in his life as a teenager, and he can't seem to get past it."

Cassi didn't reply. She felt Jared's pain distinctly, remembering only too well her own feelings when people she had cared about on her mission hadn't accepted the truth. It still hurt whenever she thought about them. A part of her wanted to reach out to Jared, but uncertainty crushed that desire. What if he didn't want her sympathy?

Jared rang the bell and waited. Finally a sound came from behind the door, and it opened slowly. Even so, Cassi was unprepared for what she saw. She had been looking straight ahead, expecting to see a man about Jared's height, but before her sat a man in a wheelchair. She tried desperately not to jerk her head down toward him. Her attempt didn't fool Carl.

"Didn't tell her about the wheelchair, huh, Jared," the man said in a raspy voice. He was very thin and had long brown hair and a droopy mustache. Cassi figured he was at least ten years older than Jared.

"Why should I?" Jared countered. "You're still a person, aren't you? Just because you can't walk—"

"Just because my legs are twisted and useless, you mean." Carl backed away from the door and motioned them inside. He turned his electric wheelchair around expertly and started into the next room. They silently followed him through the front room and down a spacious hall to Carl's large workroom. The walls were lined with low bookshelves and tables full of intricate and expensive-looking equipment.

"Put the Buddha here," directed Carl, pointing to a table between two large machines. Jared did as requested. Carl examined the statue thoroughly. "Well, just to look at it, it seems to be authentic," he said. "Except . . ."

"This mark right here," Cassi said, pointing to a spot on the lower left side of the Buddha's base.

Carl nodded. "Yes, that swirl under the flower should be longer and with a bit more of a curve like the other ones around the base. The artists of that period were sticklers for detail." He picked up a book on the table and flipped to a section that showed excellent pictures of the Buddha from every angle. "See," he pointed at one of the photos. "But . . . ," Carl's voice trailed off.

"What?" asked Jared and Cassi together.

"If I had to say just from examining it, I would say it was authentic, despite the pictures. You see, this is one of a collection of Buddhas, and it is possible for one to deviate slightly. This may not be the Buddha in the picture at all, but still a genuine one from the collection, perhaps only recently come to light." Carl moved his chair to one side and began fiddling with some equipment. "Fortunately, we don't have to rely on sight alone."

"So if it isn't real," Jared said, "then that would mean—"

"That whoever faked it has the real one," Carl finished. "Or one of the real ones, I should say. That's the only way it could be copied so perfectly. Even so, it would have taken months to get it exactly right."

"But why sell the fake one and then try to get it back?" asked Cassi. "It doesn't make sense. They probably could have gotten away with it if they hadn't tried."

"They tried to get it back?" asked Carl.

"Uh, yeah," Jared said sheepishly. "Two men attacked me at the hotel last night. Although if the Buddha is a fake, we don't know that those men were the ones who did it, or that they even know about it."

Carl's expression grew worried. "That explains your face. And I thought you and your girlfriend here just got into a fight." Carl smiled mirthlessly at his own wit.

"Cassi. Her name's Cassi."

"And I'm not his girlfriend," Cassi added. "I mean we're friends, but we really just met and . . ." She trailed off, wishing she had said nothing.

"So you've got men after a possibly fake Buddha," Carl said into the awkward silence.

"But what if it's not fake?" Cassi asked.

"Well, let's look at it from that perspective," Carl said. "Say the Buddha is real. Why would those men want it?"

"Yeah," Jared agreed. "The commission on four hundred thousand dollars would be peanuts to guys like this."

Cassi snapped her fingers. "So it *is* a fake. It must be."

"That's my bet," Carl said. He looked up at Jared's face. "But that doesn't explain why those men want it so badly."

"Maybe they're trying to cover up a counterfeit art ring," Jared said.

"That's as good an explanation as anything." Carl turned back to the table. "Uh, Jared, why don't you go out to the kitchen and get us a drink? This is going to take a while, so don't hurry." Jared shot Cassi a puzzled glance, but did as he was asked.

Carl didn't immediately go back to his equipment, but said softly, "He's a good man, Jared is. There isn't any better."

Cassi shrugged. "I don't know him well, but I know that he's kind. He came to the hospital to give my friend a blessing when she went into labor early. He helped her a lot."

"A blessing? Are you a Mormon?"

Cassi nodded.

"That explains it."

"Explains what?"

"The light I see around you, shining and white. The same one I see around Jared. I can always tell if people are good by the light around them."

"You can see auras?" Cassi asked.

Carl nodded. "Ever since the accident. I believe that on some level, all people see auras and are attracted to the purest ones. Most folks just aren't aware of it."

"Does Jared know about this?"

"No. I couldn't tell him because he'd claim that I knew he was telling the truth. Then I'd have to be baptized." He began to fiddle with the knobs on one of his machines.

Cassi was quiet as she puzzled over what Carl was telling her. Essentially, he knew the Church was true; but something had held him back all these years from being baptized.

"How did it happen?" she asked finally.

Carl looked up at her. The hazel eyes seemed much too large and beautiful for his twisted body. "Surfing accident when I was nineteen," he said without expression. "At a competition. I would have won; I was the best."

Cassi shook her head in sympathy. Then without knowing why, she asked, "You love the ocean, don't you? You miss it."

This time there was pain in Carl's eyes. "Yes."

Cassi took a breath and continued. "You know, my favorite part is the sunset, first when the rays reflect off the shining water, radiating all that beautiful gold, then the color creeps in, the pinks and reds. And finally—and this is the best part—when the sun seems to be swallowed by the ocean."

Carl nodded. "It's all I have left."

"For now," Cassi agreed lightly. "Of the ocean, anyway. But the sunrise is just as beautiful—the dawn of a new day, unblemished by mistakes. Jared tells me you're one of the foremost authorities on determining the authenticity of art. Did it ever occur to you that this talent was a gift to replace the one you lost? That and the gift of seeing auras? It could very well be your sunrise. The saying goes that whenever God allows a door to be shut, he opens one somewhere else—one that may be more difficult to pass through, but better for us in the end."

"Are you saying my life now is better than before?" Carl asked bitterly.

"Can you honestly say you would give all the knowledge, satisfaction, and recognition your work gives you for a few brief years in the surfing world?" Cassi countered. "Come on, be truthful. I grew up in California, and I know the surfing crowd, the drugs and immorality that exist. Tell me, how many white and shining auras would you see among them? And where would you fit in? Am I telling the truth?"

As Cassi talked, Carl's eyes grew wide with anger, but by the time she had finished, he was nodding. "I'll have to think about it," he said. He glanced at his equipment and then back at Cassi. "But thanks. That's one thing about you Mormons, you don't mince words." He turned back to his work.

Cassi smiled gently. *I'll bet your aura is white and shining too,* she thought silently to Carl. *There's nothing so bright as what emerges from the refiner's fire.* Indeed, Cassi felt strongly that the Lord was keeping watch over this shriveled man, and someday he would understand and be grateful.

She thought the subject closed, but Carl glanced up at her again. "You have to think too," he said. "About Jared. You may have to chase him, but he wants to be caught."

Before Cassi could reply, Jared came back into the room. "What took you so long?" Carl asked.

"You didn't have any clean glasses, so I had to wash some. I did the rest of the dishes while I was at it."

Carl's head was turned from Jared, but Cassi could see the smile that played on his lips. He had known very well that there were no clean dishes, and just as well that Jared would wash not only the glasses, but also the rest of the dirty pile.

Carl flipped a switch on the machine in front of him before reaching for the glass Jared held out to him. "Yuck," he said, making a face. "Orange juice. Couldn't you have brought me a beer?"

"Sorry," said Jared, "but I didn't see any *root* beer in the fridge." Carl snorted and Cassi laughed.

Carl moved a machine attached to an extendable arm and looked through it at the Buddha. Every now and then, he paused to change the light and jot down a few notes. Then he moved to the second machine and scribbled more on his pad. Finally, he turned the machines off.

"It's fake, all right. But someone's gone to an awful lot of trouble to make it appear real. They used paint that has almost the same emission and absorption spectrum as the original. But where I could tell was when I did the depth check with sound waves. This Buddha is not as thick as the original—or at least it's not made up of the same material. Then I checked it with this," he pointed to one of his machines. "The magnetic resonance proves that it's definitely hollow. But I'm sure it weighs the same, or it wouldn't have come undetected as far as it has. That means it's probably made out of a heavier clay."

"Or maybe it has something in it," Cassi said.

Carl threw back his head and laughed. "You've been watching too many movies," he said.

Cassi smiled. "And reading too many books."

"So it's a fake," Jared said, as if unable to believe what he was hearing.

"Absolutely. And I can do a paint analysis to prove it. The chemicals will be able to tell the age absolutely." Before Jared or Cassi could say anything, Carl laid the Buddha on its back and picked up an instrument to shave off a tiny piece of the surface glaze on the bottom. Then he wheeled across the room to dip it into his chemicals.

The minutes ticked by as they waited for the results. Carl, satisfied that all was going well, put his hand on his chair's controls and wheeled to the doorway. "Jared, call me a taxi," he said.

"Where are you going? We can take you."

Carl shook his head. "No way. Much as I like you, Jared, you're dangerous to be around. I don't know what's going on with this Buddha, but whoever is behind it has money and power, and I'm not about to get in the way. Me, I'm going to Mexico. There's a girl I met the last time I was down there, and I've been meaning to visit her. Name's Maria, and she writes to me all the time. She's not like these American girls who want money *and* a man who can walk. Money is enough for her. And she seems to like me besides. And she's one he—" Carl stopped abruptly and glanced at Cassi. "Heck of a cook," he finished lamely.

"But—" Jared began. He and Cassi followed Carl into his bedroom and watched as he wheeled erratically around the room, taking clothing out of drawers, from the closet, and even from a basket of dirty clothes in the corner by the bed.

"But nothing. Cassi here started me to thinking, and I'm not about to get killed before I finish."

Soon Carl had a pile on the bed and began to pack it rapidly into a suitcase with surprising neatness. "Shut that for me, Jared, would you?" Carl said when he was finished. "The paint test should be finished. And I still haven't heard you call the taxi."

"You're completely serious!" Jared said, ignoring the suitcase and following Carl back into the workroom. Cassi hurriedly shut the case and carried it with her.

"Look at your face and read the signs," Carl retorted. "Those men are serious. Do yourself a favor and get rid of this Buddha as quickly as possible."

"I'm taking it to New York tomorrow and giving it to Laranda," Jared said.

"Good. But keep your gun handy."

"I will, except for when I have to check it in at the airport."

"Too bad you can't get around that." Carl bent over the chemicals again and motioned for Jared and Cassi to see. They knew enough about the process to see for themselves that the Buddha was a fake.

"That's proof then," Jared said quietly. "That paint is younger than we are."

Cassi went to the phone and dialed for a taxi. "Is there anything else we can do?" she asked. "Anyone we should tell or any payments to make?"

Carl shook his head. "No. Everything's paid through the bank, and I can call the cleaning lady and the company I work for at the airport. Truth is, they've been trying to get me down to Mexico again anyway. They've got a lab there, and some museum needs me to date some items for them. They'll be happy to see me. Not to mention Maria. Come on, let's go."

By the time Jared repacked the Buddha and Cassi picked up her box, Carl was already waiting for them at the door with his suitcase on his lap. They silently made their way into the lobby as the taxi pulled up outside.

"Well, good-bye. Take care of yourselves," Carl said gruffly. "And here." He took out a piece of paper and a pen from the pocket in his T-shirt and scribbled a number, thrusting it into Jared's hands. "In case you need some fake IDs fast."

"We won't need them," Jared insisted.

Carl's lips curled. "Don't be too sure."

"Let me know what you decide," Cassi said softly, handing him her business card.

"And you let me know," he countered.

"About what?" Jared asked. The different answers he received were simultaneous.

"About baptism," Cassi said.

"About marriage," said Carl.

"What?"

Carl chuckled. "Tell you what, Jared. On the day you get married, you can baptize me." With that, he wheeled his chair down the ramp and to the waiting taxi.

"Carl," Cassi called. "About Maria. What color is her aura?"

Carl's smile was genuine. "White. Shining and white." He lifted himself into the taxi and reached down to fold his chair. A minute later he was gone.

"I knew she didn't want his money," Cassi whispered.

"What?"

As they walked back to the car, Cassi explained about Carl's gift. "I knew it!" Jared said. "I knew there was something he wasn't telling me. Thank you, Cassi!" Jared's free arm flew around Cassi in an awkward hug.

Cassi could smell his closeness, and her flesh tingled. She wished he would kiss her. Did he feel it too?

An idea formed in her mind. She still had several hours before her plane would leave; maybe he would agree to a short walk on the beach. Since they were so near the ocean anyway, it would prolong their time together without seeming too forward. "Why don't we—"

With no warning, Jared's arm tightened around her waist and his body shoved hers from the sidewalk and up against the building they were passing.

"W—what?"

"Shhh," he said. "Look there, across the street at those two men. I swear they're the ones who attacked me at the hotel last night!"

Cassi looked up to see two ordinary-looking men in casual clothing. *But they're not wearing trench coats and dark glasses!* she wanted to protest. Certainly this adventure was destroying many of the movie stereotypes she enjoyed. The men stood with their backs toward Cassi and Jared, facing across the street where Jared had left the car. It was obvious they were waiting for something. Or someone.

Cassi felt fear wrench in her stomach. *What were they going to do now?*

CHAPTER 15

The men were as tall as Jared but more muscular. They had a practiced air of nonchalance that ordinarily would have made Jared oblivious to them, but Carl's agitation and hurried departure had made Jared more alert. As he told Cassi, he thought the men might be the same ones who had attacked him. At this distance, however, he couldn't be sure.

But I was so careful when I left the hotel, he thought. *I didn't see them following in the black sedan.* It occurred to him that the pair of thugs might have used another car, one he hadn't been looking for. They could have even placed a monitoring device on his rental car. *Darn it all!* At least they hadn't caught up with him until now.

Cassi's breath came rapidly. Fear darted from her eyes, the same fear that churned in Jared's stomach. These men must have followed them from the hotel, and he had no doubt they meant business.

Jared was still pressed up against Cassi, whose back jabbed into the rock surface of the apartment building. Her hair was in his face, and he could smell its clean scent. He reached up to push her soft curls to the side so he could study his pursuers more thoroughly.

Soft? Soft curls? It was the first time Jared had touched Cassi's hair, and he could hardly believe that those tiny ringlets were soft and silky, not brittle and unpleasant as he'd expected.

"They're getting impatient," Cassi said.

Jared focused intently on the men. Now was certainly not the time to dwell on his romantic fantasy. *What can I do to save us?* he thought. Even with all his experience as a guard for Laranda's art treasures, he was not prepared for this.

The two men scrutinized each passerby, occasionally glancing at their watches and shaking their heads. Their black hair shone in the sun.

Jared knew he had to do something. Any minute now, the men would come searching for them. Or turn and see them. Touching the reassuring weight of the revolver under his arm, he hadn't any doubts as to the hardware their jackets must hide. And they certainly wouldn't hesitate to use it.

Alone, Jared felt he could outrun them. But with Cassi? Silently he prayed.

"Let's back away," he whispered. "Slowly, so we won't draw their attention." Yet even as Cassi obeyed, Jared's worst nightmare came true; the men turned. In a single motion they leapt toward the couple, but Jared and Cassi were already sprinting down the street, drawing wide-eyed stares from the people they passed. At first Jared held onto Cassi's hand, hoping to pull her along; but she shook off his grasp and wrapped both hands around the box that held her *Mother and Baby* statue. She pulled ahead of him, the sun reflecting from her hair and bringing out the red highlights. Jared shook his head in amazement. This woman sure could run!

He followed Cassi's lead and shifted the heavier weight of the Buddha to both hands. His tie flipped up at the movement, hitting him in the mouth and staying there as he gasped for air. Jared spat out the cloth and jerked his face to the side, pushing his sore body to run as fast as the woman in front of him. The men behind, unencumbered with art treasures, were rapidly closing the gap.

On they ran to the Venice Boardwalk, where they had to weave in and out of the hordes of people dressed in swimming suits, shorts, leather vests, and a variety of strange costumes. Pink, orange, and green hair dotted the crowd as often as black or blond. Jared had been on the Boardwalk only twice in his life, and the variety of individuals there amazed him. Along the strip of pavement that separated the shops from the sandy beach, jugglers, artists, trick roller bladers, disco-dancing roller skaters, musicians, and even comics plied onlookers for cash with their outrageous—and sometimes very talented—spectacles.

As they passed several mimes and a juggler, Jared felt his lungs begin to burn. He was in good shape, but not accustomed to long runs. He lagged behind, and Cassi cast a worried glance behind her.

"Quick, in here!" she yelled at him. She ducked into the opening of a nearby shop, and Jared followed. It was a clothing store, and already Cassi was grabbing several items off the racks. "Quick, get some clothes and change." Not waiting to see if he understood, she plunged into a dressing room. Once again Jared followed her lead, though he wondered at its prudence. At least it seemed that in their mad rush through the colorful crowd, they had pulled ahead of and temporarily lost their pursuers.

He changed quickly into the long shorts and T-shirt he had grabbed. They were slightly large, but Jared didn't have the time to be choosy. He wrapped his dress pants, shirt, and jacket around the Buddha's case; his holster and gun lay just under the first layer where he could reach them at will. Cautiously, he peered from the dressing room out into the small store. Cassi was there, dressed in fluorescent pink shorts and a white T-shirt three times too big, her hair tucked up under a straw hat. To someone not knowing her, she looked completely different from the sophisticated woman of before. Once again he was amazed, and silently admired her impulsiveness and creativity.

She smiled when she saw him. "Do you think they'll recognize us?"

"Not you," he said, grabbing a straw hat for himself. They went to the counter, where Jared quickly paid for the clothing. There was only one thing missing. "Do you have coolers?" he asked the clerk. "Big ones?" The man shook his head, watching Jared a little strangely.

Jared turned to Cassi and she shrugged, drawing her eyebrows together in puzzlement. "Why do you want a cooler?" she asked.

Before he could explain, the door to the shop opened. Both tensed, but it was only a couple of young boys, carrying a large cooler between them. Jared eyed it for less than a second before making his decision. Now he would show *his* impulsive and creative side to this impressive woman. "How much for the cooler?" he asked.

"No way, man. Get your own," said one of the boys, backing away.

"No, I mean it. What'll it take? A hundred? Two hundred?"

The boys stared at him in amazement. Their eyes glazed over as they tried to calculate Jared's offer versus the price of the cooler and the few beers inside.

"Two hundred," the oldest boy said. Before the boy even finished speaking, Jared pulled the money out of his wallet. He was twenty dollars short, but Cassi handed him a bill. While the boys counted their loot, Jared peeked outside the door and unceremoniously dumped the ice and beer onto the edge of the Boardwalk. In less than two seconds he was back in the store, gently placing the Buddha's case inside the cooler.

Cassi smiled as she put her box on top of the Buddha and stuffed their extra clothing around to pad the precious cargo. "Pretty good," she said admiringly.

Jared felt pleased, though he found it strange that her approval should mean so much to him. "Come on, let's go," he said. They left the shop with the cooler between them, moving quickly along the Boardwalk, but not fast enough to set them apart from the crowd.

"Don't look now," Cassi said softly, "but I see them. They're checking the stores further down the walk. They must have passed by the store and are doubling back. They'll catch up to us soon."

"We can't go back to the car," Jared said.

"The beach then," Cassi suggested. "Let's go sit down and pretend we belong. They won't look for someone who's not moving."

They angled out for the sand, but found that the two men had separated. While one checked the Boardwalk and peered into the stores, the other scanned the beach. He approached them from behind, and Jared tensed. He could see the thug's hand in his jacket pocket and the telltale bulge of his gun. The man had a hooked nose and was definitely one of the men who had attacked him at the hotel.

Jared lowered the cooler slowly and turned to Cassi. "Behind us," he muttered, pulling his hat as far down as possible to hide his battered face.

"Kiss me," she said suddenly.

Kiss her? Now? While the idea was something Jared had been entertaining in his private fantasies since he had seen her helpless in the hospital, this moment hardly seemed the time for romantic advances.

"The movies," Cassi hissed softly. At her words, Jared remembered the many films he had seen where the hero always grabbed the heroine and kissed her, making them invisible to the bad guys. Cassi wasn't being romantic; she had simply read the same books and seen the same movies he had. Could it work?

Jared pulled Cassi close. He felt her arms go up and around his neck, and despite the seriousness of their situation, he enjoyed her soft touch. Their lips met, tentatively at first and then more firmly, like real sweethearts. Jared's heart hammered against his chest, and he wondered if Cassi could feel the pounding. He could always explain this as terror of the men who chased them, but in his heart he knew Cassi's closeness was the real cause.

The kiss continued, and out of the corner of his eye Jared saw that their pursuer was upon them. Was it possible this man had also read the spy books? Would he look closely at the entwined couple? Jared would have held his breath as the man passed, but since he was already doing so as he kissed Cassi—which, he reasoned, had to explain the sudden dizziness in his head—he couldn't do anything but peek out from under his eyelashes.

To his relief, the man averted his gaze from the necking pair. Jared noticed that everyone else also avoided looking at them, just as he normally avoided looking at others who made in public.

Jared lifted his head. "He's gone." Relief passed over Cassi's face. But now that the danger had passed, if only temporarily, Jared felt the desire to kiss Cassi again.

"Now what?" Cassi asked, her face flushed.

Jared shrugged. He scanned the beach, tensing abruptly. "Here he comes again," he whispered. He grabbed Cassi again and lowered his lips to hers. After a long moment, he dared to peek beneath his lashes and saw that it was not their pursuer after all, but someone dressed similarly. A mistake; but what a sweet mistake!

Jared didn't want to let Cassi go, but he knew it wasn't right to continue kissing her under false pretenses. Still, he kissed her tenderly once more before breaking away.

"He's gone," he said, searching her face for emotions.

Cassi stared at the sand and bit her lip. "Let's go that way, nearer to the ocean," she said, motioning in the direction opposite the one the thug had taken. Apparently the man was heading to their car, so that avenue was closed to them.

They walked along the beach in silence, carrying the cooler between them. Jared felt the sand slip into his loafers, but he didn't care. Cassi seemed to have the same problem with her sandals, and she stopped a moment to remove them. At long last, they emerged on an unfamiliar street, far away from where they had parked their car. From there they called a taxi and began the drive back to the hotel.

"You missed your flight," Jared said, showing her his watch.

Cassi shrugged and stared out the taxi window at the passing buildings. Her eyes were veiled, and Jared wished he dared ask what she was feeling.

"I'll get another flight," she said. "Tonight or tomorrow."

"Come with me to put the Buddha in the hotel safe, then I'll go with you to the airport. Or we could have dinner and go tomorrow. We still have to find some way to retrieve your luggage out of my rental car."

Cassi nodded silently. "We don't have to have dinner," she said. "I can go tonight."

Something about her words reminded him of how Cassi had reacted when Sam Boader had asked her out. Jared had thought then that she didn't recognize the man's intentions. Like Boader, Jared had only suggested dinner to have more time alone with her. Was it possible that she misunderstood Jared's intentions?

Before he could decide, the taxi drove up to the hotel. His attention was diverted immediately as several marked and unmarked police cars with flashing lights blocked parts of the drive. He paid the driver with the bill Cassi had shoved into his hand as she jumped out of the car to question an elderly hotel employee who stood outside with a few interested bystanders. Jared arrived as the man began to talk.

"It's like they've gone crazy," he said, scratching his white head. "You see, we had a break-in at the hotel safe. It set off all the alarms, but we weren't able to stop the thieves. Strange thing is, they didn't touch nothin' in the safe. Not a thing." He leaned toward them conspiratorially. "But the real shocker was when the Feds showed up in them fancy unmarked cars of theirs and blocked the drive." His chin jutted out in the direction of the offending vehicles. "They hadn't known about the break-in . . . just came to demand that we open the safe to show them something. But whatever they was lookin' for, they didn't find it either. They went up to some guy's room on the fourth floor and tore it apart, though. I heard someone say something about him being a Buddhist or something. I don't envy that guy when they catch up to him. They looked real upset."

"Thanks," Jared said. The man nodded and ambled away.

"Come on." Cassi tugged softly on his arm. They walked down the street until they were well away from the hotel.

"We'll go to another hotel," Jared said, shifting the weight of the cooler they carried between them. "We can't go back there."

Cassi stopped in the street and stared at Jared, her expression filled with concern. "Linden," she said. "I told him you bought the Buddha and that you'd be here for a couple days. I said you'd probably keep it in the safe. Could it be that *he's* behind the attempted theft? And why is the FBI involved? Oh, Jared, I'm sorry!"

She had tears in her eyes, and Jared could see how it hurt her to think that her good friend and mentor was involved. Jared hastened to reassure her. "We don't know Linden's responsible, not really. It could have been anyone." Jared thought for a minute. "Hey, it could have been that couple who helped me last night when I was attacked! When I called Laranda, the man could have heard me tell her that the Buddha would be in the safe. Maybe he was working for someone!"

"You think so?" Cassi asked hopefully.

"Could be. Anyway, it seems as if there are at least three parties after the Buddha: the men at the beach, the men who broke into the safe, and the Feds."

"But why? Because it's counterfeit? There has to be something more." Cassi's voice sounded scared. "Jared, maybe we should just take it to the FBI at the hotel and be done with it."

Jared thought it over. He had seen too much in his life to believe it could be so easy. He shook his head. "No. Tomorrow I'm going to the funeral, and then I'm taking this statue to Laranda. She can do what she wants with it while I take a vacation. Maybe I'll join Carl in Mexico."

His comment brought a smile to Cassi's lips, but when she spoke, her voice was serious. "And what are you going to do with the Buddha during the funeral? They'll be there, you know—all three of the parties who want that ugly thing. If you're carrying a box, you'll never get anywhere near without getting caught."

"I'll stash it somewhere," Jared said. "It's not as if it's really worth nearly four hundred thousand."

Cassi was silent as they continued to walk down the street. "I'll stay with the Buddha," she said. "I'd like to help."

Jared hesitated. "I don't know."

"Please! It could be my fault, some of this. I told Linden about the hotel safe. Please let me help." Then her eyes widened. "You don't trust me, do you? After all this, you don't trust me!" Her expression was one of anger—and something else Jared couldn't identify.

"I do trust you," Jared said truthfully. She might not see him as a potential suitor as he wished, but he felt that Cassi would never betray him when it came to the Buddha. "I just don't want you to get hurt."

"I won't. We'll go to some motel where they won't think to look for us. We'll register separately, under different names, and then wear disguises. If worst comes to worst, we'll give them the Buddha."

"Oh, Cassi, you've read—"

"Too many books. I know. But the kissing worked, didn't it?" A blush covered her cheeks. Could it be she had felt something when they kissed?

"Okay," he said. "But we go to the store to buy our disguises first. Then we'll put them on before we go to the motel."

Cassi laughed. "You're as bad as I am!" She bit her lip thoughtfully. "We need more money, though. Cash, so they—"

"Won't track us."

Cassi looked up defensively. "Well, they do it in the movies."

"It's a good idea. What do you suggest?"

"We go to Renae's," Cassi said without hesitation. "I still have enough cash to pay for another taxi, and if we hurry we can get there before the banks close. Even if we don't make it in time, they have a teller machine. They'll give us cash, and we'll write them a check and ask them to hold it until we catch our plane tomorrow—on a different flight than the one you've already scheduled."

"We?" Jared felt doubt and hope war within him. He wanted to be with Cassi, but he felt guilty at the danger he was putting her in.

She shrugged. "I've always wanted to tour the Empire State Building and go inside the Statue of Liberty."

"But—"

"Please, Jared. I feel responsible, and I can help."

It wasn't quite the answer Jared had hoped for. Something more along the lines of, "Oh, Jared, I just want to be with you" would have been more appealing. But perhaps this latter argument, though welcome, wouldn't have been as compelling. Certainly Jared wouldn't put her in danger simply because she liked him. As it was, he had no right to stop her from trying to correct her mistakes, however real or imagined they might be. Jared had always been taught to honor women's abilities and wishes.

"Okay, Cassi," he said finally. He only hoped he could keep her safe, and that in the meantime, she would grow to care about him. As for his own emotions, Jared wasn't quite sure how he felt, but he knew he was more attracted to Cassi than he had ever been to anyone in his whole life. Was that love? Jared didn't know the answer.

CHAPTER 16

As the taxi neared Renae's house, Jared leaned over to whisper in Cassi's ear. Goose bumps arose on her neck and she was glad that her hair, released now from the straw hat, hid the reaction. All too vividly, she recalled their kiss on the beach. His lips had been tender, his face sincere, though Cassi knew he was just playing a part. The intensity of her own emotions had surprised her.

That was what had led her to stay with Jared. He needed her. At Venice Beach he would have been caught but for her, and maybe she could help him again. Of course that wasn't the only reason; the real truth was that she wanted to be near him. But how could she say such a thing to a man she had only known for four days? No, better let the guilt she felt for giving information to Linden appear to be her argument. It was safer not to expose her feelings.

"I just thought of something," Jared was saying. "The hotel might have an address for Renae. We could be traced."

Cassi shook her head and whispered back. "The room was in my name. I don't think she could be traced."

"What about Linden?"

"He only knows her first name and that she was an old friend of mine. He can't trace us on just that, can he?"

"I don't know. I guess it depends on who he's working for."

Cassi bit her lip, her thoughts racing. Her trust in her boss had been shattered, and she didn't know if she wanted to pick up the scattered pieces. Or try to. How could Linden have used her as he did? And what if he could somehow trace her? What if the taxi driver was found and questioned? Her heart thumped heavily against her chest as she considered the possibilities.

A glance out the window told her they were traveling through a residential area a couple of blocks from Renae's house. Abruptly, she leaned forward and tapped the taxi driver on the shoulder. "Excuse me, we've changed our minds. Please stop here. She pointed to a corner house on the left. The driver hit his brakes and came to a stop. Cassi fumbled in her purse for the money. As she handed the driver the rest of her cash over the seat, her other hand slipped down and retrieved the paper she had given him with Renae's address. "Just in case we change our minds and want to visit after all," she said with her best innocent smile. She hoped that if questioned later, the driver would not be able to remember Renae's exact address.

They waited until the driver was gone before resuming their trek to Renae's. The air was warm, typical for June, yet the hottest part of the day was gone. The close-set houses around them had landscaped yards and a few children were out playing, giggling together in their carefree games.

"Do you have a house or an apartment?" Cassi asked.

"I own an apartment near work," Jared said. "I've been meaning to get a house, but . . ."

Cassi knew only too well what he was thinking. It had been hard for her at first to decide to buy a house; she had always expected it was something she and her husband would do together. But that husband hadn't come along, and now that she had been in her house for a year, she was grateful she hadn't waited. It was lonely at times, but the neighbor children made it less so, and the few ward members nearby often included her in their activities. It was second best, perhaps, but immeasurably better than a single's apartment. She kept busy and was generally happy with her life.

"I have a house," she said. "Much like these. It's nice getting away from the main part of the city."

"I'll have to come see it sometime."

Cassi nodded and wondered what Jared was thinking. Was he saying it to be polite, or did he actually want to come? Why couldn't men say what they really meant?

She looked at her watch. "Plenty of time left. There's Renae's house now." She pointed to a large house in the middle of the block. Even from four houses down they could see the huge sign announcing baby Jared's birth. Four children tumbled on the front lawn in what appeared to be an exciting game. Cassi and Jared quickened their steps. Soon the children saw them and ran down the sidewalk.

"Oh, Jared, Cassi, people are bringing us food tonight! We're out waiting for them," Janet said, reaching them first. "And all because Mommy had a baby. This afternoon they brought a cake *and* cookies! I wish Mommy could have a baby every day." Cassi and Jared laughed.

"Don't let your mother hear you say that," Cassi said, picking up the little girl.

The noise level increased as the other children arrived and excitedly pulled Cassi and Jared into the house. Jared picked up Sandy, whose legs were too short to keep up.

"Mommy, Daddy, look who's here!" Scotty yelled the minute they were in the door.

Renae lay on the couch in the front room reading a magazine while baby Jared slept peacefully in his swing nearby. She looked up curiously at Cassi, taking in her large T-shirt and disheveled appearance. Then her gaze swung to Jared, eyeing the scrapes and bruises on his face. "What's going on?" she asked, sitting up.

"We need some help from you," Cassi said hurriedly, sitting on the sofa next to Renae. "We need some cash, real fast, and we can't use our credit cards or checks because we're afraid they can be traced. We thought we could write a check to you, and you could exchange it for cash. But we need you to hold the check until Thursday morning. Can you do it?"

"Yeah, sure. If we have what you need. But what's going on?" Renae was on the edge of her seat, gazing at Cassi anxiously.

"Okay, we'll tell you—but isn't Trent home? He'll probably want to hear our story, too."

"Yes. Scotty, go get Daddy in the garden and tell him I need him. Then all of you kids go into the toy room to play. I don't want you to come out unless one of you is dying. I mean it! The Bartons aren't coming with dinner for another hour. When they do, I'll call you."

"Awww, Mom," the children murmured, but they did as they were told. Trent arrived in seconds, and soon Cassi and Jared were telling their story. Renae and Trent shook their heads in amazement.

"So you see, we just have to get the Buddha to my boss in New York, and we'll be out of it," Jared said. He handed Trent a check for two thousand dollars. "If you could give us the cash for this check and hold onto it until Thursday morning, when we'll already be in New York, it would really help us out. We probably won't use it all, but we have to buy plane tickets, pay for a motel tonight, and plan for incidentals."

"You can stay here tonight," Renae said quickly.

Cassi shook her head. "Jared has someplace he has to be tomorrow at nine, and then we need to be near the airport. Besides, we don't want to put you guys in any danger. I don't know how they could trace us here, but . . ." Cassi shrugged.

"Is there anything else we can do?" Trent asked.

"Well, you could call the company I rented the car from and ask them to pick it up," Jared said. "Don't you go there; it might be dangerous. Just tell them to send Cassi's suitcase and bag to her house and charge any of the extra expenses to me. Tell them I had an emergency." He drew out a card and scribbled the address of where he had left the car on the back, then handed it to Trent. "Oh, and could you call our hotel and have them send my things, too? Unless the FBI has confiscated them."

"Will do," Trent said. "I'm only too glad to repay you for helping Renae yesterday. I'll go to the bank right now. I should be back within a half hour." He gave them a wave and walked out the front door.

Renae eyed Jared. "You look tired, Jared. And your face looks horrible. Would you like some new bandages?"

Jared shook his head. "I don't think so. Cassi did a good job of bandaging me."

"Cassi did?" Renae looked at Cassi with raised eyebrows.

"Well, I wasn't going to let him bleed to death," Cassi retorted. "Even *my* bandaging is better than nothing."

"You will stay to eat at least, won't you? One of my visiting teachers is bringing dinner, and if there's not enough, I have some pork chops in the refrigerator that we can cook." She winked at Cassi. "You like pig, don't you?"

Cassi glared at Renae. "Some pigs are what they seem," Cassi said. "I don't think we'd better stay for dinner, had we Jared?"

Jared was looking from one woman to the other, obviously puzzled. "We ought to eat something, Cassi," he said. "We haven't eaten since breakfast."

"Well . . ." Even as she hesitated, her stomach growled loudly enough for the others to hear.

"Oh, come on, Cassi. I can start the pork chops now, and they'll be done before Trent returns." Renae stood up. "And I think I'd also better get you something else to carry your statues in," she added, eyeing the cooler. "That's kind of awkward now that you're not at the beach."

"Please, let me make the pork chops," Jared said. "I promise not to burn your house down."

"Yeah," interjected Cassi. "You shouldn't be up so soon after having a baby. In fact, I don't even see how you can walk at all after that!" She wrinkled her nose, recalling the agony Renae had gone through only the day before.

Renae laughed. "After the first one I couldn't walk without pain for over a week, but it's not so bad after the first time, except the after-birth pains are worse. I'm taking Tylenol for those. But you're right, I shouldn't be up too much. The doctor said I lost more blood than usual. So go right ahead and do the cooking. I'll get the dufflebags; it won't take but a minute to find them." She started slowly down the hall. "Just help yourself in the kitchen. If you need something, yell."

Cassi followed Jared into the kitchen. She opened the refrigerator to search for the pork chops while he found a pan and some rice.

"You like to cook?" Cassi asked when Jared started to whistle softly.

"Yes, don't you?"

Cassi blanched at the question. She didn't like to cook. No, she *hated* to cook. At home she mostly ate frozen or canned foods, or ate out. When she did try to cook, she ended up with a lot of food burned to the pans and spent hours cleaning them. Consequently, she didn't understand how anyone could enjoy cooking. The recipes always used words that made no sense at all, and she might starve to death before finding out what they meant. On her mission, she had finally decided that cooking was an innate gift that you either had or didn't have. And she didn't.

"No, I don't," she said. It wasn't in her to lie, even though she didn't want to admit the whole truth to Jared. "It takes a lot of time."

"Well, when I was growing up, my mom made each of us learn to cook. We each had a night to make dinner. At first I burnt things a lot and had to resort to hot dogs, but eventually I got the hang of it."

"My mom always did all the cooking at home. She never asked me to help," Cassi said. "Hey, I bet that with eight kids your mom never had to make dinner, right?"

Jared smiled at her crookedly. "That's right. My mom's no dummy. She never did any dishes or vacuuming after we got older, either. Smart woman!" Jared's voice was full of admiration, and Cassi envied his mother.

"I guess I'll have to have at least seven children," Cassi said. "Then I'll never have to cook dinner."

"Ah, but who will teach them? And what do you do until they're old enough to cook by themselves?" Jared added several extra dashes of garlic to the pork chops.

"Eat canned," Cassi replied immediately. "And teach them to read. Maybe put them in a cooking class. Or make their father do it."

Jared shook his head. "You're serious. You really hate cooking, don't you?"

"I detest it! When they were passing out the cooking genes in heaven, I accidentally got the cookie-eating genes instead." Once it was all out in the open, Cassi felt better, even though she knew most men wanted a wife who cooked, and the fact that she didn't would not work in her favor. But it wasn't as if Jared was actually interested in her as a woman, so what did she care what he thought? He was just an arrogant pig who knew how to cook pork chops! "And I hate vacuuming, too," she added for good measure. "I let it go for months, until you can actually see the dirt on the carpet."

"With kids you wouldn't be able to do that," Jared said.

Cassi took his comment as an insult. "Well, I don't have any kids, do I?" She turned around and stomped out of the kitchen, muttering under her breath, "I think I hear the baby crying."

She went back to the front room to find that she hadn't imagined hearing baby Jared's cry. His eyes were clamped shut, his tiny mouth opening and closing in little sobs. "Shhh," Cassi said as she approached the swing. She sat down in front of the infant. "Jared, it's okay, sweetie. Mommy's coming right back."

Little Jared didn't stop crying, even when Cassi wound his swing and set him rocking. She looked around for Renae, her heart going out to the helpless baby. Finally, she could stand it no longer and carefully scooped him out of the swing and held him close to her chest. Immediately the baby stopped crying and opened his eyes. They were a deep blue, and seemed much wiser than any Cassi had ever seen.

"See? I told you everything was okay. You gotta trust your Aunt Cassi." She bent her head and kissed the soft cheek. She noticed that little Jared's skin was partly peeling, and she faintly remembered hearing that this was normal for newborns, not something to be concerned about. She kissed him again and held him even closer.

Cassi was still sitting on the floor next to the swing, cuddling the tiny miracle, when Renae came back into the room with two dufflebags.

"He was crying," Cassi said. "He wouldn't stop until I picked him up."

Renae smiled. "Well, he's used to being snuggled inside my stomach. Babies always like lots of cuddling."

"He's so precious." Cassi touched the little hand, and the baby instinctively grabbed her finger.

"You'll have your own someday," Renae said.

Cassi looked up with tears in her eyes. "But I can't teach him how to cook," she said, knowing that to Renae, her comment sounded irrational.

Renae snorted. "So what? I can't teach my children to appreciate art or make their beds. They don't speak proper English, and I can't help Scotty with his math. Does that make me a bad mother? We can't all be talented at everything."

"I guess you're right," Cassi said, smiling. "I never thought of it that way. I guess I could always hire someone to do the cooking."

"Now you've got it." Renae threw two dufflebags on the floor by Cassi, then reached to take the baby and settled with him on the couch.

"Thanks." Cassi retrieved the bags and went to the cooler in the middle of the room. She laid the statues in the separate bags and padded them with clothing. She made sure that Jared's gun was near the top of his bag, just in case. "Maybe I should change back into my clothes," she murmured.

Renae laughed. "Don't. You look so cute, like a teenager or a tourist. Oh, that reminds me, did you see the makeup and lotion I put in the smaller bag?"

Cassi shook her head and felt in the bag where she had already put her *Mother and Baby* statue. "Thanks. It would be kind of awkward to buy something like this with Jared."

"I know. That's why I put in some extra underclothes, too. For both of you. Still in the packages. They're from our one-year clothing storage. And I put in some cash, too."

"You don't have to do that. I can just give Jared a check, and he can give me some of the cash you're giving us. Besides, his employer will reimburse us both."

"Well, keep it just in case. You might need it."

"Thank you so much."

The sound of a car in front of the house made them both start. "It couldn't be Trent yet," Renae said. "Maybe the Burtons are early with dinner." She went to the edge of the window and peeked out. She gasped. "Cassi, two men are getting out of a car. They're wearing suits. They're talking and looking at the house. They're coming up the walk!" Renae's eyes were wide as she turned to face Cassi.

Cassi's heart pounded. "Linden. He must have said something about you, and they found out who you are. But they can't know for sure that we're here. Then again, what if they search?"

"Quick, out the back way," Renae said, heading toward the kitchen. "Cut through our neighbor's yard—there's a break in the fence—and go to the grade school. Trent'll meet you there later with the money."

Cassi grabbed the dufflebags, straining slightly against the double weight. Jared looked up from the stove as they rushed into the kitchen.

"Men outside," Cassi said. She handed him the Buddha and motioned to the back door.

"What about Renae?" he asked.

"They don't want me," Renae said. "I'm just going to slip down the hall and warn the children not to say anything. Now go!"

As the door shut behind them, Cassi heard the doorbell echo through the house. *Please, Father,* she prayed. *Please watch over Renae and the kids. And please help us!*

CHAPTER 17

During the time they had been in Renae's house, the weather had changed. Dark, ominous clouds now filled the sky, and a warm wind was blowing. Jared glanced at Cassi and saw perspiration streaking her face; they had been running nonstop since leaving Renae's house. Now they were at least a mile away and probably safe. By continuing to run, they were only drawing attention to themselves.

"Stop," Jared puffed, wiping the sweat from his own brow. "We should stop."

Cassi nodded and slowed to a walk. "Do you think they're okay?" she asked.

Jared knew what she was talking about. He too was worried; he would never forgive himself for running if something happened to Renae and the children. "I think they will be. From what Renae said about their actions, they didn't seem to be in a hurry. It's probably just a routine check."

"Yeah. That's got to be it." Cassi sighed. "It must have been Linden. I must have told him that I went to high school with Renae. I guess they did some research and found out where she lived."

Jared didn't have any answers. Under the circumstances, he thought it best to change the subject. "Where did you learn to run like that?" he asked.

Cassi smiled. "I did track in high school, and I've kept up the habit of running six days a week. It's something I enjoy."

"It sure took me by surprise at the beach. I was worried about having to pull you along, but you ran faster than I did."

"I may not cook, but I can run!"

At her words, Jared recalled how helpless Cassi had been in the kitchen. The revelation that she couldn't cook, and even hated doing so, had shocked him. It had hit him abruptly that this woman, to whom he was quickly becoming attached, was far from the typical stereotype of a wife who lived to cook for her man. Before he could decide how he felt about the matter, Cassi had stomped out of the kitchen. Jared followed unobtrusively, amazed that she had heard baby Jared crying. How did she know? Could it be that even though she didn't have any cooking instincts, she still had a strong second sense about when a baby needed her? And what did it matter if she couldn't cook, as long as she was there for her children? What was more important?

Jared had continued to watch Cassi trying to calm the baby. When she glanced around helplessly, he had ducked back into the hallway. He peered around the wall again as the crying stopped, to see Cassi with her long, perfectly curled hair, cuddling the infant against that ridiculously oversized T-shirt. A feeling of awe had crept over Jared. She didn't know about babies, yet she had all the instincts of a good mother. That had made him completely forget about her inability in the kitchen.

"It's not exactly your fault," he said to her now. She looked at him curiously. "I mean, it's hard to do something that you weren't raised doing. Like having family prayer and scripture study, for example. If your family didn't do it when you were young, it's harder for you to establish that tradition in your own family, or even realize its importance sometimes."

"So you're saying it's my mother's fault that I can't cook?"

Jared smiled. She did have an innate ability to get down to the crux of the matter. "Well, not exactly. You're an adult now and have to make your own decisions about life. I just think that things like cooking would've been easier if you'd been taught."

Cassi looked at him, and her brown eyes seemed soft. "Thanks, Jared. I appreciate that. But you know, I still hate cooking."

"Well, I'm not too hip on running."

She grinned. "I could teach you. You'd probably enjoy it."

"And I could teach you to cook. *You'd* probably enjoy it." They both laughed.

A large drop of rain fell suddenly and splattered on Jared's nose. Cassi laughed even harder until she too was pelted with the warm drops. She breathed in the pungent scent of the wet pavement. "I love that smell," she said. "It's so earthy."

"Is the school nearby?" asked Jared. Cassi nodded and pointed ahead. Jared could see a large building in the distance. "I think we'd better run again."

"Don't you like the rain?" Her voice was almost challenging.

"Not particularly."

She lifted her face to the sky. "I love the rain." Then she sprinted ahead, and Jared followed. Together they ran toward the building. The rain came down harder, and soon Jared's hair and T-shirt were soaked. He looked at Cassi to see that she was equally drenched. Parts of her hair were plastered against her head, yet she had not lost any of the end ringlets. A sneaking suspicion that her hair was natural crept over Jared. Impossible! He would wait until it dried to judge. At least he knew for sure that no gel from her suitcase in L.A. would save her now.

They reached the school and set the dufflebags against the building where the rain wouldn't reach them. Then Jared settled down to wait.

"Come on," Cassi beckoned to him, going back out into the rain.

"Are you crazy? You'll get sick."

"Oh, that's only if the rain is cold. You said as much yourself when Sandy was all wet, remember? As long as it's warm outside. I've always played in the rain during the summer, and I've never once gotten sick. We have to wait for Trent, so we might as well enjoy ourselves."

She looked inviting standing on the wet blacktop with her T-shirt plastered to her slender curves. Jared stood up, allowing Cassi to grab his hand and pull him to the set of swings in the school yard. In moments both were sailing back and forth in the air above the blacktop. As their laughter echoed out over the deserted playground, Jared could almost imagine the laughter of little children accompanying them. The burdens of the last two days slipped from his shoulders, and he looked at Cassi gratefully. Her mascara was coming off in black smudges and little rivulets, but she had never looked so beautiful to him. She was so impulsive, so free, so full of life. It almost seemed as if he had known her forever. Then it came to him; perhaps he had!

When they tired of swinging they tried the teeter-totter, but she weighed so much less than he did that they had to give it up. They went to the merry-go-round, where Jared pushed Cassi on the large wheel. She had wiped the black mascara from her face, and now Jared noticed the tiny black beauty mark near her right eye. There was another just above her lip, and he found himself wanting to kiss it. He hesitated. She seemed almost like a wraith in the darkening day, a mythical creature that he couldn't, or perhaps shouldn't touch.

"What's wrong?" Cassi asked him. She leapt off the merry-go-round to stand next to him.

Jared was all too aware of her and fought the emotions boiling inside him. "Nothing. I . . . we should check on the statues." Jared couldn't bring himself to tell Cassi of his growing feelings for her. What if she scorned him? He remembered Léon's accusations against her and felt his confidence plunge even further. *No*, Jared decided. *I'll wait until this business with the Buddha is over, and then I'll find out how she feels.*

As they reached the place where they had left the bags, Cassi looked up at him with a guarded expression. A voice seemed to say in Jared's head, *Kiss her.* He felt startled, remembering how he had felt when a similar voice had warned him away from his hotel room. If he had immediately obeyed, it would have saved him problems, and he had vowed not to make the same mistake again. But this was different, wasn't it? He couldn't expose his feelings so easily. Jared hesitated, and the moment was lost.

"Cassi!" A shout from behind made them turn. Trent ran across the blacktop that separated them. It was still raining, though more lightly now, and Trent's hair dripped water into his eyes. He shoved the brown locks back from his forehead.

"Here it is," he said, handing Jared an envelope. "I got some smaller bills, too, to make your transactions less noticeable." He grinned. "I think I'm getting into this. I've half a mind to go with you myself. But I can't leave Renae."

"Is everything okay at home?" Cassi asked anxiously.

"Yes. The men wanted to know if we'd seen you, and asked us to call them if you contacted us. They didn't even come into the house. They seemed worried about you, Cassi. Are you sure they're the bad guys?"

"No, I'm not. We don't know who to trust. That's why we're going to take the Buddha to Jared's employer and be done with it. Right, Jared? Then we can forget it ever happened."

Jared wanted to disagree. Despite the problems, he was glad he had met Cassi. He wasn't sure that he wanted their adventure, however dangerous, to be over.

Trent nodded. "I guess you guys know what you're doing. Oh, I almost forgot. Here's a dinner Renae told me to make for you. It's just sandwiches and stuff, but it should tide you over."

"Thanks, Trent," Jared said as Cassi accepted the proffered sack. "We'll call you when we get to New York."

"There's a convenience store across from the front of the school," Trent said. "You could call a taxi from there."

"I've got my cellular," Jared said.

"Couldn't that be traced?" Trent asked.

"Oh, right," Jared said, chagrined. "I'm not sure if they could, but it's best to be certain. I guess we'll go call from the store."

They said good-bye and watched Trent jog across the school yard. Cassi sighed wearily. "Thank you, Father," she whispered loud enough for Jared to hear. Jared knew she was relieved for Renae's safety.

"And help us get through the rest," he added. Cassi looked at him and smiled.

*****

On the drive back to L.A. Cassi fell asleep in the taxi, her head resting on Jared's shoulder. He removed his jacket from his bag and put it over her damp T-shirt. His fingers also touched the gun in the bag, bringing the reality of their situation to him vividly. He closed his eyes and prayed fervently for help. As he did so, he remembered the prayer he and Cassi had shared aloud at the school building. How wonderful it was to share faith with a woman as wonderful as she was! It was something he could never have dreamed of doing with the calculating Laranda.

He finished his prayer and brought a hand up to stroke Cassi's soft locks. "How can I tell you how I feel?" he asked softly. "And is what I feel even real?" The ringlets of sweet-smelling hair twisted around his fingers, and he marveled at them. He had been so very wrong about her. She wasn't the vain creature he first imagined, but just herself, unadorned and simply beautiful.

Jared's eyes closed. With a full stomach from Renae's sandwiches and a comfortable position next to Cassi, he allowed himself to slide into a contented sleep.

*****

"Jared, wake up. We're here." Cassi's voice brought Jared back to consciousness. He shook his head to clear the fogginess and reached for his wallet to pay the driver with the cash Trent had given him. Then he hefted the Buddha and stepped out of the car, looking around. They had asked the driver to take them to any motel in downtown L.A., and he had obliged by dropping them off at an intersection that held four of them. They walked purposefully to the nearest one.

"What about our disguises?" Cassi asked with a little smile, remembering their earlier plan. "I don't think I can walk another step, unless I have to."

Jared sighed. "Me too. Maybe we were exaggerating a little this afternoon. They didn't know we were at Renae's, and with all the motels in L.A., they certainly won't know which motel we're at."

"Good. Let's leave it for tomorrow."

Jared nodded and opened the motel door for her.

"We need two adjoining rooms," he said to the night clerk at the desk. He had vowed not to compromise Cassi again, but wanted at least some way to check on her welfare. The clerk didn't look twice at them as he accepted money in exchange for the keys. Nor did he question the fake names Jared gave him.

Jared led Cassi inside one of the rooms and opened the connecting door. "Well, pick which one you want," he said.

"Any one that has a bathroom," Cassi said. She threw him a self-conscious look and darted into the bathroom behind her. Jared hurried through the door and into an identical room.

Cassi was moving around in her room when he emerged. He walked to the door. "I guess we'd better turn in."

She yawned. "Lots of work tomorrow. It's the Buddha's big day."

He smiled and with a wave returned to his own room, shutting the connecting door behind him. Before throwing himself on the bed, he kicked off his shoes, leaving his clothes on and his gun nearby, just in case he had unwanted visitors in the night. For long moments he lay there, not moving or letting himself feel anything.

The door from Cassi's room opened. In the moonlight coming from his half-shuttered window, he could see her face, framed by the curls he adored. She still wore the large T-shirt, with the cuffs of her long shorts peeking out beneath.

"Jared?"

He sat up in the bed. "Yes?"

"Could I leave the door open?"

A smile spread over Jared's face, and he was grateful the dark masked his features. "Yes, Cassi."

"And Jared?"

"Yes?"

"Do you mind . . . could we say a prayer together?" Her voice shook slightly, as if she was afraid of what he would say.

A feeling of rightness came so strongly over Jared that for a moment he couldn't answer. He stood up and met her at the door. "That's a great idea. Thank you for asking." He hesitantly took her hand and knelt on the worn carpet.

"Would you like me to offer it?" he asked.

"Please."

Jared prayed aloud and the Spirit filled the room. Afterward, he couldn't help himself as he leaned over and hugged Cassi, kissing her once on the forehead. With spiritual insight, he admitted to himself that the feelings he had for her went far beyond the simple physical attraction he had felt earlier at the school.

"Thank you. And good night." She got to her feet and padded into her own room, leaving Jared's arms empty but not aching. Although he wasn't sure how he would do it, he would win her yet.

But first he would have to get rid of the Buddha.

CHAPTER 18

Light filled Cassi's motel room, and she reluctantly pulled herself out of bed. The nightmares that had tortured her during the previous night were gone, but their effect remained. She felt as if she had been fleeing for weeks, when in reality this would only be the second day. Admittedly, this was the most exciting thing that had ever happened to her, and part of her was enjoying the adventure—especially being with Jared.

Cassi tried not to think about the man in the room next door. She stifled her thoughts and went into the bathroom to shower. He had not so much as tried to kiss her since the beach—on her lips, anyway. His kiss on her forehead the night before had been more like a comforting gesture given to a child. At the school, she had thought perhaps he was beginning to care about her, though at the last moment he had pulled away from her instead of kissing her as she had expected. Perhaps like her high school boyfriend, Tom, he too had been put off by her rashness.

She sighed. "Well, I am who I am." Even so, she wished she hadn't made him play in the rain; perhaps her action had made him see her more as a child than a woman.

She dressed in her light green dress of the day before, the one she had worn to Carl's house. The top part was wrinkled, but the crinkled broomstick skirt seemed no worse for traveling scrunched in the cooler and dufflebag. She felt her face soften as she thought of the gruff Carl. "I hope you're with the woman who loves you," she said aloud.

Her thoughts filtered relentlessly back to Jared. He would be going to the funeral today and leaving her behind. She was frightened at being alone with the Buddha, yet she wasn't going to let him know; she had already admitted enough of her fear by asking him to keep the door between their rooms open all night. She had finally closed it this morning before going to shower.

As Cassi left the bathroom, a knock sounded. She stiffened before she realized it was coming from Jared's room. She tried uselessly to run her fingers through her wet hair; the shampoo and conditioner supplied by the motel left much to be desired. Besides, it hadn't been her day to wash her hair, and when it dried it would be frizzy. Sighing, she went to the door and threw it open.

"Breakfast," Jared said with a big smile. "Sleep well?"

Cassi grimaced. "Between the bad guys chasing us, I guess."

"You too, huh?" He looked at her sympathetically. His face looked much better today, and he had removed some of the bandages. His black eye was fading into a dark greenish-yellow. He wore the same semi-dress clothes of the day before, complete with his tie that they had somehow managed not to lose in the confusion of the day before.

Cassi took the carton of food he handed her, recognizing it as an egg sandwich from a fast-food restaurant. On top of the carton were several large bills. "You never know if we might get separated," he explained.

"Thanks." She paused. "Uh, did you see the underclothes Renae put in for you?"

"Yes. Remind me to write and thank that woman. She's one in a million." He looked at Cassi. "Are you going to be okay? I need to leave for the funeral now. I've already called a taxi."

"But what if those men are there? I mean, if they found Renae, it's a sure thing they'll know about your friend's funeral."

Jared frowned. "I know, but I can't think how to get around them. I'll call Larry on the way to see if he sees anything unusual. At any rate, I made flight reservations for us at one, so I'll be back before then. Since I won't be staying for the graveside part of the service or the luncheon like I'd planned, we can take that earlier flight. I called and scheduled us under false names. I'll pay cash when we arrive so we won't have to show our IDs. It's not a direct flight, but we should be in New York around nine or ten, L.A. time. It'll be three hours later there."

"And we'll take the Buddha to Laranda?"

He nodded. "I'll call and see if she's home. But first we'll stop at my apartment. I have something there I want to show you."

"What?"

He smiled enigmatically. "You'll see."

Cassi's curiosity was piqued, but she tried not to show it. What could be so important that he would want to go home before getting rid of the dangerous Buddha? "They're probably watching your apartment," she said.

"I know. We'll figure out something." He looked at his watch. "I'd better go. I should be back in less than two hours."

"And if you're not?" Cassi hated the words but couldn't help saying them. She looked earnestly up at Jared. His bruised face showed only too clearly that the people after the Buddha meant business.

His hand reached out and stroked her cheek. A strange expression was on his face, one that Cassi had seen before at the school yard when she had expected him to kiss her. Since that was obviously not what it meant, she felt confused. She looked away.

"I'll be back, Cassi," he said, his voice rough with . . . emotion? Cassi was unsure. "One way or another, I'll be back." Cassi thought his words were more bravado than anything. She shook her head; sometimes men weren't very rational.

With a little wave, Jared left, leaving Cassi to wonder at how much the separation pained her and how much she wished he had kissed her good-bye. She sighed again loudly. She couldn't just throw herself at the man, could she?

There was, however, something she could do. Cassi hurried to the phone book to look up an address. Jared wouldn't approve of her leaving the motel with the Buddha by herself, but she had her own agenda. In minutes she was out the door, lugging both statues in one dufflebag and clutching Jared's money in her hand.

Luckily, the place she was headed to was nearby. Even so, Cassi was out of breath when she arrived. The Buddha, while only slightly taller than her *Mother and Baby* statue, was much wider and heavier, and Cassi was not used to carrying so much weight.

She looked up at the store name to be sure she had the right place, then plunged inside a completely different world. Wigs, costumes, and various makeup supplies filled artful displays. This wasn't just a

Halloween store, but one that specialized in disguises all year round.

"May I help you?"

Cassi turned to see a hovering clerk. The woman was about Cassi's age, though the amount of makeup she wore made it difficult to tell for sure. "Uh, yeah. A friend and I want to dress up. Like old people, maybe."

"Man or woman?"

"What?"

"Is your friend a man or a woman?"

"A man."

The clerk nodded and took Cassi around the store, showing her the different products. Cassi settled on a subtle paint for their hair, glasses, and skin makeup that made realistic wrinkles without actually affecting the real skin underneath.

"It's more expensive than the other," the woman said about the skin makeup. "But at least you'll not be damaging your own skin." Cassi nodded and paid for her items. It cost half of the money Jared had given her.

Next, she went to a secondhand store and bought old clothing and a bit of stuffing to pad their waists. She smiled in satisfaction as she spied an old cane to use with Jared's costume.

Back at the motel, Cassi wet her hair and pulled it into a knot in the back, securing it with pins she had bought at the store. With a bemused smile on her face she changed quickly into the old lady dress, padding her waist and chest to make her figure seem more realistic. Underneath, she wore the thick hose she had found at the second-hand shop. The odd pattern made her legs look old. Last of all, she sprayed her hair with the gray tint and applied the wrinkle makeup to her face and hands.

"Why, I look just like my grandmother!" Cassi exclaimed. She could hardly believe the transformation. In her mind, the steel-colored hairdo was an improvement over her own frizzy curls.

She left the bathroom and set about packing her few belongings into her dufflebag with her statue. Then she went into Jared's room and did the same with his belongings. She hesitated when she saw the T-shirt they had bought for him at the beach. She held it near her face, careful not to let it touch the drying makeup, and breathed in Jared's smell. She walked back to her room, still cradling the shirt to her now matronly bosom.

A banging at the outer door startled her. She shoved Jared's T-shirt into her bag and went to the door. "Who is it?" she asked in a craggy voice.

"It's Jared."

Cassi opened the door. Before she could say anything, Jared pushed his way in and walked around the room. "Where's Cassi?" he said, turning on her.

"Right here. It's me," Cassi said in her normal voice. Jared peered at her.

"Cassi?" He started laughing.

"I fooled you! It really works!" Then she sobered. "Why are you back so early?"

Jared's face fell. "I called Larry, and he said some men claiming to work for the FBI came by. They're going to have men all over the funeral watching for me. He also said he noticed a lot of people just sitting around in cars outside the church and in front of his house. The men Larry talked to said those men weren't theirs. I didn't get any more information because I was afraid of a wire tap or something." Jared crossed to Cassi's bed and sat down. "I won't be able to get close enough to Sister Martin to even say good-bye."

Jared's voice was expressionless, but Cassi could feel the pain behind his words. She sat next to him on the bed. "I'm sorry. She must have meant a lot to you."

"She was like a second mother," he said, looking down at his hands. "All these years since my mission she was always interested in what I was doing, like she really cared. She was a true Saint."

"Had she been sick for very long?"

"For the last year or so." Jared looked up at Cassi. "Logically, I know she's better off with her husband in heaven and with the daughter she lost, but I feel as though I'm betraying her by not being at her funeral."

His blue eyes filled with unshed tears, and Cassi reached out to lay a hand on his. "That makes sense," she said. "They say funerals are for the living, not for the dead. You know, to help them deal with their grief and to say good-bye." She paused, unsure of how she should continue. "You were with her at the hospital when it really mattered. And I think she knows how much you wanted to be there today. But from what you tell me, I also think she just might be more interested in what we're going to do with the Buddha than who's at her funeral."

Jared stared at her for a long moment before replying. Cassi held her breath. Had she gone too far? To her relief, Jared started laughing. "You're crazy, you know? But you're also right! I think Sister Martin would've loved you."

"Good, then let's get you ready, old man," Cassi said, pointing to the bag of clothing and makeup on the dresser. Jared groaned but complied. When he was dressed, Cassi began applying his makeup.

"So what made you decide to do this?"

"Well, we talked about disguises yesterday, and I got to remembering how in the movies the bad guys are always waiting at the airport. I figured that if they are waiting for us, we would be recognized."

Jared laughed. "I think you've got that covered. You could walk past your own mother and not be noticed!"

"Don't move," Cassi admonished. "How will I ever get your face to be uniformly wrinkled? It's hard enough hiding your wounds and bruises."

"I can't help it. You always make me laugh. Did anyone ever tell you that you're funny?"

"And impulsive, crazy, and unpredictable. That's why I'm not married, you know. The men I've known can't handle such spontaneity." Cassi purposely made her voice light, hoping he wouldn't see through the guise. The pain of having lost the only boy who'd ever asked her out because of her impulsiveness hadn't dimmed over the years since high school. Maybe it would have if she had dated other men, but though she had many male friends, not one had ever been romantically serious about her—at least not that she was aware of. Cassi sighed and turned from Jared to mask her emotions. "Come see how you look in the mirror," she ordered gruffly.

Jared didn't move, but sat watching her. "Cassi, look at me." She turned toward him hesitantly. "It was their loss," he said softly.

A warm feeling spread through Cassi. "Thanks," she said. "Maybe it was."

*****

The elderly couple moved slowly down the large corridor in the airport, searching for their gate number. They looked no different from the other old people in the crowd around them, except that their step was perhaps a bit more spry than it should be at their age.

"Don't look now, but they're checking ID at the gate," Cassi whispered to her distinguished-looking older companion, who bent slightly over his cane. She saw Jared look up at the men and down again quickly.

"What should we do?" she asked, adjusting the glasses that were a part of her costume. The men at the departure gate had guns at their waists and bored expressions.

"I don't know." Jared made a gesture as if checking for his own gun, the one he wasn't carrying. Not wanting to risk checking it in for the flight, in case they were being watched, they had stopped and mailed the weapon to his apartment in New York.

"Have you ever taken drama?" Cassi asked.

Jared shook his head. "Let's just go back the way we came," he said. "Looks like we'll have to go see Carl's fake ID friend after all." Jared turned around, only to see the two men who had attacked him at the hotel. He spun back to face the gate. "The men from the beach," he muttered.

Cassi felt her heart begin knocking in her chest as fear washed over her. Though they hadn't yet been recognized, they were boxed in. The men they were running from were specialists, and surely they were trained to look for disguises; it was only a matter of time before they discovered Cassi and Jared. There was only one thing to do. She shoved her dufflebag at Jared. "Get on the plane if you can, and wait for me."

She took three quick steps away from Jared and started screaming in what she imagined to be an old lady's voice. "Thief, thief! Those men stole my purse!" Cassi pointed vaguely at the men who had attacked Jared as people flocked to her. The two men backed off slightly. "Thieves! Stop them! Make them give it back! Oh, what am I going to do?"

The two men checking ID at the door raised their heads at the commotion, and Cassi beckoned to them. Silently she referred to them as FBI men, though she didn't know exactly who they were. One left the door and came to stand with Cassi.

"What seems to be the problem?"

"Those men took my purse! I was just going to get on that plane there when they came up behind me and . . ."

"We didn't take her purse," protested the man with the hooked nose. His companion nodded vigorously.

"You did too!" Cassi didn't feel any qualms for either of them. These were the men who had beaten Jared and chased her on the beach.

"Hey, don't I know you?" The FBI man said to the thug.

The men began to back away under the agent's intent stare. The FBI man motioned for his companion, who took a few steps away from the door, herding the few passengers with him so as to not let any get by without showing their identification. Cassi saw that as the man approached, Jared slipped behind his back and into the short corridor leading to the plane.

"Don't you work for Big Tommy?" asked the first FBI man.

The thugs nodded. "We ain't done nothing wrong, and you can't take us in. This old lady's crazy."

"Ain't done nothing wrong, you say? What a joke! Part of the biggest organized smuggling ring in the country, and you say you ain't done nothing wrong!" The second FBI man stopped talking, noticing the intent expressions on the faces of the people around him. Their irritation at being delayed vanished as they sensed something interesting happening, something that didn't concern them but that reeked of juicy scandal. Several took out their cameras.

"You just stay out of our way or we'll take you in," the FBI man growled at the thug, turning back to the door leading to the plane. "Come on now, folks, just get on the plane. No, don't show me your ID unless I ask for it," he added. "Let's hurry this along. I know what I'm looking for. Without a blasted passenger manifest, it does me no good to check all of you."

The rest of the passengers consisted mostly of a tourist group from Japan and several American women. There was a tall American man, too, and he was the only one the FBI man asked for identification. The lack of a passenger manifest worked in their favor, Cassi realized. Without the manifest, the FBI agent would have no way of knowing if Jared had managed to sneak on the plane. Surely they wouldn't be so lax during the flight Jared had originally booked under his real name.

"Maybe it wasn't them who took my purse," Cassi said to the first FBI man uncertainly. "I think maybe it could have been someone else. Please, young man, could you help me to my plane?" Cassi pulled her ticket from the pocket in her dress and showed it to him.

"What about your purse? We could call the police."

"Oh, it was an old one anyway," Cassi said. "And I don't keep anything irreplaceable in it. I'm not stupid. I know how these purse snatchers are; they always target old ladies. Besides, I don't even own any credit cards. Now, please, help me to my plane."

"Sure, right this way." He looked at Cassi as if an idea had suddenly occurred to him. His watery eyes grew suspicious. "But you'll need to show me some ID."

"But someone just stole my purse!" Cassi protested as they neared the door and the second agent. "My word, don't you young fellers listen? My identification was in there. To think that now I'm going to have to go to the drivers license bureau to get another one. I tell you, this is the *last* time I visit my grandchildren in L.A. This city is barbarous! Why, the last time I was here . . ." Cassi droned on until both men's eyes glazed over.

The first man looked at his companion, and both shrugged. "Go on in," the man said. "And next time, hold on to your purse."

CHAPTER 19

Jared sighed with relief when Cassi boarded the plane. Her face was wrinkled and white from the concealing makeup, but her eyes danced with excitement behind the spectacles. She had obviously enjoyed her own performance.

"Well?" he asked as she slipped into the seat beside him. He shook his head back and forth in an exaggerated motion as she told him.

"It really must have been a routine check," she said. "They weren't sure we would take this plane, or we'd never have gotten away with it. They hadn't even gotten a passenger manifest yet."

"I hoped they wouldn't guess we had changed flights," Jared said. "This morning I reserved a seat for you on the direct flight I had planned to take. I hoped they'd expect us on that one." He paused. "But that was a very dangerous thing you did."

"I don't think so. They were probably FBI at the door, don't you think? If they'd discovered me, then at least you would have been free to choose another route. I didn't have the Buddha, and for all they know we aren't even together. Right?"

Jared thought for a minute. "Maybe so. But what if they weren't FBI? And speaking of that, I'm having second thoughts about simply giving them the Buddha. They're supposed to be the good guys, right?"

"That's the way it should be," Cassi said, leaning back in her seat. "But in the movies—"

"Yeah, I know." Jared grinned at her. The rubbery makeup on his face stretched to accommodate the action.

"Oh, no," Cassi said suddenly.

"What is it?"

"I've got an itch on my cheek." She moved her cheek furiously under the makeup, but to no avail. Jared laughed. But now that she mentioned it, he felt an itch begin on the backs of his hands where he also had makeup to make them appear old.

"Me too," he said.

*****

The plane ride passed uneventfully, though both were uncomfortable under their disguises. They were nervous when changing planes in St. Louis, but saw nothing out of the ordinary. As they circled the Kennedy airport in New York, Jared marveled that the long hours had passed so quickly with Cassi. They had talked the entire flight about their lives and plans for the future. One particular thing had impressed Jared.

"I want to have my own gallery," she had said. "One where I could sell beautiful and artistic things to ordinary people. I don't want to cater just to the rich. I know it wouldn't bring as much money, but it would be real, a place that people could learn in and feel comfortable visiting."

Jared had entertained such a notion himself for the past few years, though he hadn't gone beyond the dreaming stage. "I know what you mean," he replied. "I'd like to have art classes for children. To teach them about real art."

"Exactly," Cassi said.

How different she was from Laranda, who had simply laughed at his idea when he had suggested it! Jared's boss had neither time nor patience for children, who certainly wouldn't increase her bank account. Thinking of Laranda brought a sour taste to Jared's mouth, and he put her firmly from his thoughts.

They took a taxi from the airport to Jared's apartment. Cassi sat close to him, her wrinkled face staring out the window at the passing lights. He touched her knee. "I'm glad your little play-acting back in L.A. worked," he told her. "I don't think I could have forgiven myself if anything had happened to you."

"You're not responsible for me," she said with a wicked grin. "Can't you see these wrinkles? I'm old enough to take care of myself.

Eh?" She slapped the seat near the driver's shoulder, and he agreed enthusiastically.

Her nonchalance reminded him that somewhere in her past she had lost at least one male suitor because of her impulsive behavior. Jared honestly believed that letting Cassi go had been the other man's loss, because one thing he knew was that besides being a lot of fun, sharing time with Cassi had brought him closer to heaven than he'd been in a long time. When they had been together on the plane, he could almost imagine that they actually were an old couple, grown comfortable with each other over long association, and deeper in love each day. Jared couldn't imagine anything more satisfying.

He continued staring at Cassi and found her beautiful. Even in disguise, she radiated an inner light. *The Spirit,* Jared thought to himself, finally pinpointing the source. The understanding deepened his interest. Surely here was a woman like the one Sister Martin had talked about on her deathbed. But how could he show Cassi that he cared? How could he open his heart to her? It wasn't something Jared was good at; he had learned well from Laranda.

Cassi's voice broke in on his reverie. "Is this your apartment?"

Jared looked up from the stopped taxi and nodded. "It is." He paid the driver as Cassi got out of the car. Then he glanced around quickly, but saw no one running toward them with guns. It seemed their disguises were perfect.

"It's beautiful," she said when he joined her. "I mean, as far as apartments go." The six-story building was gracefully built out of gray brick. Each window had a built-in planter box, many of which were filled with blooming flowers, though they were difficult to see in the dark despite the bright streetlights. The front of the building had a small yard in front, filled with greenery and more flowers.

"Wait until you see my apartment."

"Which floor is it on?"

"The fourth. On the left side." He pointed.

"Do you grow flowers?" Cassi strained to see the planters above her.

Jared shook his head and grinned. "Tomatoes, a little parsley, and even a pumpkin."

Cassi laughed. "Mormons will be Mormons, even in New York apartments."

"That's right," he said, laughing with her. "Come on." They went up the cement stairs together, and Jared used his key to open the outer door. As planned on the plane, they went not to Jared's apartment but to his next-door neighbor's, Meela Sanders. After many rings, they finally heard footsteps approaching.

"Who is it?" a sleepy voice called through the door. Meela was a single mother of a little boy and was careful about opening the door to anyone, particularly after one in the morning.

"It's me, Jared."

The door opened, then started to shut again as Meela spied the old couple. Her brown face twisted in consternation. "You aren't Jared."

Jared quickly put his foot in the door. "Yes, Meela, it's me. I'm just in disguise, see?" Jared reached up to his face and pulled a piece of the makeup off.

"You have Jared's voice," Meela said hesitantly. She reached a slender hand through the chained door and touched a slight bulge on Jared's nose. She pulled it suddenly, and it snapped off in her hand. She chuckled. "Why so it is, Jared old boy. Come on in." She shut the door, removed the chain, and opened it again, waving them inside. "But who's this?" she asked as she locked the door behind them.

"This is Cassi. We met in L.A. She's helping me with something."

Meela nodded, studying Cassi as if trying to determine whether she was actually old or just made up like Jared. "Are you in trouble, Jared?" Meela asked, still watching Cassi. "Some men came by yesterday with Mrs. Fackly. They were looking for you and gave me a number to call if I saw you."

Jared sighed. Mrs. Fackly was the building supervisor, and also the woman who cleaned his apartment. "May we sit down?"

Meela nodded and led the way to the living room. Jared and Cassi explained everything to her, interrupting each other to add specific details.

"So you need to give your boss this Buddha, and then you're done with it?" Meela asked.

"That's right. I called Laranda before we left the airport, but no one answered. I didn't dare leave a message in case someone else gets it first. So I guess I'll take the statue to her first thing in the morning. Laranda will probably call the FBI or whoever. The statue is obviously a fake."

"May I see it?" Meela asked.

Jared nodded and pulled the Buddha out of its protective case, setting it carefully on the coffee table in front of them.

"Boy, is that an ugly thing!"

Cassi nodded. "My thoughts exactly."

Meela looked at her. "You're not old, are you." It was more of a statement than a question.

"No, I'm not. I'm twenty-nine."

"Twenty-nine?" Jared had thought her younger than that, but found himself relieved that she was closer to his own age of thirty-three. Cassi nodded.

"So what do you want me to do?" Meela asked.

"Just give us a place to stay tonight. And a place to wash up. I don't dare use my apartment in case someone comes looking for me."

"That's fine. Just don't wake Mikey up." Mikey was Meela's five-year-old son. She looked at Cassi. "Are you hungry, or would you rather wash up first?"

Cassi scratched at her cheek. "Wash, please." As Meela led Cassi into the bathroom, Jared walked out onto the balcony off the kitchen, stopping only to take a flashlight and a knife from a kitchen drawer. He stepped easily over the rail that separated his balcony from Meela's. It took him ten minutes and the help of the knife to open the sliding glass doors to his apartment. Carefully, he searched the apartment in the dark, but found nothing out of the ordinary. Everything was exactly how he had left it. Daring to use the flashlight, he went to his closet and took out his spare gun and a change of clothing. With a satisfied sigh, he slipped back over the rail to Meela's, leaving his glass door open a sliver; he still had something to show Cassi.

As he entered the kitchen, Meela and Cassi were talking, cradling mugs of hot chocolate. "Just be grateful your hair isn't wiry as well as curly," Meela was saying. "We African-Americans spend a combined fortune trying to straighten our hair."

Cassi laughed. "I see what you mean. I guess I need to be grateful for what I've got, even though it's always messy."

"I like it that way," Jared said. Cassi had washed the gray paint from her hair, and already little ringlets were sticking out at different angles. Without thinking, he reached to touch a lock.

"Get away, you lecherous old man!" Meela said. "At least until you've grown a little younger." She shoved Jared in the direction of the bathroom.

A short time later, Jared emerged dressed in jeans and a T-shirt. Meela and Cassi were still at the table. For the first time, Jared noticed that Cassi also wore jeans and a fresh blue T-shirt. "Meela lent them to me," she said, noticing his stare.

"You can keep them," Meela said. "I haven't fit into them for years, ever since I had Mikey." She patted her hips for emphasis, though she was by no means heavy. Everyone laughed.

"I guess it's time to go to bed," Jared said.

"Wait! You said you were going to show me something," Cassi said. "Don't you remember?"

"I haven't forgotten. I was just testing your curiosity. And I've already checked out my apartment. No one's there."

"Are you going to show her 'Life'?" Meela asked.

Jared nodded. "Yes."

"What is it?" asked Cassi.

"Oh, no, I'm not telling," Meela said, stifling a yawn. "This is something you've got to see for yourself. I'm going back to bed. The couch folds down into a bed when you're ready, Cassi. It's got fresh sheets and a blanket. Jared, you can use the spare bed in Mikey's room. Just be quiet."

They watched Meela leave. "She's really great. Have you known her long?"

Jared nodded. "Five years. Just after she had Mikey. Her husband died shortly after they moved here, so I help out around the house when I can. She joined the Church two years ago. She used to smoke and drink a lot, but she's come a long way." Jared stopped and stared at Cassi.

"What is it?" she asked.

He grinned. "You looked exactly as you did the first day I saw you in front of the auction pamphlets."

She groaned. "I'd hoped you didn't remember."

"I couldn't believe someone could be so nonchalant about what the stuffy buyers thought."

"I just got caught, that's all. Boy, that seems like a lifetime ago, doesn't it?"

He chuckled. "It does at that. A lifetime in five days."

"So, are we going to your apartment or not?"

Jared smiled at her impatience. Still he hesitated. What he had to show her was something special, and so much a part of him that he feared she wouldn't see its true value.

"I spent a lot of time working to get 'Life' just right," he said, walking toward the balcony. "It's . . . it's . . . special," he finished lamely. Words were not adequate to describe "Life." For some reason, Cassi's opinion meant more than he had ever guessed. He almost changed his mind about showing it to her, but Sister Martin's words came back to him: *Open your heart and let her in.*

"Come on." He led the way over the railing and into his apartment. "Wait here," he whispered at the glass door. Cassi obeyed, and Jared swiftly rechecked the apartment for intruders. Once again he found nothing. He motioned Cassi inside the living room and shut the door behind her, making sure the heavy curtains were securely covering the glass. Only then did he dare to switch on the flashlight he had brought from Meela's.

He led the way reverently to the second bedroom, where he had placed his sofa and a few chairs in a large semi-circle as people often do around a television. But there was no TV in the room—only his collection, which he had nicknamed "Life." After making sure the blinds and curtains were tightly drawn over the windows, Jared switched on the table lamp next to the sofa, using the lowest of three settings.

Cassi gasped and shook her head in amazement.

CHAPTER 20

"Life" was the perfect title for what Jared was showing her. The collection consisted of over fifty pieces of art, similar to her *Mother and Baby* statue. The sizes ranged from a few inches to nearly a foot tall. All had realistic coloring and intricate detail, and most portrayed the family in activities common to real life. Jared had organized them in twelve groups. In the front, a father read to his children while a mother nearby nursed her young infant. To one side, a couple knelt with their offspring in prayer. Another grouping showed the children's daily bath, and still another depicted various couples entwined in passionate embraces. Cassi's experienced eyes picked out the statues' flawless lines and calculated the value of the collection, while her heart felt the impact on quite a different level.

"It's perfect," she said.

Jared chuckled in the dim light. "I think so. I hoped you'd like it."

"Like it? I love it! I want it! It must have taken years to find all these pieces."

"Six, to be exact," Jared said.

Cassi was silent. Her own small collection paled by comparison. Only in the last few years had she started to buy a few expensive pieces for herself, like the *Mother and Baby*.

Her heart nearly stopped beating. The *Mother and Baby* statue! Instinctively she understood that Jared had wanted it, not to sell at Laranda's gallery as she had supposed, but to put here with others of its kind. But, no! It was hers, and she wasn't selling.

Cassi examined each piece of the collection, caressing them lovingly with her eyes and giving credit where she knew it was due. Without a doubt, Heavenly Father had inspired those who had made these antique items, long before the Church had been restored on the earth. That Jared had recognized their subtle value, when the world didn't give them much notice, said a great deal in his favor. Cassi felt that by looking at his collection, she was looking at his heart; she knew him much better than she had before, perhaps better than she had ever known anyone.

She shook off the feeling. "Thank you for showing me this. I will never forget it."

Jared smiled at her in the lamplight. She could see that he was pleased with her reaction. "Let's go," he said. "We can see it again tomorrow."

He switched off the lamp, and they retraced their steps to the living room where the sliding glass door next to a long couch led to the balcony. Before they could open the glass, they heard someone at the door. Cassi felt Jared grab her and pull her back.

"Quick!" he whispered. "Hide!" As he spoke, he ducked behind his couch, dragging Cassi with him. He pushed her closer to the floor and hovered in a squat above her, poised to jump. Cassi felt a sense of protection, though she didn't know what Jared might do if the people on the other side of the door were armed. They waited tensely as the sound at the door increased and a key turned in the lock.

A key! Who had a key to Jared's apartment? Cassi was curious, but she knew that now was not the time to ask. Besides, Jared seemed just as puzzled as she was. His body, pressed against her back, was tense, and she could feel his heart pounding through their shirts and his warm breath on the back of her neck. In another situation, she might have enjoyed his closeness.

The door to the apartment opened, and they heard footsteps. A tiny ray of light flicked around the room. "He ain't here," a gruff voice said after a while.

"He ain't in the bedroom either," a second voice said a bit louder.

"Shut up, would ya?"

"I tell ya, he ain't here. He must have missed his flight. You know, I'm thinkin' of getting into a new line of work. These late nights are gettin' to me. And this job's been full of dead ends. First we have to rob a hotel safe to find an item that ain't there, and nearly get caught by the Feds; then we spend most of tonight checking out an airport for a guy that ain't coming. Why is this stupid Buddha so important?"

"I don't know," rasped the first man in an odd voice that Cassi wouldn't readily forget. It reminded her of Carl's gruff voice, only deeper and without the warmth that characterized Jared's friend. "And it ain't our place to ask," the craggy voice added. "We just do as we're told and get paid for it. This new boss of ours seems okay, if a little uniformed."

"Yeah. And gives a better view than our old one, at any rate." Both men chuckled, and Cassi felt shivers run up her spine.

"Come on, let's get out of here," said the man with the strange voice. "We're wastin' time."

The door slammed shut, and Cassi breathed a sigh of relief. But neither she nor Jared moved until they were positive the men were really gone. Finally, they were confident enough to go back through the adjoining balconies. Jared took her hand and led her through Meela's dark kitchen to the living room. He let go of her hand and sank to the couch. "They had a key. Where would they get a key?"

Cassi plopped down beside him. "I don't know. It doesn't make sense. Those guys are the ones who broke into the hotel. Could they be working for Linden?"

Jared moved closer to Cassi. "I don't know, but I'll sure be glad when this is all over."

"Me too." Cassi leaned back on the couch. Jared had flung his arms across the top, and her head lay on his arm. She felt her heartbeat become ragged as it had when the thugs were searching Jared's room, only now it was for quite another reason. She lifted her head so he could move his arm, but he didn't move.

"Cassi." His voice had a strained, nervous sound.

She turned toward him. "Yes?"

"I . . . thank you for coming to New York with me." He was so close that Cassi could see him, even in the dark. On his bruised face was the expression she had seen so many times, yet misinterpreted; for each time she saw the look, he would either change the subject or move away instead of taking her in his arms and kissing her. Cassi didn't want him to retreat now. She wanted to know how he felt about her, even if it meant risking her own feelings.

She took a deep breath. "I like being with you." She had been going to say, "I just wanted to be with you," but at the last second had changed her mind. There was a difference between admitting you liked someone and throwing yourself at him.

"I like being with you, too." He moved his face closer and their lips touched, gently at first and then with more intensity. Cassi felt her emotions soar. He was kissing her—not to fool any chasing thugs, but because he liked her. Yes, her, Cassi Mason! His feelings were plainly visible in the way his lips moved against hers.

His arms went around her, and their kiss deepened. It wasn't like the clumsy smooching Tom had given her in high school before dumping her after the prom, or like the dainty pecks Cassi's men-friends gave her when they had business lunches. This was a whole-hearted kiss that sparked fire in her soul. She felt dizzy and clear-headed all at once, and she didn't want it to end.

She twisted her body on the couch to slide closer to him. As she did so, her foot kicked the coffee table with such force that a sharp pain began in her foot and traveled up her leg. She broke away from Jared with a swift intake of air, just as a loud crash came from in front of them.

"What?" Jared flipped on the lamp beside the couch, only to verify the sick feeling in Cassi's stomach. Her kick had caused the Buddha to topple to the floor.

"Oh, no!" she cried as they both leaned over to see the damage.

Jared grabbed her hands as she reached for the statue, looking into her eyes. "Cassi, it's okay. Remember, it's counterfeit. And even if it weren't, it's insured. What's important is that your foot's okay."

Cassi felt relief. *Thank heaven he's not angry,* she thought. "It's fine now," she said aloud, grimacing. "But I'm sorry."

He smiled. "It's my fault. I should have known better than to kiss you when we were all alone in a dark room like this. I really am a gentleman— I think. I have to remind myself of that a lot since I met you."

"You do?"

"I do." He gazed at her seriously, as if wanting to say more.

Cassi felt a blush tinge her cheeks and looked away. He released her hands, and once more she reached for the Buddha. It had fallen on the back of its head, leaving several large cracks and a small opening in the thin neck. As she lifted the statue, tiny objects about the size of large peas streamed from the fissure.

Jared scooped up several and held them on his palm. "You were right," he said with wonder. "It is filled with something."

"The movies were right, you mean. I can't believe it! Are those diamonds?" The objects seemed to pick up the lamplight and reflect it back tenfold. Cassi set the Buddha to the side on its face so that no more of the gem-like objects could fall out. Then she gingerly picked up one of those that had fallen on the gray carpet.

Jared shrugged. "If so, then they're the biggest cut diamonds I've ever seen."

"This must be worth a fortune!"

"A lot more than four hundred thousand greenbacks, I'd say."

Cassi snapped her fingers. "Smuggling! Those FBI men at the airport said something about the thugs who chased us being involved in smuggling. That's why they wanted the Buddha."

"I must have outbid their man at the auction," Jared said excitedly. "That's how we got involved. Laranda is going to go nuts when I tell her about this. She has a buyer all set up for this ugly thing. When she learns it's a fake, she's going to hit the roof!"

Cassi's smile vanished. "That means Linden knew all along. Do you think he's the one who was trying to smuggle them into the country?"

Jared shook his head. "You don't know that, Cassi. If he was the buyer, then he'd have let you bid more on it, don't you think?"

"Then why didn't the smuggler's man bid more?" Cassi countered.

Jared shrugged. "There are still a lot of unanswered questions."

Cassi stared at the diamond in her hand. She tried to calculate its worth along with the hundreds of others that were still inside the Buddha. These would be able to buy her a gallery and anything else she had ever dreamed of having. What if she and Jared were to simply disappear with all of them? She grimaced. What was she thinking? She dropped the diamond on the carpet and rubbed her hands over her face. "I don't know anything anymore. I don't know who I can trust—except you."

Jared took one of her hands in his. "You *can* trust me, Cassi. You can." He squeezed her hand for emphasis before letting it go. "Now help me get the diamonds back inside the Buddha. I know where Meela keeps the tape; that'll keep them inside until I get to Laranda's."

They taped the Buddha and repacked it in its case. Then Jared opened the couch bed for Cassi. "I guess we'd better turn in." He took a few steps toward the hall.

"Jared?" Cassi said.

"Yes?"

"Did you even think about keeping them? The diamonds, I mean."

He came back and stood beside her with a lopsided grin. "Yeah. I thought of buying us some fake passports and going to Europe somewhere to live a life of luxury. In my fantasy, I even bought a Ferrari for me and three fur coats for you. Of course, I knew I wouldn't do it. Temporary happiness may be bought, but I'm shooting for eternity."

"Me too. Only I thought of buying a gallery," Cassi admitted. "I couldn't wear all three fur coats, you know."

Jared laughed. "Art. It's in your blood. I like that." He hugged Cassi and kissed her quickly, as if he was almost afraid to let himself get carried away again. "Good night, now. I'll see you in the morning. Tomorrow, after this is all over, we'll go out to eat or something. I'll show you all my favorite haunts in New York."

"New York has something other than buildings?" Cassi asked with fake innocence. She had been to New York many times in her job, and she knew the city better than a casual visitor. It may not have the same charm that California held for her, but it had its own particular beauty.

"You'll see," Jared promised. He gave her a wave and disappeared into the hallway, looking as handsome as any man Cassi could remember.

"Three fur coats!" she whispered. That meant Jared had thought about staying with her even after this adventure was over. It was more than Cassi had dared hope for. Her greatest fear was that once the Buddha mystery had been solved, he would disappear from her life forever as quickly as he had come into it. She didn't want to entertain that thought. These past few days had been wild and at times scary, but she wouldn't have given up a second of her time with Jared.

Was she in love? Cassi didn't know enough about it to be certain. She had never believed it could happen so fast, but she felt that what they had could possibly develop into a strong bond like the one shared by her parents.

With a smile, she switched off the lamp and knelt by her bed in prayer.

*****

The next morning, Cassi awoke to the smell of bacon. She sniffed several times and sat up in bed before she could convince herself she wasn't dreaming. She hadn't had a bacon and egg breakfast anywhere other than in a restaurant since she had left home at age eighteen. Slipping out of bed, she pulled on the jeans Meela had given her and tucked in the ends of the huge T-shirt they had bought at Venice Beach. The long folds had served better as a nightdress than as a shirt. Giving it up, she made her way to the kitchen, expecting to see Meela.

"Jared!"

"Good morning, sleepyhead."

Cassi groaned. "How did you get up so early?"

"It's not early for us New Yorkers. We're three hours ahead, you know. Would you like some breakfast?"

Cassi nodded. "It smells wonderful. Ordinarily I wouldn't have been able to get out of bed at . . ."—she glanced at a clock on the wall above the table—"seven-thirty after such a late night, but that smell is heavenly."

"Sit down."

Cassi did as she was asked. She studied Jared as he put the finishing touches on the breakfast. He was already dressed in the jeans of the night before, but this time he wore a dress shirt with his jacket on top; he must have sneaked back to his apartment again for another shirt. That reminded Cassi of his collection of statues, and how she would like to see them in the daylight. Of course, that could wait until they got back from Laranda's.

"Here you go," he said, placing a steaming plate in front of her.

"Aren't you going to eat?"

"I had some already, before you came in. Besides, I called Laranda and she's meeting me early at the gallery. We open at nine, and I wanted to show her the Buddha before then. Without interruptions."

"But . . . are you going right now?"

"Yeah. I thought I'd get it taken care of and then get back here as soon as possible, so we can go out like we planned."

Cassi's hand tightened on her fork. They had come so far together, and now he wanted to finish it himself. Why didn't he want her with him? "The police or whoever might need me," she said.

"Then I'll bring them back with me." Jared sat down at the table and looked at Cassi. "Please, Cassi. I can't explain it all right now, but I have to go alone. You're not mad, are you?"

She wasn't mad, but hurt—and not about to admit it. "No," she said tersely.

"I know this may sound strange, but Laranda is . . . well, I don't have time to explain it properly. Please, just trust me on this. Besides, those people looking for us could be waiting there, and I don't want to put you in any more danger. I've done that too much as it is." He paused. Cassi busied herself with her food, though she had suddenly lost her appetite. "And we promised to call Renae and let her know we got here okay," Jared added hopefully.

Cassi nodded, trying to mask her feelings. "All right, Jared. I'll stay." She wanted to add that he'd better have a good explanation, but worried she might burst into tears before she finished the sentence. That would only embarrass both of them. Besides, she had no real right to question him; ultimately, the Buddha was his problem.

"And someone's got to say good-bye to Meela and Mikey for us. They should be getting up in an hour or so. I'll call you when everything's clear. Then you can go and wait in my apartment, or go for a walk or whatever. Meela's got my extra key around here somewhere— just in case I lock myself out—so you won't have to go through the balconies again." Jared talked so fast that Cassi could tell he felt bad about leaving her alone. She did feel happier knowing he trusted her in his apartment with his "Life" collection. Maybe that made up for how he was acting now.

"All right. Then go already," Cassi said.

Jared looked down at her, hesitating as if wanting to say more. He touched her shoulder awkwardly. Cassi's eyes met his, and a tingle flooded her body. "I'll be back," he said.

After he left, his words rang out hollowly, almost ominously in the quiet kitchen. Instead of feeling comfort, Cassi felt more agitated than when Jared had first said he was going without her. She finished her breakfast and washed the dishes sullenly.

"He made this breakfast simply to bribe me," she made the fork say to the knife in the sudsy water.

"That's a man for you," replied the knife. "They never say what they really mean or want, they just cover up with bribes and suggestions. Why can't they be more like women?"

"Those creatures?" interjected the plate. "They're even worse, falling for men they've only known for six days."

"Well, he kissed her!" the cup said.

"She kissed him!" countered the spatula.

Cassi sighed. This was getting her nowhere. Besides, she was quickly running out of dishes to talk for her.

"At least I'm not talking to myself," she said, "only dishes. Whoops, there I go again."

After finishing the dishes, Cassi went down the hall to the bathroom to clean up. She discarded her large T-shirt for the blue one Meela had lent her the night before. Unlike her other clothing, it smelled fresh and clean.

The minutes ticked slowly by. Cassi paced from the living room to the kitchen and back again, trying not to wake Meela. At eight o'clock, she could stand it no longer. She had to talk with someone or go crazy, time difference or no. She sat down on the couch and dialed Renae's number in Covina. It rang three times before anyone answered.

"Hello?" said a groggy voice.

"Renae, it's me, Cassi."

"Where are you? Are you in trouble?" Renae's voice sounded more alert now, and Cassi could hear Trent in the background.

"No. I'm sorry for calling so early. It's just that I'm upset. Oh, I should have waited."

"No, Cassi, I'm glad you called. I've been waiting to hear from you. In fact, I tried to call you at Jared's but there was no answer—hasn't he ever heard of an answering machine? Anyway, I've got so much to tell you. You see, I talked to Linden."

"You *what?* You didn't tell him where I was, did you?"

"No. I don't know where you are, so how could I tell him? But shut up for a minute and let me tell you what happened. After you and Jared left, Trent and I got to thinking that despite the many movies to the contrary, those men claiming to be from the FBI probably were who they said they were, and most likely they're on the good side. Anyway, I called the number they left me and asked to know more about what was going on. At first they wouldn't tell me, but then

Linden called me last night and told me everything he knew. You see, he's been working with the FBI to crack down on this new smuggling ring. He says they believe someone's using the Buddha to smuggle something important. Only it's not the main cartel who usually does a lot of the big-time smuggling—Big Tommy, or something—meaning that the established smuggling cartel is mad at the newcomer."

Cassi moaned. "With us stuck in between."

"Right. Now you're starting to see the picture."

Knowing about the diamonds, the story Linden had told Renae made sense. "But all that shouldn't matter now," Cassi said. "Jared went to give the Buddha to Laranda, and she'll call the police. Oh, I wish we had done that back in L.A.! It wasn't until I saw the diamonds last night that—"

Renae gasped. "Diamonds? You saw them?"

"Yes, but—"

"And Jared went to give them to his boss?"

"Yes." Cassi felt fear clutch at her throat.

"Oh, Cassi that's what I'm trying to tell you. They suspect Jared's boss *is* the smuggler! And now that Jared knows about the diamonds—"

"She'll never let him go without . . . Oh, Renae, what am I going to do?" Panic flooded Cassi's mind. "Jared must have suspected. That's why he wouldn't let me go with him to give her the Buddha. Oh, I've got to do something!"

"Cassi, calm down. Linden and his friends flew to New York yesterday. They should be there. They'll help Jared."

"But what if they aren't there in time? Renae, I can't let him die!" Cassi started crying. Renae was saying something else, but Cassi was beyond hearing. She dropped the phone back onto its cradle.

Deep sobs wracked Cassi's body. At that moment she knew that despite the short time she had known Jared, she loved him. Loved him! And she couldn't let him die! "Think!" she said aloud, knocking her hand on the side of her head to clear it.

"Is everything okay?"

Meela stood in the doorway. Cassi jumped up from the couch and ran to her side. "It's Jared; he's gone to Laranda's. Only I just found out that she's the one behind all this. The Buddha is full of diamonds. Oh, Meela, you've got to help me!"

"What can I do?"

The woman's calm question helped Cassi control her emotions. "Tell me where the gallery is, and . . . do you have a gun?"

Meela nodded. "Everyone in New York has a gun," she said. She went to the kitchen and reached into the cupboard above the refrigerator. She drew out a small box and opened the lock with a key from a chain around her neck. "Are you sure about this?"

"I have to try to help him, Meela. I just have to. Please."

Meela gave her the small pistol and a handful of bullets. "I don't keep it loaded."

Cassi stroked the new-looking bluing on the gun. It was a Ladysmith .38 Special and, despite her aversion to guns, it felt good in her hand.

"I've never fired it—except for when I got the permit," Meela said. "Do you know how?"

"My brother's a police officer," Cassi said. "His hobby is anything to do with guns. He made me learn a few years ago." She put the bullets in her pocket and tucked the gun in her bra between her breasts. Then she pulled on the big white T-shirt from Venice Beach on top of the blue T-shirt. "I won't load it now," she said. "I wouldn't want it to go off before—" She shrugged. She hoped she wouldn't have to load the gun at all. "Can you see it?"

Meela shook her head.

"Thanks, Meela. I appreciate it. I hope we'll meet again."

"I'm calling the police," she said.

"That's a good idea. And pray, too, would you?"

Meela nodded. Cassi gave her a quick hug, then turned to the door.

"Wait, Cassi, let me write down the directions for you. And take these." Meela threw her a set of keys. "They're Jared's. I'm sure he has one for the gallery there."

Cassi caught the keys and shoved them into the pocket with the bullets. She waited impatiently while Meela wrote down the directions to the gallery. Finally, she was out the door. "Oh, please let me be on time," she prayed as she ran down the hallway. "Oh, please."

CHAPTER 21

The June morning was warm, and already the traffic was heavy. People filled the sidewalks, trying to avoid the gaze of others who crossed their paths. Normally, Jared would purposely go out of his way to smile or say hello to his fellow New Yorkers, but today he was too busy watching to see if he was being followed. There had been a car parked outside his apartment building, and he had run quickly around the back and weaved through the side streets to be sure he wasn't followed. Now he tried to hum and act natural, but he felt his apprehension etched clearly on his face, as plainly as though he were guilty of some crime.

Jared felt awful about leaving Cassi behind, yet he knew it would be a mistake to take her with him. Not only would this last part of their journey be the most dangerous—for surely the people chasing them knew where he was headed—but it would also involve Laranda. To himself he admitted that his beautiful boss was the real reason he didn't want Cassi along.

Laranda's face, cold and calculating, came to his mind. Funny that it was never her great beauty he remembered when he was separated from her. It was always her business sense and her impartial judgments, her hawklike stare and her blatant propositions that echoed in his memory. Only when he was with her did he recognize her exquisitely sculptured features and flawless porcelain skin.

Cassi, with her slightly olive-cast skin and dark eyes and hair, was Laranda's opposite in every way. She was as beautiful inside as she was on the outside, as kind and soft as Laranda was hard and cruel. Jared felt a need to protect Cassi from Laranda, a woman of the world who would not look too kindly upon being scorned by Jared in favor of another woman. Laranda had put up with his refusals when there had been no love interest in his life, confident that he would eventually fall to her wiles. But with Cassi around, Laranda would no longer have any hope. Jared had heard many times that hell had no fury like a woman scorned, and he could well imagine that Laranda's brutal wrath would be boundless.

"You will give in to me one day," she had said once, smiling her perfect smile.

"Only if you convert to my religion," Jared replied jokingly. It was always best to keep things light with Laranda.

"Is that what it would take?" she asked with arched eyebrows. "Maybe I'll convert you instead." She had cast him one of her sensuous looks that made him back away in self-defense, dragging his traitorous body along.

Jared didn't fool himself that Laranda wanted him for his good looks or inner qualities, but simply because he had put himself out of her reach. He had known all along that any relationship between them would have been temporary for her and painful for him; he had the potential to love, whereas Laranda had suppressed such tendencies long ago.

"She may be successful," Jared muttered to himself, "but she will end up alone." His words reminded him of what Sister Martin had said about having posterity, and how grateful she had been to have her family around her when she died. "I don't want to die alone," he said. It suddenly dawned on him that since he had gone to the hospital to help Cassi, he hadn't felt alone—not once. The longings he usually felt for a family life out of his reach had utterly vanished.

Jared quickened his pace. *The sooner you give Laranda the Buddha,* he told himself, *the sooner you can be with Cassi.* A smile spread over his face and he laughed, thinking of how Cassi also admitted to talking to herself. How alike they were!

Cassi! He could feel the touch of her lips even now. The night before, when they had kissed, Jared had admitted to himself that he was in love, though part of him still fought the notion. He hadn't planned to give in to his desire to kiss her at all, except that once again he had felt the promptings of the Spirit. This time he hadn't paused to think about getting hurt, or why the Spirit would want him to kiss a woman in the dark. Perhaps it had been to find the diamonds—or maybe it was simply time he showed Cassi his true feelings. But in the end, the Buddha had fallen, and during the ensuing discovery of the diamonds, he hadn't been able to tell her of his . . . love? Was it really love? Wasn't it too soon to know?

Jared forced his mind away from thoughts of Cassi and back to Laranda and the Buddha. Despite the tension between him and Laranda, they had also been longtime friends. He respected her business sense almost entirely, though he occasionally disagreed with her methods. She had been a good boss, giving him leeway with his purchases and helping him gain confidence. Unlike most of his previous employers, she was willing to take a risk if the odds were right. On his end, Jared had done the extra research that had made those risks pay off. He had earned his position, but Laranda had given him the room to prove what he was worth.

What would she do when he brought her the diamonds? Jared knew she would want to keep them, but in the end, she would have to turn them in. Even her greed would not overrule her logic. Jared himself had rejected the idea of keeping even a portion of the diamonds; because he was a Latter-day Saint, it was completely out of the question. In Primary he had been taught to ask, "What would Jesus do?" whenever a decision faced him. Thus, his course was clear.

Jared came to a stop, shifting the weight of the Buddha. He was near the gallery now, and he needed to scope out the situation. There were at least three different groups of people after the Buddha and its precious cargo—the FBI, the thugs who had attacked him and chased them on the beach, and the men who had broken into his apartment and robbed the safe at the hotel. "Unless two of them are working together," he muttered.

At any rate, he would be a fool not to take precautions. He began walking again, but more slowly. Sure enough, two men stood separately on either side of the gallery steps. At this distance Jared couldn't be sure, but he thought he recognized the hooked nose of one of the men who had attacked him at the hotel.

"Newspaper?" a young boy asked. He stood near a corner magazine stand with a stack of newspapers. Inside the stand, the boy's father sold magazines and gum, as well as more newspapers.

"Thanks." Jared handed the boy his money. He opened the paper and stood slightly to the side of the stand, studying not the print but the gallery. With each passing minute, more people arrived in the busy streets, as many businesses opened at eight. With this natural cover, Jared felt confident he would not be spotted until he was closer to his goal. Then he noticed several cars parked across the street from the gallery. A few had people still inside them—an unusual occurrence at this hour, when most people were hurrying to work or to complete their daily errands. Also, there were several cafes whose outer tables held more customers than normal. Something was definitely amiss.

How could he get to the gallery without being seen? Two alleys led to the back of the gallery, but Jared spotted men he didn't recognize at both entrances. He continued to puzzle over the possibilities, but every idea came back to the alleyway nearest him. Somehow he would have to get past the guard.

Jared's attention wandered over the passing people, searching for an idea. His eyes fell on the boy selling newspapers. The youngster awkwardly helped his father by stopping people in the street as they passed. Most ignored him, cursing because he was in their way. Jared waited until the boy drew near. "You there," he said.

"You want another paper?" The boy eyed the one already in Jared's hands.

"No, I want to hire a messenger."

"For what?"

"There's a man standing in the alleyway, over by the art gallery. I want you to deliver a message to him."

The boy's eyes grew calculating. "How much?"

"Ten dollars."

"Really?"

Jared nodded. "Will you do it?"

"Sure thing. What's the message?"

"Tell him someone wants to meet with him about the Buddha. I know what's in it, and I want to make a deal. Got it?"

"Someone wants to meet him about the Buddha, you know what's in it, and you want to make a deal. Easy. But aren't you going to tell him where to meet you? Or do you want me to bring him here?"

"No, not here," Jared said quickly, nearly kicking himself for the oversight. "There's too many people." He looked around furtively for the child's sake. The boy's smile grew. "Tell him to go inside the café across the street, to table ten, and I'll call him with further instructions." The boy's eyes widened. Jared pulled out the money and handed it to him. Then he added, "I'll leave another ten in the plants at the base of this tree for when you get back." Jared squatted down beside one of the trees that occasionally dotted the street and began making a hole in the greenery at the tree's base, making sure that none of the passersby could see what he was doing. Not only would the extra money urge the child to deliver the message quickly, but would assure that his attention would be elsewhere when Jared slipped into the alleyway.

The boy dropped his few papers on the ground near his father's stall and raced down the street. Jared quickly finished burying the money and followed as closely as he dared. Just before the boy reached the man, Jared slipped into the first open door he spied, a bakery. Delicious aromas tantalized Jared's nose, and he felt hungry. He had eaten a little this morning when he had cooked breakfast for Cassi, but he had been too agitated to eat a full meal. He walked to the counter.

"May I help you?" asked the elderly lady.

"A croissant please," he said, twisting his head around so he could look out the window. He had expected to see the man walking across the street by now, but he was nowhere to be seen. Was it possible Jared had missed him?

He paid for the pastry and sidled up to the window near the door, careful to stay slightly to the side so that anyone walking casually by wouldn't notice him. There was still no sign of the man.

The crusty bread filled his mouth and somehow brought memories of Cassi. Why couldn't he get her out of his mind? That morning he had awakened early, thinking to leave before she had a chance to object. But as he passed the living room, he had peered in to see her sleeping soundly, and he knew he had to say good-bye.

She had been disappointed about his decision to see Laranda alone, and maybe even hurt; but Jared told himself he would explain later. He would make her understand that he had only been trying to protect her.

The man Jared had been waiting for appeared suddenly, but not crossing the street as Jared expected. He was right outside the bakery window with the boy. Jared drew back further from the window, reaching under his jacket for his second-best gun, which he had retrieved from his apartment. Miraculously, the man didn't see him.

"He was just over there," the boy was saying, "but he's gone now. You'll just have to go to the . . ." The voice trailed away, and Jared dared a peek out the window. The man and boy walked over to the tree where Jared had left the money, and the child reached down and brought up something in his hand. The man nodded, satisfied, and left, crossing the street in the direction of the café. The boy stared after him for a moment, then ran to show his father the money he had earned.

Jared was out the door in an instant, stuffing the rest of the bread in his mouth and walking quickly to match his pace with the people on the sidewalk. There were more people now to blend in with, but he sighed with relief when he was able to duck into the deserted alleyway. It wouldn't be long until the thug realized he had been tricked, and Jared had to be inside the gallery before his pursuer came looking for him.

In less than a minute, Jared was at the end of the alleyway, only to come across another man as he turned the corner. They saw each other at the same time.

"You!" the thug said in a gruff voice that sounded strangely familiar. He held out his hands menacingly. Jared darted around him and ran toward the back door of the gallery. If he could only reach it in time! But the man's hands reached out and grabbed Jared's dufflebag, pulling him to a stop.

"You got the Buddha?" the man rasped.

Those four additional words were enough for Jared to place the voice. This was one of the men who had been at his apartment the night before! Anger welled within him, and with a burst of energy he tore the bag out of the man's hands and punched it toward his exposed stomach.

"Umph," the man grunted.

Jared hit him again, this time in the head. There was a loud pop, and the man reeled as the hard case inside the bag made contact. He took a couple of steps backward and roared with anger. Fists clenched, he came at Jared, his eyes murderous. Jared dropped the Buddha, thinking that its condition hardly mattered anymore. It was a fake and worthless, shattered or not.

He feinted and then jabbed at the man's face, hitting flesh. Jared was smaller than his opponent, but what mattered now were the long hours he had spent at the gym each week. His reflexes were sharp and his punches hard. The man he fought was also experienced, but unlike that night at the hotel, there was only one to fight. Now Jared's trimmer build worked to his advantage as he made a smaller target for the man's potentially lethal strokes.

He stepped to the side to avoid a blow, feinted twice, and then scored on the man's jaw. Enraged, the thug came toward him, punching without pausing. One of his blind punches hit Jared in the stomach and another in the chest. He gasped in pain but didn't step back. He fought for all he was worth. The man retreated slightly and Jared pressed his advantage, no longer feinting but simply trying to make each punch score, while dodging the ones thrown at him.

Finally the man gave a grunt of pain and dropped to the blacktop, still breathing but unconscious. Jared's hand ached from the blow that had felled his large opponent, and his sore chest heaved. He threw the bag with the Buddha on top of the man and dragged them both to the back door of the gallery. With his key he opened it and pulled the man in, locking it securely after him and rearming the gallery's alarm system. They were in the packing department, and Jared quickly found some tough string to tie the man's hands. He might be out for awhile, but it was possible he would come to and sound the alarm to whoever was his employer. He needed to stay inside the building until the police arrived.

Slow clapping brought it to Jared's attention that he wasn't alone. He turned to see Laranda sitting calmly on one of the packing tables. "Very good, Jared. I knew you would make it here."

"This man tried to get the Buddha," Jared said.

She shrugged and slid off the table. She wore a red, shiny, skin-tight dress that flaunted her ample bosom to good advantage; it was not only immodest but embarrassing to Jared. Her neck, ears, and wrists sported expensive diamond and white-gold jewelry. He averted his eyes from the gaudy display.

She glanced at the man on the floor, then turned to Jared. "He doesn't matter. You do. I underestimated you."

"What?" Jared asked. Laranda wasn't making sense.

"Give me the Buddha," she said, ignoring his question.

He handed her the dufflebag. "Uh, it got a little beat up."

Her expression was bemused. "How do you expect me to sell a broken statue?"

"It's a fake, so we should get reimbursed." The words tumbled out of Jared's mouth as she opened the bag. "And that's not all; there are diamonds in it. Someone's using the Buddha to smuggle them, probably from India where the Buddha came from, or maybe from somewhere else. I don't know. But we need to call the police. I should have done so before, but I didn't know about the diamonds until last night."

Laranda paid no attention to his rambling. She drew the Buddha out of its case, significantly more damaged than the night before. Diamonds flowed into her hands. A calculating smile covered her face. "They are beautiful, aren't they?" Her voice echoed eerily in the large room. She rolled them around on her palm, watching the full range of colors they reflected. Some seemed to glow like icy fire, as if reflecting Laranda herself.

Jared felt suddenly cold inside. He glanced around for the first time, realizing that the room was empty of the regular employees. "Where is everybody?" he asked.

Laranda tore her eyes away from the diamonds with apparent difficulty. "Taking the day off," she said. She turned back to the diamonds, inverting the Buddha to let them all slide into the case.

"But—" Suspicion crept slowly over Jared. "I'd better call the police," he said.

Laranda laughed. "Come with me. I've something to show you." She picked up the case of diamonds and walked to the large vault in the corner of the room. Without looking to see if Jared followed, she twirled the dials. "We can't call the police," she said. "I've yet to complete the deal with my buyer."

Before Jared could object, she opened the heavy door and stepped in. She walked quickly to the back and unlocked a drawer with a key, stepping to the side. "Open it," she directed.

Jared did as he was told. He gasped and drew out a Buddha identical to the first, except that it was uncracked and whole. Understanding flooded through him.

"You!" he said, staring at Laranda. "You had the second Buddha made!"

She nodded. "By copying the original that I bought a few years ago in India."

"Then you—" Jared's eyes swung to the diamonds she carried.

She smiled her icy smile. "Of course, Jared. Of course, it was me." With one hand she shut the drawer with the Buddha and turned abruptly, leaving the vault.

Again Jared followed her. "But how did you know I would get it at the auction? I mean, there was another man who seemed very interested, and a woman who might have outbid me."

"The man bidding against you was the one who sold us the diamonds," Laranda said. "He was there simply to make sure you bid the proper amount—which, incidentally, is only one third of what I have already paid. The woman was unimportant. As the price of the Buddha went above its real value, all others would lose interest. Wasn't that so?"

Jared nodded. "But just in case, you told me to get it no matter what the price. You couldn't risk that someone would find out about the smuggling."

Laranda shrugged and ran her fingers through the glittering stones in the case. "These diamonds are worth much more than I paid for them. Much, much more." She smiled once more at Jared, then jerked her head toward the doorway that led to the gallery itself. "Ivan!" she shouted. A man appeared with a gun. Jared's idea of calling the police and turning Laranda in vanished even as it formed.

"Yeah, boss?"

"Untie your useless companion back there. I'll hold your gun while you free him. Then come and guard this man for me while I decide what to do with him."

"They work for you?" Jared's betrayal knew no end. Not only had Laranda used him to buy the Buddha, but she had sent thugs first to rob the hotel safe in L.A. and to then search his apartment.

"I didn't want you to find out," Laranda said. She leaned back against a table and rubbed a long fingernail over her red-painted bottom lip. Her other hand held the gun steadily. "I hired them to steal the Buddha, only you didn't put it in the safe like you promised."

Jared snorted. "You didn't give me a chance. When I went to put it there, the safe had been broken into and the Feds were there."

"How nice of you to avoid them for me."

He gritted his teeth. "I wish I hadn't."

Laranda laughed, sounding genuinely amused. "And you kept away from my competition, too; that was smart of you. They are very unhappy that I've taken over a lot of their business."

A horrible thought came to Jared's mind. "You mean this isn't the first time?" he asked. He had been hoping to convince Laranda of the uselessness of her situation, but now his hopes were failing fast.

"No, I've been doing it for several years now. Only it appears everyone's catching on. Fortunately, this is my biggest and best deal, and when it's done, I'm going to lose myself in Europe. I'm quite wealthy now, you know."

Jared found he wanted to touch her beautiful throat, but to choke, not to caress. "How could you do this—"

"To you?" she finished. "Oh, come on now, Jared. This isn't personal. You never let it become that, did you?" She shook her head in mock sadness. "It's too bad you found out about the diamonds. I had thought to leave you in charge here while I retired in Europe, but now I'm going to have to kill you." Her voice was calm, but her eyes sparkled with excitement.

"You wouldn't!" But Jared couldn't be sure of anything about Laranda anymore. He considered reaching for his own gun, but knew he wouldn't be able to use it on her—even if she didn't kill him before he drew it out of its holster.

"Oh, Jared, don't be silly. Of course I would." She laughed again. "Ivan, aren't you finished yet? I've got things to do."

That reminded Jared of how Ivan and his companion had broken into his apartment. "A key. They had a key to my apartment! Where did they get that?"

"Oh, I had a copy made when I borrowed your car a couple of years ago. I thought it might come in handy some day. Only I'd origi-nally had a different idea in mind."

Jared shook his head in disbelief. They had been friends! He had trusted her!

Ivan lumbered over. "I've untied him, but he won't wake up yet. He must have been hit pretty hard."

"Yes, Jared's a man of many talents." Laranda handed Ivan the gun. "If he makes a move, shoot him." She moved closer to Jared and put her hands on his chest caressingly, moving them further inside his jacket. "Ah, here it is." She slipped the gun out of his holster. Jared's face fell, and Laranda laughed. "You didn't think I would forget this, did you? I'm not stupid."

"You were never that."

She looked at him as if trying to see his sincerity. Then she walked behind him and tied his hands. "You could come with me, you know. We would be happy in Europe together."

"Until you tired of me," he said.

She didn't deny it. "At least you would be alive."

Jared thought hard, but he knew there was no way he would ever go with Laranda, especially now that he knew how evil she really was. She stood for everything he was against; and even to save his life, he couldn't—no, wouldn't—give in to her. "Laranda, I can't. For crying out loud, we don't believe in the same things. Take friendship, for example. I thought we were friends, but I wouldn't even treat an enemy the way you're treating me."

"Your religion again?" sneered Laranda, drawing back from him as if she had been slapped, her beautiful face twisting in anger. "There is no God, Jared. When are you going to understand that? The only thing you get out of life is what you can grab, and that's what I'm doing. As for you, even if a God existed, he couldn't save you now." She whirled around and walked toward the door Ivan had come in, trying to move more quickly than her skin-tight dress allowed. She reminded Jared of an animal stalking its prey.

CHAPTER 22

Cassi ran nearly all the way to the gallery, feeling as though everyone was staring at the uncomfortable bulge between her breasts. Only as she reached the corner of the gallery's street did she pause to catch her breath and take stock of the situation. It was an older, yet well-kept part of town. The streets and sidewalks were crowded, and she couldn't tell for sure if there was anyone watching the gallery. How awful it would be if she tried to save Jared but ended up leading the thugs to him, or to have the FBI stop her before she could arrive! She couldn't just walk up to the gallery, could she? For an instant, she wished Linden was around so he could help her. How wrong she had been to suspect him!

"He's not here, so he can't help," she muttered aloud. "It's up to you to save Jared. Oh, I wish I'd never seen that stupid, ugly Buddha!"

"Want a paper?" asked a boy in front of her.

"Huh?" Cassi focused on him.

"Do ya want a paper?"

"No, thank you." Cassi shook her head and lifted her gaze back to the gallery down the street.

"I know about the Buddha," the boy said.

Cassi looked down at him sharply. "What did you say?"

"The Buddha. I heard you talking to yourself about it. And I know something about where it is."

"You do? Tell me!" Surely this was a joke. This little boy was just trying to panhandle her. Cassi sighed. Once again her habit of talking to herself was proving painful.

"First, I want to know whose side you're on."

"The good side, of course," Cassi said. She knew that what she was saying might seem nonsensical, but how else was she supposed to explain it to this child, who may or may not have some information to help her?

"People are watching the gallery," the boy said suddenly. "See those two men in front? There's another one here by the alley, and one in front of the alley on the other side, too. I've been watching them, and they haven't moved. Even before that man came along."

Cassi's hopes rose. "What man?" If this boy had seen Jared, maybe he could tell her how he slipped past the men and into the gallery.

"You tell me."

She stared at the boy, praying silently. She came to a decision. "Okay, I'll tell you. My friend, Jared, came this morning to the gallery. He was dressed in jeans, a white button-down shirt, and a tan jacket. He was carrying something in a green dufflebag."

"The Buddha?" the boy asked eagerly.

Cassi nodded. "He was supposed to take it to his boss at the gallery, but many people have been after him for it, so he had to be really careful. He thought if he could just get it to her, she would call the police and it would be okay. But I just found out that she's the one behind the whole thing! The Buddha is fake and full of smuggled goods. Jared doesn't know about his boss, and I'm afraid when his boss finds out he knows about the Buddha, she'll kill him."

The boy nodded. "I thought he was good. The man guarding the alleyway talked to me real mean-like, but your friend was nice. That's why I didn't tell that I saw him sneak down the alleyway when I sent the bad guy to the restaurant."

"What?" Cassi was confused. "Tell me, quickly, from the start." The little boy obliged, and Cassi learned how Jared had arrived at the gallery unseen, without alerting the thugs. Or were they FBI? No matter; Cassi had to get into the gallery before the police arrived. Too much could happen before then. Too much could go wrong.

"The man wouldn't fall for it again," Cassi said aloud.

"No," agreed the boy. "But I know a way to the back of the gallery, if you want me to show you."

"Yes, please."

"Come on, then."

The boy set his papers down by his father's stand and motioned to

Cassi. She followed him down the street until they were uncomfort-ably close to the alleyway. Then he slipped into a small store. It was a bakery shop, full of mouthwatering smells. At another time, Cassi would have enjoyed the visit; but now she felt impatient.

"I've come to use the bathroom," the boy shouted to the old lady who was helping customers at the counter. The woman smiled and nodded, and the boy grabbed Cassi's hand and led her up some stairs and down a hall. "We pay the lady a fee each month to let us use her bathroom. It's easier than having to walk blocks to find a free one. It's no good shutting the newspaper stand for so long. This way I can watch it alone for a few minutes while my pop goes, and we don't lose out on the sales."

Cassi wanted to ask what a bathroom had to do with getting to the back of the gallery, but she decided to wait and see. Obviously, this observant child knew what he was doing. He led her into the bath-room and opened a small window. "It's a tight squeeze," he said, "but I think you can make it." Cassi peeked outside. Below the window was a stone ledge that might have once been a high wall before the buildings grew to meet it. Now it was simply a narrow space between the bakery and the back of the building behind it. It would be a tight squeeze for Cassi, but she was willing to try anything to save Jared. The only problem was that instead of continuing to the alley, it was blocked ahead. Evidently, builders further down the street had decided that even those few inches were too much space to waste, and they had built their second and consecutive floors out on top of the wall.

"But it ends," Cassi objected.

The boy smiled. "Come on, I'll show you." In a flash he climbed onto the sink, slipped out the window, and landed on the ledge. With much less grace, Cassi followed, wondering idly if the old woman at the bakery counter would worry when they didn't return within a reasonable time.

She had to walk with her feet forward and her body twisted side-ways to get through the tiny space. Sometimes it became tighter, and she felt the rough stone of the building rub against her back and chest. At last, they reached the place where the ledge was blocked, about three store lengths down from the bakery itself. Cassi watched in amazement as the boy scrambled up a rope ladder hanging against the side of the building. She climbed up after him, grateful to be facing it so she wouldn't have to attempt the four-story climb backwards.

When she arrived at the top, the boy was sitting near the edge of the building, staring down into the alleyway next to the gallery. If she stretched her neck, Cassi could just see the man guarding the street. He had copper-colored hair and wore suit pants and a dress shirt. He turned her way, and Cassi drew her head back quickly.

"This is my favorite place to come," the boy said. "From here I can watch what they unload at the gallery, or I can walk to the front and watch the street—that's more interesting."

Cassi nodded. "Like watching the world without them knowing it. I like to do that, too." She put her hand on his shoulder. "Thank you for showing me this."

He shrugged. "Getting down shouldn't be too hard. I'll just switch my rope to the other side."

The rope was anchored by a huge screw hammered into the top of the building. "Did you do this yourself?" Cassi asked.

"Yeah. I used to use the fire escape ladder that goes down into the alley, but it broke partway and now it's hard to climb." He paused and looked at her almost guiltily. "I don't hurt nothin' up here. I just come to watch people or feed the birds."

"Of course." Cassi watched him as he moved the rope to the other side. As it was anchored to the roof near the other side of the building, the rope didn't quite reach the top of the stone wall that emerged again below. It seemed a long way down, yet Cassi was determined to make it.

"I guess I'd better go. What's your name, anyway?"

"Donny."

"Well, I'm Cassi, and I'm very grateful." She leaned down and kissed the boy on the cheek. He turned red but looked pleased.

"It is drugs?" he asked suddenly, unable to hide his curiosity. "Inside the Buddha, I mean."

"No, diamonds. Great big ones."

"Wow!"

Cassi smiled, glad that he was properly impressed. "That's what I said when I saw them." She turned to go.

"You climb on down," Donny said behind her. "When you're on the ledge, I'll tell you when it's safe to run across."

Cassi made her way quickly down the rope, keeping as close to the building as possible. She couldn't see the man guarding the alleyway, so he shouldn't be able to see her—yet. When her feet reached the end of the rope, she braced them against the wall and used just her hands on the rope, wishing she'd worn tennis shoes instead of sandals. She had to drop the last two feet and nearly fell off the wall and into the alley, but at the last moment her hand found an indentation in the side building, and she was able to balance herself.

She looked around, rubbing between her breasts where the gun had jabbed her when she dropped off the rope. More than ten feet below her was the blacktop floor of the alleyway. The stone wall stretched the length of the gallery and slightly beyond, where it was once more blocked by stores or businesses. To her left were tall buildings without windows, built directly up to the wall. Cassi could see why the men guarding the alleys didn't see any reason to post another man back here; the alleys seemed the only way to the back of the Garrettson Gallery.

Unless, of course, you knew a curious boy named Donny. Cassi smiled.

"Pssst," came a sound from above. "Go now, he's turned away. Good luck!"

Cassi immediately ran across the wall, hugging to the buildings on her left so she wouldn't fall. "Why didn't I take gymnastics instead of drama in high school?" she muttered. Into her head flashed a scene of women doing flips and dancing on a beam much smaller than the wall she was on.

After she passed the alleyway, Cassi breathed a sigh of relief and slowed down. The last thing she needed at this point was a broken ankle. At the back of the gallery there was a large garbage bin; she jumped on top of it and then lowered herself to the ground. She turned to wave at Donny, who still watched her from the roof. He waved back. Cassi ran to the back door and quietly inserted a key. The first one she chose didn't work, but she found the right one on the second try.

CHAPTER 23

A loud crack at the back door halted Laranda in mid-flight. Her exquisite head turned on her white neck, and the rest of her body followed. "What!" she said, bringing up Jared's gun.

Jared also turned and saw Cassi at the back door. His heart constricted and his eyes began to water. "Run, Cassi!" he shouted.

"No, don't! I'll shoot him!" Laranda countered. She pointed her gun at Jared. "Come here, and lock that door behind you."

Cassi cast Jared a frightened look but did as she was ordered. Laranda slowly approached her, transferring the gun's aim to Cassi instead of Jared. He considered running for her, but a sharp jab in his back assured him that Ivan was on the job. Laranda moved past Cassi and punched in a code on the alarm. If she didn't do so, the alarm company would call or send someone over. After she finished, Laranda waved Cassi over to stand with Jared.

"Who's this?" Laranda asked.

Jared didn't answer. He was still in shock that Cassi had come. He wished desperately that she hadn't, though he really should have expected it, knowing her impetuous nature.

Cassi lifted her chin. "I'm Cassi. And you must be Laranda. I've heard a lot about you."

"That's funny, I haven't heard a thing about you."

Jared finally found his voice. "She's not part of this, Laranda. Let her go."

Laranda turned on him. "So you care about her. Is this what kept you so long in L.A.? Has our Jared finally found a bride? How sweet." She eyed Cassi up and down, from her curly hair to her sandaled feet.

She shook her head, obviously not impressed, but Cassi didn't quail under her stare. "You always were a sucker for permanented hair," Laranda continued with obvious scorn. She brought a hand to her own shoulder-length locks, as smooth as they were blonde.

"I know you're behind all this smuggling with the Buddha," Cassi said, lifting her chin defiantly. "But Jared gave you the statue, and now you have what you want. Just let us go."

"You know so little about what I want, girl!" Laranda's voice was harsh, but Cassi didn't draw back.

"I know what you're doing is wrong," Cassi said.

"Why, because God says so? Don't tell me you're a Mormon, too."

"I am." There was pride in Cassi's eyes, and Jared wanted to hug her. Instead of being daunted by Laranda's presence, Cassi was standing up to her, and holding her own very well. It was plain to Jared that Cassi had all the important qualities that made a woman truly beautiful, while Laranda's perfect beauty was only skin deep.

"So that explains what Jared sees in you. The poor fool."

Jared wanted to protest, to tell the creature in front of him that it was not only Cassi's religion that captivated him but her kindness, her intelligence, her beauty, and most of all her impulsiveness. The fact that she was a member of the Church was icing on the cake. Jared had no doubt that she would have accepted the Church had she not already been converted years ago.

He was about to tell Laranda the truth, but something warned caution. Learning through hard experience, Jared bit back the words that had come to his throat. Laranda had their lives in her hands; it was better not to taunt her with his growing love for Cassi.

Jared threw a warning glance at Cassi, yet her eyebrows were already furrowed in thought. He knew that like him, she was busy trying to find a way out of this mess. Somehow he knew they had to get clear; he couldn't let Cassi share his fate when she had come to save him. But how? Maybe he would have to rethink Laranda's offer in order to save Cassi.

Jared began to pray, his faith unwavering. Just then the phone rang.

CHAPTER 24

In two seconds, Laranda crossed to where her cordless phone lay on a table. She scooped it up with her free hand, her long nails making a scraping sound in the sudden quiet of the vast room. "Hello? Ah, yes, Peter, I have your merchandise and am waiting for you."

Cassi was relieved to have those green eyes turn away from her. Even without the sharp eyes, Cassi felt her presence dominating the room. Laranda's shimmering red outfit was glamorous, if revealing, her skin was smooth and white, her hair flawlessly groomed. Cassi was only too aware of her own borrowed jeans and the oversized T-shirt, both of which were becoming quite grubby. She stifled the urge to pat her hair into place, a useless gesture since her wild hair wasn't going to start behaving just because it was in the presence of a beautiful woman.

The large packing room was both strange and familiar to her, as it resembled the shipping room in Linden's gallery. Several long tables and enormous shelves of packing supplies were the most prominent features in the room—besides the exquisite Laranda.

"I'm sorry," Jared mouthed. His hands were tied behind him, and a big man pointed a gun at his back. Cassi felt some satisfaction in knowing she had been right about Jared's trouble—only somehow she wasn't helping exactly as she had envisioned.

"Who's the bruised guy by the door?" Cassi asked.

Jared's jaw twitched, and she noticed that the cut above his left eye had reopened. "One of Laranda's thugs," he said. "He was one of the men at my apartment last night. I—I wish you hadn't come."

I surprised him by coming, Cassi thought.

"Shut up," Laranda growled, the phone still pressed to her ear. She waved her gun threateningly. Then, with no warning, she shrieked into the phone. "What do you mean, we're being watched? Oh, the Feds?" Her voice became scornful. "Don't worry about them. I've got the real Buddha to show them if they show up. They can't prove anything without witnesses." She paused and smirked meaningfully at Cassi and Jared. "Well, if you won't come here, I'll come to you. Give me a few hours to get rid of those who are watching the gallery. Where? Okay, I'll be there. And I'll want the money in the same manner as before." She paused and then laughed. "Of *course* I trust you—at least as much as you trust me."

Laranda hung up the phone and threw it onto the nearby table with more force than necessary. She picked up some string and approached Cassi in a cloud of expensive perfume, working the thin rope back and forth in her hands. Fear beat at Cassi's insides, but she steeled her face to show nothing. She was all too aware that Laranda held their lives in her hands; and the woman's heart seemed as perfectly cold as her white, flawless face and icy green eyes implied.

"Let her go," Jared said, his voice calm but as hard as Cassi had ever heard it. She saw the burning rage in his eyes, and the fierce inner struggle to contain it.

Laranda laughed, a tinkling, free sound. "I don't think so." She tied Cassi's hands behind her back and laughed as she winced from the pain. With hard fingers she gave Cassi's body a cursory search, yet she didn't find the gun in her bra, and the bullets made a bulge too small to worry her. Laranda's smile mocked her, as if the woman also searched for and found expected physical and emotional flaws. Cassi felt naked under her gaze.

It seemed a long time before those cold eyes left hers and turned to the man near Jared. "Ivan, put them in the vault and lock it. They'll be all right there for a while; there's enough air for at least an hour, don't you think?" She flashed her white teeth. "Make yourselves comfortable. I may not be back for a while."

Ivan motioned for Cassi and Jared to precede him to the wall vault, which was twice the size of a large elevator. Cassi went in first without help, but Ivan shoved Jared in after her, clicking the heavy door into place behind him.

"Oh, Cassi, why did you come?" Jared asked, recovering his footing.

"Linden called Renae and told her he was working with the FBI, and that they suspected Laranda was behind the smuggling. I was worried about you."

Jared leaned against a shelf where various art objects sat and hit his head against the metal. "I can't believe I trusted her. We've been friends for over six years. And sure, she has her faults, but I never imagined she could use me in such a way."

Cassi didn't think it odd that Jared had not seen Laranda's true nature. In her life, she had seen that physical beauty often blinded men to a woman's other attributes. Her heart ached for Jared, though; he was obviously in pain at the woman's betrayal. He sank to the floor, looking miserable.

"Don't you want to know how I got here?" Cassi asked. He managed to look interested, so Cassi recounted her adventure with Donny. In turn, Jared shared how he had come down the alley and described his fight with the nameless man who lay unconscious by the door. Both were in better spirits when they finished.

"Jared, I'm really sorry about Laranda," Cassi said. "I remember how I felt when I thought Linden was on the wrong side. It was as if suddenly the whole world had changed, and I didn't know who to trust."

"But I should have seen it coming," Jared said. "Oh, I wish you hadn't come and were safe back at the apartment!" He paused, and a determined look passed over his face. "I do appreciate the effort, though. You know, I think I may have a way out of this situation."

His face became so grim that Cassi was frightened. "Look, the FBI should come soon," she reminded him. "Renae said that Linden and others flew to New York yesterday. Just wait a while and see what happens."

"Yes, but Laranda has the real Buddha. She'll just have Ivan take us to the attic or somewhere while she shows it to them, then knock us off at her convenience. No, I've got a better idea." Jared stood up and walked to the vault door. Sheer determination had replaced his misery.

"Wait!"

Jared paused and looked back at her, one eyebrow raised questioningly.

"I have a gun. Meela gave it to me."

"Where?"

Cassi looked down at her chest, feeling a blush tinge her cheeks.
Jared smiled. "Is it loaded?"

She shook her head. "I've got the bullets in my pocket."

He nodded. "Well, hang onto it; it might come in handy." He
turned and kicked at the door with his feet. "Come on, Ivan, open
up! I've got something to tell Laranda!" Jared screamed his request
several times before the thug opened the door.

"Did you say somethin'?" he asked.

Cassi thought it was amazing that Ivan had heard anything at all
through the thick door. A miracle, perhaps.

"I need to talk to Laranda privately. Please ask her if she can spare
a minute."

Ivan nodded and shut the vault again. While they waited, Cassi
began to rub the twine that bound her hands against a metal shelf
where the finish was uneven. The twine was strong but would not
hold up to her efforts; one by one, the strands making up the rope
were severed.

Ivan returned shortly and ushered Jared from the vault. This time
he left the door halfway open, placing himself just outside it. He
obviously didn't expect the discussion between Jared and Laranda to
take long. Meanwhile, Cassi felt the last of her bonds break away. She
moved to the door, keeping her hands behind her. From her position,
she could both see and hear Jared and Laranda.

"What do you want?" Laranda's voice was impatient. "We've said
all we have to say."

"No, we haven't," Jared said. "I'll go with you to Europe, if you
still want me." Laranda started at his words, but no more than Cassi
did. What was he doing? She reached under her shirt and retrieved
the gun. Carefully and quietly, she pushed in six bullets with shaking
hands. She had never liked guns, though her brother had always been
fascinated with them and had taught her to load and fire them. Even
under his patient tutelage she had never felt very comfortable with
any weapon and, until now, had never wished to be.

"You want to go with me?" Laranda asked. She stared intently at
Jared. "So your virtue disappears when faced with death, huh? I
thought it might." She sidled up to Jared until their bodies were
touching. "Or is it me you will miss?"

"We've been friends for six years," Jared said. "Why wouldn't I miss you?"

Laranda laughed. "I could use your help getting the diamonds to my buyer. I've got four men outside from an opposing cartel, and most probably the Feds as well. But how can I trust you? Of course, I do have your girlfriend, don't I?"

"But she could never live up to you, Laranda," Jared said. At the words Cassi's jaw dropped, and her heart throbbed painfully. What was he saying? Surely this was an act. Unless he was unaware that Cassi could hear. Was it possible that Jared cared for Laranda despite her betrayal? Could it be that maybe he was trying to save Cassi's life, but in such a way that assured his continuing association with the woman he loved? Cassi's stomach turned at the thought.

"Untie me, and I'll show you what I mean," Jared continued.

Laranda laughed one of the low, sexy laughs that Cassi had never been able to master. She watched as Laranda found a packing knife on the counter and cut Jared's bonds. With Ivan watching carefully for foul play, Laranda put her arms around Jared's neck and kissed him. Jared's arms slipped around Laranda; he was kissing her back!

Cassi felt betrayed. Only last night, Jared had kissed her in much the same way. Did it mean nothing to him? Did she mean nothing to him? Another part of her argued that Jared was simply trying to free them, and playing his role convincingly so Laranda wouldn't suspect. Cassi felt her grip on the gun loosen and desperately tried to hold it tighter. Her fingers refused to obey, and the gun slipped from her hand.

As her gun hit the floor, things happened quickly, though Cassi felt as if the world moved in slow motion. The impact made her weapon fire, hitting Jared. She saw him wince and grab his left shoulder. At the same time, Ivan whirled around to face Cassi, bringing up his gun. A shot rang out, but Ivan, not Cassi, fell to the floor. She blinked in surprise, but had no time to dwell on what had happened. Then she saw Jared reach for the gun that Laranda had set on the table and turn it toward the door leading into the main part of the gallery, a place Cassi couldn't see from the vault. As he did, another shot was fired and Laranda, still standing next to Jared, slumped against the table. Jared fired, and Cassi scrambled toward the door and her fallen gun, driven physically as if by an invisible hand.

She felt comfort and strength flow from the hand to her body and recognized divine help. She picked up the gun and held it in front of her as she sprang from the vault.

Jared and a hook-nosed man were facing each other, holding their guns ready. The intruder stared at Jared with hard black eyes, and any moment Cassi expected his gun to kill Jared. Beside the thug lay a motionless companion. Cassi recognized the men as those who had chased them at the beach and whom the FBI agents had accused of smuggling at the airport. *They must be the thugs from the opposing cartel.* The thought only had time to flit through Cassi's mind.

"Put it down!" she shouted. The man glanced at her and back at Jared. "Don't be stupid," she sneered. "I will shoot, and gladly." She meant every word, and at this range, it would be impossible for her to miss—even without her brother's training. Something in her face must have convinced the man of her sincerity, for he slowly lowered the gun and tossed it to the floor several paces in front of him. Cassi retrieved it quickly, still pointing her gun at the man's gut.

"Jared!" Near the front table several yards away, Laranda held her stomach where a darker patch quickly spread through the glittering red of her dress. Jared gently lowered her to the floor, wincing noticeably as blood poured from his own wound.

At that instant, the back door sprang open and five men charged in, each heavily armed. Cassi felt a wave of fear as she watched additional men emerge from the hallway. "FBI!" someone shouted. "Put down your weapons!"

Cassi began to shake. As much as she wanted to obey the command, all the guns pointing at her struck such fear in her mind that she couldn't move. Tears slid unchecked from her eyes to her cheeks.

"Wait!" Linden bounded toward her, gathering her into his arms.

"Linden!" She sobbed against his shoulder as he loosed her fingers from the two guns.

"It's okay now," he murmured against her cheek as he stroked her hair. "It's all over. You're safe."

"Jared?" Cassi asked. She knew it had been her gun that had fired on him when she dropped it. Was he all right? Did he know she was responsible?

With an arm around her, Linden took a few steps toward Jared and Laranda. A man had tied a cloth around Jared's shoulder to staunch the flow of blood, and now he sat on the floor with Laranda's head in his lap. Her dress was soaked with blood.

"Please stay with me, Jared," Laranda pleaded. "I'm scared. It hurts so much. Stay with me. You love me, don't you?"

Cassi saw tears in Jared's eyes as he stroked Laranda's blonde locks. "Hold on, Laranda. Help is coming. Yes, I love you. Hold on!"

Pain burst through Cassi's heart, and she buried her face in Linden's chest. "Take me home, Linden," she said through her tears. "Please. Please, just take me home."

CHAPTER 25

With an arm around her, Linden hustled Cassi past the armed FBI agents and down the steps of the gallery to a car parked across the street. "She'll answer questions later," he said brusquely to the only man who dared stop them. "You have the diamonds and the smugglers, and that's enough for now. I've helped you, now let me through." Linden's voice was rigid, and Cassi wasn't surprised when the man allowed them to pass.

Outside, an ambulance drove up and men rushed from it into the gallery. Cassi averted her gaze from them and allowed Linden to settle her into his car. Seconds later, he stepped on the gas and sped around the corner, leaving the scene behind. He drove on in silence, his sharp eyes occasionally darting to Cassi.

"Well?" he asked finally.

She looked up. "I'm sorry, Linden. You were right. I shouldn't have gotten involved. It's just that we didn't know who to trust." Another tear rolled down her cheek. With the three little words Jared had uttered to Laranda, Cassi's dreams had been shattered. But then, how could she have ever expected to compete with the beautiful Laranda? Still, she found it difficult to believe that Jared had chosen to stay with the heartless woman, even in her time of need.

Linden stopped the car against a curb in a No Parking zone. His brown eyes were kind as he looked at Cassi. "No, I'm the one who should apologize. I should have told you everything from the start. The Feds made me promise silence, and I agreed, thinking I was protecting you." He shook his white head and frowned, making him look older than the sixty years he claimed.

Cassi bit her lip. A vision of Jared dressed as the gray-haired man on the plane came to her, cutting deep. In the short time they had been together, they had shared so much. How was she to go on alone?

"How did they know about the Buddha?" Cassi managed to ask.

"A man who works for the auction alerted the FBI that the statue wasn't quite as it should be. He was certain enough that they began to look into it and found a lot of evidence pointing to smuggling. At first we suspected a major smuggling cartel to be involved—Big Tommy's gang—but they weren't bidding on the Buddha. In fact, we're pretty sure that only after Jared bought the Buddha did the cartel know which object even had the diamonds in it."

"That explains the note I received," Cassi said.

"What note?"

"A plain white sheet, no markings. It said, 'Do not bid for it, if you want to live.'"

"They were probably trying to scare Laranda's man away. Everyone else would have considered it a joke."

"Some joke," Cassi frowned. "How strange they should know about the diamonds when Jared didn't." Even saying his name made Cassi ache.

"You might be surprised at the things they know. In this case, Big Tommy and the FBI had opposite problems. The cartel knew who was doing the smuggling—the Garrettson Gallery—and the general price range, but not which item was being used; we knew about the Buddha, but not the person responsible."

"Until Jared bought it," Cassi said almost bitterly.

"Even then, it could have been a mistake," Linden said.

"You never intended for me to buy the Buddha, did you? You gave me enough money to make it appear that I was a serious buyer, but not enough to win the bid. It was all just a cover-up."

Linden nodded. "I'm sorry, Cassi." He put his worn hand on her shoulder. "I promise you it will never happen again."

Cassi sighed. "I know you did what you thought was best."

"I'm having serious regrets about either of us being involved at all," Linden said. "The FBI didn't inform me, but from what I can gather, it seems Miss Garrettson has been intruding on Big Tommy's operation for a few years now. Meaning the cartel would be more concerned about revenge than simply getting the diamonds. They probably would have enjoyed stealing them, then sending Jared's body to Miss Garrettson in pieces or something."

Cassi blanched at the thought. She sighed heavily. "Well, it's all over now. Can we go home? To San Diego?"

Linden nodded. "You'll have to answer some questions, but I think I can get that delayed with a few phone calls." He patted his cellular phone in his suit coat pocket. "Meanwhile, they'll have your friend Jared and Miss Garrettson to question here—if she lives. That ought to keep them busy. Is there anything you need, or should we go straight to the airport?"

"My *Mother and Baby*," Cassi said. "I left it at Meela's. My dress, and some shorts." The fluorescent pink shorts from Venice Beach were one of the few mementos of her time with Jared; they were every bit as important as her statue, even if the memory was now painful. "We have to go to Jared's apartment building."

She was about to give directions, but Linden already knew the way. "We staked it out for a while and even had the other residents questioned," he said, pulling out into traffic. "No one had any information."

"We came in last night dressed as an older couple, and stayed with his neighbor."

"We know that now. That's one of the reasons we went blazing into the gallery when we did. You see, Jared's neighbor called the local police, but they didn't believe her. So she finally contacted us—we'd left a card with each person we questioned in the building. Then, right when we were on the phone with her, we saw two members of the smuggling cartel go into the gallery. Needless to say, we were on their heels. When the guns went off, we were already at the doors."

Cassi nodded. "The guys guarding the alley by the gallery . . . were they yours?"

"No. They were with the cartel. They're in custody now. You'll have to tell me, though, how you and Jared got past them—and us."

"I will, Linden, on the plane. Okay?" Cassi shut her eyes, and tears again spilled over.

"Sure."

Cassi felt grateful for Linden's sensitivity in not pressing her at the moment. Time would help to get her unstable emotions under control. But would it heal the wound in her heart?

Linden pulled up outside Jared's apartment building. "I'll wait here," he said, pulling the phone from his pocket. "I've got some calling to do, anyway—the Feds and the airport."

Cassi nodded. "Thanks." She hopped out of the car and ran up the stairs. The outside door was locked, and she no longer had Jared's keys. She pushed the buzzer to Meela's apartment. There was no answer. In desperation she pushed the supervisor's number. Instead of answering the call, a middle-aged woman emerged from her down-stairs apartment. Jared had told Cassi that each person owned their own apartment, but together they paid the supervisor to maintain the halls. Jared also paid the woman to clean his apartment, so perhaps she had a key. Cassi knew that from Jared's she could probably get into Meela's apartment. It was also possible the supervisor knew where Meela had gone.

"May I help you?"

"Yes, please. I need to get in touch with Meela. I left something in her apartment, and I'm flying to San Diego this afternoon."

"I don't know where she is." The woman moved to close her door.

"Please, I need to get into her apartment. You could go with me to make sure I don't take anything. You clean Jared's place, don't you? I need to go there, too—to leave him something. Please, won't you help me?" Cassi knew her voice was beginning to sound desperate, but she didn't care.

The woman's eyes narrowed. "Look, I don't know you from Mr. Magoo, and I'm certainly not going to open Jared's apartment for you. You'll have to talk with him."

"I can't. He's in the hospital. I—" Cassi broke off. She wouldn't be doing herself any favors by admitting she had shot Jared. "He was shot and—" Cassi was nearly crying again. Hopelessness flooded her; she just wanted to get her things and get as far away from New York as she could.

"Cassi! Are you okay?"

Cassi turned to see Meela coming up the stairs behind her, a little boy in tow. She nodded numbly. "But Jared got shot. In the shoulder. He's in the hospital by now. Laranda also was shot. I've come to get my stuff and leave something at Jared's. I—it's my fault he was shot."

Meela put an arm around Cassi and pushed her through the door. "It's okay, Mrs. Fackly. I know her. I'll take care of it from here." The older woman nodded but stayed where she was, watching them get on the elevator.

"So what happened?" Meela asked when the door closed.

"Is Uncle Jared okay?" asked the little boy.

"I think so," Cassi began, trying futilely to hold back her tears. "Laranda had us prisoner, and then I dropped the gun and it went off, hitting Jared. Right then, some men came through the door and shot the guy who was guarding me—they must have thought he was the one firing. Then Jared went for a gun, and they shot Laranda. In the stomach. Jared shot one of them and stood facing the second man, a guy with a hooked nose. I grabbed your gun and held it on the guy." The words brought back to Cassi the utter terror she had felt, especially that the hook-nosed man would shoot and kill Jared.

"Then what happened?"

"The man gave up his gun and the FBI showed up. Laranda was hurt pretty bad, and Jared was still bleeding when I left. He was crying. I—I think he loves her."

Meela looked at Cassi with understanding. "I'm sorry, Cassi," she said. "I was praying for you."

Cassi gave her a watery smile. "Well, we got out of it alive, anyway. I think the Lord did help us. It seemed that I felt someone helping me get the gun and hold it on the smuggler."

Meela opened the door to her apartment. "I'm going to call the hospital and see how Jared's doing."

"I don't know which one he's at."

The other woman shrugged. "I'll find him." She went to the kitchen and pulled out her phone book.

Cassi grabbed her dufflebag and followed Meela into the kitchen. She walked quickly out onto the balcony and stepped over the railing. The sliding glass door to Jared's apartment was still open a tiny sliver, and in a few seconds she was standing before Jared's "Life" collection. Carefully, she drew her statue out of its case.

Ever since she had seen Jared's collection, she had known that the *Mother and Baby* statue belonged with others of its kind. She ran her fingers over the realistic features of the mother's face. The woman's full blue-checked skirt swung out to the side, and one could easily imagine the mother dancing with her baby next to her chest in a tender embrace. Its sweetness made Cassi's heart ache, yet she forced herself to set the statue down among a small group of children who were also dancing. A man with what looked like a fiddle stood to the side, one foot raised as if keeping time with the music.

Cassi sobbed as she touched the baby's face in parting. She didn't cry because of the money, for she felt Jared's honor would cause him to reimburse her. Nor did she cry because the statue was no longer hers. She cried because of her love for a man she had just met, and for the seeming hopelessness of her situation. For good or for bad, he was in love with Laranda.

"I love you," she said softly. She knew that the statue would tell him as she couldn't, and in a way that would not embarrass him or compromise his feelings for Laranda. And who knew? Perhaps Laranda would change her ways and make him happy as Cassi wouldn't have the chance to do.

She wiped the tears away with both hands, gathered up her dufflebag, and turned her back resolutely on the rare collection. Then she slipped, unnoticed, back into Meela's kitchen.

"He's not there?" Meela was saying into the phone. "Well, maybe he hasn't arrived yet. Yes, I've already called the other hospital. What? You've found them? How is he? And the woman? Oh. I understand. Yes. Thank you."

She hung up the phone and turned to Cassi. "Jared's going to be all right. They're examining his shoulder now. They'll probably keep him for a day or so."

"And Laranda?"

"They wouldn't give me any information over the phone. It must be serious."

"Could you maybe get someone there to give Jared a blessing? And Laranda, too. Jared would want that."

"Good idea. And what about you?"

Cassi's eyes watered. "I'm going home. I just have to go home." She paused, knowing she was running away. "Could you tell Jared that I'm sorry for shooting him? I feel that it's my fault, what happened to Laranda and all."

"I'll tell him, but it sounds to me like you actually did good. If those thugs had gotten control, you would have all been dead."

Cassi shrugged. "Maybe." She didn't think Jared would look at it that way. Not when Laranda might be dying. "Thanks for everything, Meela."

"You're welcome. If ever I can do anything for you . . ."

Cassi hugged her and shook hands with the solemn Mikey. When the door shut behind her, she walked to the elevator without looking back, feeling that Jared and everything to do with him was gone from her life forever.

CHAPTER
26

"Aren't you done yet?" Jared asked the doctor impatiently. They had given him medication, but even so the doctor's bandaging made pain shoot up his arm and through his chest.

"We'll need to check you in for a few days," the doctor said. "You've lost a lot of blood."

"No. I've got to find Cassi."

"She's in surgery now. You can't go to her."

For a moment Jared's heart jumped anxiously, until he realized the doctor was talking about Laranda. "No, not her, someone else," Jared said. He shut his eyes against the pain. In an instant, it all came back. He had been kissing Laranda—so different from the warm and vibrant Cassi— and had felt strongly that he should reach for his gun on the table behind her. Doing so seemed a dangerous thing to do, yet he had followed the prompting. As he leaned forward and to the side, reaching for the weapon, he felt a bullet rip into his shoulder. He hardly had a moment to realize that if he hadn't reached for the gun, the bullet would have hit him in a more vital place near his heart, perhaps killing him. The rest had happened too quickly for words, and even now he had trouble sorting out what had happened before the FBI agents raced into the room. Jared had clearly seen the fear on Cassi's face and had wanted to run to her, but one arm hung uselessly at his side and dizziness had quickly overtaken him.

And Laranda! Jared felt new tears in his eyes as he remembered how the blood had soaked her shimmering dress, and how she had clung to him, asking him if he loved her.

Yes! Jared had always loved Laranda—not for the woman she was, but for the woman she could have become. He loved her as a friend and as an admirer, though he knew that even before the shooting she had been planning to use and betray him again. Admittedly, his respect and trust in her had evaporated, but he couldn't shut off his feelings of love so quickly. She had been alone and desperately in need; Jared wouldn't turn his back on her.

With Laranda's blood flowing onto the floor, Jared had glanced up at Cassi, hoping for comfort. He found none. Her tear-streaked face was abnormally white, and her body shook violently. An older man had his arms around her, and she leaned heavily against him. Though he longed to go to her himself, Laranda's pitiful cries made him feel that he should stay with her. He had expected Cassi to come with them to the hospital, but to his surprise, she had begged the stranger to take her home, with an expression on her face that Jared had never seen before—lonely, sad, devastated. Jared would have gone to her then, but the man hurried her out of the room. Who was he? Where were they going? Surely home didn't mean San Diego . . . didn't she care about what happened to Jared? *No, there's been a misunderstanding!* he wanted to shout at Cassi's retreating back.

The ambulance had come then, and Jared had been in too much pain to think coherently. Finally they had given him some medication, and he had pulled himself together enough to give Laranda a priesthood blessing. At the hospital, she was rushed into surgery, and there was nothing more he could do. His only thought now was for Cassi.

"Is that it?" Jared asked. The doctor had finished taping Jared's shoulder, and was fitting him with a sling for his arm.

"Yes. The nurse will take you to your r— Hey, where are you going?"

Jared was running out the emergency room doors before anyone could stop him. He had to see Cassi; he needed to tell her how he felt. He hadn't stopped for his shirt, and he knew he made a strange sight, especially with his blood-stained jeans. Indifferent to the stares, he ran down the street, searching for a taxi.

"Stop!"

Jared turned to see one of the FBI men behind him. It was Fred, the burly, brown-haired man who had been assigned to question him. "We're not through with you yet!"

Jared stopped, breathing heavily, and waited for Fred to catch up. "Look, I need to find Cassi, the woman who was with me. Please, help me!" he panted.

Fred nodded. "Linden, the guy with her, called us. She went to get her stuff at an apartment somewhere, and then they're going to the airport."

Jared blinked in surprise. How could she leave him, when there was so much left to say? Panic rose in his throat. "But don't you have to question her or something?"

Fred shrugged. "They'll do it in San Diego. Linden says she's pretty shaken up just now, anyway. It's better to let her rest for a while."

Jared wanted to curse himself for not going to Cassi after the shooting. Her expression had clearly shown how much she needed him, and he had failed her. All because of his loyalty to Laranda. "Why don't *I* get to rest first?" he asked, saying the first words that came to his lips.

The man's mouth curved in a half-smile. "You're a man. You don't have that luxury."

Jared hardly heard the words. "Please, I've got to find her before she leaves. Will you take me?"

The man studied Jared's face for a moment before replying. "Is she really worth all this?" At his nod, the man motioned for Jared to follow him. "But afterwards, you'll have to come back to the hospital like a good boy."

"Agreed."

Jared stared anxiously out the window as the car rolled through the crowded New York streets. Not for the first time, Jared wished he lived somewhere less busy. After what seemed an eternity, they arrived at his apartment building. Jared pounded on Meela's door. "Where's Cassi? Is she here?"

"Jared! You're supposed to be in the hospital."

"Where is she?" Jared wanted to shake the answer out of his friend.

"She's gone—went home to San Diego. She asked me to tell you she was sorry for shooting you."

"Shooting me? What do you mean?"

"She said she dropped the gun just as the smugglers came into the room, and it went off, hitting you."

"Oh, I thought it was Ivan."

Meela shook her head. "No, it was Cassi. And she feels that what happened to Laranda is all her fault."

Jared snorted. "It was an accident. And Cassi probably saved us all. I was dizzy by then, and might have missed that guy at the door. She swung the balance. If it weren't for her popping out of the vault when she did, we'd have all ended up dead."

"I tried to tell her, but—"

He grinned, ignoring the pain rippling through his shoulder. "You should have seen her, Meela! She barked an order at that man, and he knew she was serious. She would have shot him. What a woman!"

"How's Laranda?"

Jared shrugged. "She's in surgery now. The doctor says it doesn't look good, but I think she's too tough to die. I gave her a blessing in the ambulance. What happens will be the Lord's will. Regardless, she brought this upon herself."

"My thoughts exactly," Meela said. "But Cassi said you were crying. She feels responsible for Laranda being shot. She said you love Laranda."

"What?" Understanding dawned on Jared as he suddenly saw his actions from Cassi's point of view. After the incident was over, he had stayed with the woman who would have killed them both, ignoring Cassi. He had even reassured Laranda of his love. He and Laranda both understood that it was a friendship love, not romantic, but had Cassi? And had she also misinterpreted his words when he told Laranda that Cassi could never live up to her? It was true; Cassi could never be the cold-hearted, money-grubbing user that Laranda exemplified. He had to find her and explain.

"The airport. Let's go to the airport!"

Fred nodded in agreement.

They arrived at the departure gate fifteen minutes too late. The plane to San Diego was already in the air. Jared was pale and dizzy from the effort of running. He reached out to the wall to support himself with his good arm.

"I'd better get you to the hospital," Fred said.

Jared dumbly let the man lead him back to the car. Cassi had left him! She hadn't waited to see if he was all right, or even to bid him farewell. Jared felt betrayal that seemed many times worse than what Laranda had done to him. One thing he knew was that he loved Cassi. Loved! And it wasn't just a passing thing; it was eternal. At least it was supposed to be. She should have trusted him, believed in him.

Jared continued to torture himself with her memory: the smell of her; the way the sun had brought out the auburn highlights in her incredible hair; her brown eyes, so deep that he felt himself absorbed every time he looked at her; the vitality embodied in her ready smile; their shared prayer at the hotel; her kissable lips; her impetuous behavior. The list seemed endless. How could he go back to what his life had been—dull, monotonous, unfulfilling—before he knew Cassi? It wasn't something he wanted to think about. Since he'd met her a whole realm of new possibilities had emerged, and he had wanted to explore them to the fullest.

In his mind, he could see her face when he had kissed her the night before. There had been an underlying passion that he had never felt before, and certainly not when he had kissed Laranda today. It was love that made all the difference. But Cassi obviously didn't share his feelings, or she would have trusted him more completely. Now that the mystery of the Buddha was solved, she was gone.

Logically, Jared knew that his thoughts didn't add up, for he also remembered how she had come to save him at the gallery, risking her own life. He remembered how she had admitted only last night, before their kiss, that she enjoyed being with him. So, what was the problem? Was it all his fault because of his actions today with Laranda? Surely Cassi could have waited for him to explain. Misery like none he had ever known descended upon him. He had opened his heart as Sister Martin had advised, and had only succeeded in getting it broken.

"You could go to San Diego when you're better," Fred commented, not looking at Jared, yet obviously sympathizing with his pain.

"But she left me!"

"When a deal at work doesn't go right, do you just dump it?"

Fred had a point. Jared wasn't one to give up easily. He would go to San Diego, if only to hear from Cassi's own lips that she didn't love him. At least he would know the truth. Determination filled his heart, replacing the misery. He hadn't come this far to lose the only woman he had ever loved—at least not without a fight.

"You're right," Jared said. They drove in silence for a moment before Jared thought of something else. "How about stopping at my apartment for a shirt? It's on the way. The sooner I look like normal, the sooner the doctor will release me."

Fred sighed. "Only if you promise that we'll go straight to the hospital afterwards. I think you're bleeding again." He jerked his head toward Jared's shoulder. Sure enough, a large patch of red stained the fresh bandage. "What we men go through for a beautiful woman."

Jared had to agree.

On the way home, another thought occurred to him. He had never actually told Cassi how he felt about her. It was entirely possible that she was blind to his love, and that his actions with Laranda after the shooting had only doused any inkling he had given her. Despite his own hurt, tenderness for Cassi swelled in his heart, once more swinging the pendulum of his emotion. He smiled grimly. His own feelings were a rougher ride than any roller-coaster he had enjoyed as a child.

At the apartment, he put on an old shirt and packed a few items for the hospital. He didn't plan on staying more than one night, and that only because he had promised Fred; but it was best to be prepared. As he emerged from the bedroom, he stopped, noticing that the door to his "Life" collection was ajar.

"I could have sworn I left this door shut last night," he said to Fred.

Fred motioned Jared back and drew his gun. He approached the door cautiously. "Is anyone there?" he asked. No one answered. In true police fashion, he charged into the room. After a moment he called out, "There's nothing here but a bunch of statues."

Jared walked into the room. Instantly, he saw that something was different. On the floor in front of his collection lay a box he remembered only too well. His eyes swept over "Life," quickly finding the addition: Cassi's statue.

Wonder filled Jared's mind; Cassi had given him her *Mother and Baby!* He instinctively knew her action meant much more than what it might appear on the surface. One could argue that she let him have it in payment for shooting him, or that she simply believed the statue belonged in the collection; but Jared knew how much she loved the statue. This was her way of telling him she cared! Perhaps she had honestly believed he loved Laranda, yet had wanted him to know how she felt—just in case it mattered to him. This statue told him more than Cassi herself could have.

"She cares," he said, hardly daring to believe. "Fred, she cares!" Jared jumped into the air and hollered again, "She cares!" With sudden inspiration, he knew what he had to do now—and he would do it just as soon as he got out of the hospital. Jared smiled, then frowned as the room went suddenly dark. He felt Fred's arms catch him as he fell into unconsciousness.

CHAPTER 27

The house was quiet. It had been that way for a week, ever since she had returned from New York. Cassi sat in her TV room, staring at the blank screen, the only light coming from the lamp beside the couch. Through the open window came a light summer breeze, rustling the leaves of the various plants that dotted the room. Not another sound broke the lonely silence.

Why didn't Jared call?

She had heard nothing from him since the day of the shooting. He had not even sent a check for the *Mother and Baby.*

Could she have killed him with that bullet? She didn't really believe he was dead, but it remained a possibility. Infection could have set in, or something equally as bad.

At first, holding on to the thin hope that he would contact her, she tried to slip back into her life as if nothing had happened. After four days of silence—and she refused to allow herself to question Linden on the matter—she had asked her boss for vacation time, and had come home near tears. That was the day she had finally unpacked the dufflebag Renae had given her and found the T-shirt Jared had worn at the beach. She clutched it first to her heart and then to her face, breathing in his fragrance. In her mind, she remembered vividly how she had hidden it in her bag when Jared had come back early to the motel from the funeral. It was all she had of him, and now she was grateful for it.

She threw herself onto her bed and cried, her face buried in the shirt. "How can it hurt so much?" she asked over and over. "I only knew him six days!" The protest only grieved her more; he had seemed perfect for her in every way. "Except, of course, that he loves another woman," she had replied, trying to stop the flood of tears. The comment served only to break her heart anew.

She put on Jared's shirt that day and hadn't taken it off in the three days since, except to shower. Eventually, she knew she would get over him; but until her heart healed, she wanted to wallow in her sorrow, feeling the bittersweet pain. No matter what the consequences, she agreed with the saying that it was better to have loved and lost than never to have loved at all. At least she now knew what love was.

The phone rang shrilly in the silence of the spacious room. Cassi picked it up, trying to stifle the hope that flared in her breast.

"Hello?"

"Hi, Cassi. It's Renae. How're you doing?"

Cassi sighed. Since her adventure in New York, Renae had called her every day. "I'm fine. And no, he hasn't called."

"Why don't you call him?"

"I can't. Besides, what would I say? 'Hi. I'm completely crazy about you, couldn't you propose?' Is that what you're suggesting?"

"No, but you could tell him how you feel. I can't believe you left New York without saying good-bye. Did you ever tell him how you felt?"

"No, unless a bullet to the shoulder counts."

"Cassi, that wasn't your fault!"

"Yes, it was. For all I know, he's dead."

"No way! Don't worry, he'll call."

"It doesn't matter; he loves Laranda."

Renae snorted. "Bull. I don't believe it. I saw the way he looked at you."

"Well, he's in New York with her, and I'm here alone. Isn't that plain enough?"

"Maybe he's recuperating."

"Renae, give it up. For heaven's sake, I shot the man and—"

"You said he kissed you, though. That meant something."

Cassi sighed again, this time more loudly. She had needed someone to talk to during those first days back from New York, and Renae had been available. Now Cassi wished she hadn't been so open with her. "He kissed Laranda, too."

"But that was to save you!"

"I don't buy that."

"Well, think about this," Renae said. "What if you were in Jared's place? What if it had been Linden instead of Laranda who had betrayed *you*? And what if Linden had been shot and was clinging to you, begging you to stay with what might be his dying breath? What would you have done?"

Renae's words hit Cassi like a slap. For a few seconds, she was unable to breathe. "I—you mean . . . Linden . . ." Thoughts whirled in Cassi's head, tumbling against one another in a battle to be heard first. She let the phone slip to the couch.

Cassi stood and paced the room restlessly. "If it had been Linden," she murmured, shaking her head in wonder. Seeing the situation from Jared's point of view was shocking. Laranda was his friend, just as Linden was hers; he could no more leave her to die alone than she could have left Linden. Jared's love for Laranda could be the same type of love she shared with Linden. Which could also mean that Jared's loyalty to Laranda didn't mean he had used Cassi or led her on; it only meant he was a good person whose sense of right wouldn't let him take the easy way out.

She had it nearly worked out in her mind when she spied the phone on the couch. Renae's voice was yelling something, and Cassi quickly picked up the receiver and put it to her ear.

"Then why hasn't he called?" she asked abruptly.

"Oh, Cassi," breathed Renae. "I was worried there for a minute. What did you ask?"

"If he doesn't love Laranda, why hasn't he called?"

"Why haven't you called him? It's the same thing."

"I left him my *Mother and Baby.*"

"You *what?* You left him a six-thousand-dollar statue?" Renae whistled in amazement. "Good girl. That must have said something."

"So now it's his turn, right?"

"Maybe he doesn't have your number or address."

Cassi wasn't accepting that excuse. "I'm in the phone book, or he could call Linden at the gallery."

Renae was silent for a moment. "I hate to say it, Cassi, but you're right. It's his turn now." She paused a moment more before adding, "Maybe he's an arrogant pig, after all."

Cassi chuckled for Renae's benefit, though pain shot through her at the thought. "Hey, thanks for calling, Renae. I really have to go." Cassi wasn't lying. In actuality, dozens of little matters begged for her attention, though she knew she wouldn't be completing any of them in the near future. Her heart wasn't in it. "Besides, don't you have some kids to take care of or some practicing to do?" Renae was taking guitar and voice lessons two nights a week, and was now busier than ever.

"Yeah, all right. But call me soon, huh? Maybe I'll come for a visit. The kids are asking for you."

"I'd like that. Thanks for calling. 'Bye." Cassi hung up.

The utter silence immediately overwhelmed her. She took a last look at the room, with its border of green, trailing plants, then turned out the light. The loneliness to which she had long been accustomed crept over her like something completely new. How easy it had been to adjust to Jared's constant companionship, and how heavy the loneliness seemed now!

She shrugged the thought aside, knowing she had to get on with her life, but at the same time knowing she would never again look at things in the same way. Love had changed her. Sighing deeply, she turned on the light in the hall that led to her bedroom. Perhaps she would read a bit before trying to sleep through the nightmares she knew would come, as they had every night since the fateful day she had shot Jared. Sometimes in her dreams he died, and in others he pointed an accusing finger at her as the ravishing Laranda at his side laughed gleefully. Cassi would run away, but always behind her ran the hook-nosed smuggler waving a gun.

She shivered. "I need a blessing," she whispered. The thought spread comfort through her. "Yes, a blessing." She started for the phone but the doorbell rang, sounding loud in the stillness of the night. Involuntarily, Cassi flinched. Who could it be at this time of night? A little smile played on her lips. Wouldn't it be funny if it were her home teachers at the door, right when she needed them? She turned on the entryway light and opened the door.

"Jared!" Cassi's shock was complete. There he stood, looking more handsome than she remembered with his blond hair and piercing blue eyes. Closer inspection, however, showed that his face was haggard and also pale, except where a beard had been growing for several days. His left eye was still greenish, and a sling held one arm securely against his chest.

"May I come in?" he asked. His eyes ran over her as if searching for a hidden sign.

Cassi realized she was still wearing his T-shirt, and for a moment she considered slamming the door and running to change so he wouldn't suspect the extent of her suffering. But almost immediately she discarded the idea; she had never been one to hide her feelings, and regardless of the circumstances, she loved him.

"Yes, of course, please come in. What are you doing here?"

Jared bent down and awkwardly picked up a medium-sized box with his free arm. Cassi rushed to help him. "What's this?" She took the box from him and led the way to her living room. The box was moderately heavy, but Cassi could handle the weight without much effort.

Jared shifted his feet nervously. With no warning, he fell to his knees on the soft carpet. "Oh, Cassi, I've missed you so much!" To her amazement, his voice shook and tears formed in his eyes. He grabbed her hand with his good one and continued, "I love you! I think I've loved you from the moment I first saw you standing in front of those pamphlets at the hotel, dressed in your jeans and T-shirt, with your hair tumbling around your shoulders. I should have told you how I felt the night we broke the Buddha. I guess I knew then for sure how I felt, but I was afraid I'd be moving too quickly for you. Then, after the shooting, you left and I thought you didn't care. But then I saw the statue you left, and I knew. Oh, Cassi, please give me a chance to show you how much I love you. I can't live without your crazy impulsiveness brightening up my life. I know we can work things out. Please, marry me!"

Cassi's jaw dropped. This was her favorite daydream turned real, and for once in her life she was speechless.

"I'll give you all the time you want to consider it, and as long an engagement as you need to be sure. I'll wait as long as it takes; we've got eternity." He stopped talking and simply looked up at her, waiting for an answer.

Cassi took a deep breath. "Yes," she said softly.

"Yes? Just yes?" he asked. "No exclamation of love?" Then he added hurriedly, "That's okay, I'll take yes. But is it yes you'll think about it, or yes you'll marry me?"

She laughed and practically threw herself against his uninjured shoulder, feeling his arm circle around her. "Yes . . . I'll . . . marry . . . you," she said between kisses. Softly she added, "I love you."

Jared threw back his head and laughed. He hugged her again and again, as if afraid to let go. "I hoped so. I've been praying so hard this last week. But wait!" He jumped up from the floor and retrieved the box Cassi had set on the flowered loveseat. He gave it to her. "Open it."

She eagerly opened the flaps to reveal six shoebox-sized cartons inside, cushioned by white packing peanuts. Puzzled, she looked up at Jared to see that he had gone to her front porch and was carrying in another box. "Go ahead," he encouraged.

She pulled out the first carton and opened it. Inside lay three of the smaller pieces of Jared's "Life" collection, nestled in thick tissue. She put it down and removed the lids of three more boxes. "Your collection," she said. "What—why?"

"It's your engagement present," Jared said softly. "The minute I saw that you had given me your statue, I knew I would give you all of mine, along with my heart. I've brought all fifty-three—no, fifty-four with the *Mother and Baby*. I meant to use them as bribes, just in case you wouldn't marry me, but—" He shrugged, smiling.

Tears formed in Cassi's eyes. He had given her his most precious material possession, as well as himself! She stood up and hugged him again, loving the way his good arm tightened possessively around her. "It's perfect," she said.

"Oh, I'm going to get you a ring, too. Make no mistake; I want the world to know you're mine. Until we go to pick it out, this will have to do." Cassi chuckled. The exquisite collection was worth well over forty thousand dollars, much more than any ring would cost. She lifted her lips to Jared's.

After a long moment, he sighed. "Much as I don't want to, we have to stop. You've got a porch full of boxes that we should really bring in."

Cassi laughed and walked with him to the door. As promised, lined up along her porch was the rest of the "Life" collection. But something beyond that caught her attention. In front of her house sat a large moving van. "What?" she asked, blinking in surprise.

"You don't think I'm going to risk a long-distance relationship with the most beautiful woman in the world, do you?"

"You're moving?"

He nodded. "To be near you until we are married and decide where to have our gallery. Actually, it was Carl's idea. He called me from Mexico three days ago, while I was still in the hospital. I was worrying about what to do, and he suggested just packing it all up and appearing on your doorstep. It sounded like a good idea, so I put the apartment up for sale, Meela helped me pack, and here I am. Uh, you don't know a place where I can store some of this stuff, do you?" He eyed Cassi's garage. "That looks about the right size."

"Wait, wait, wait, wait, wait!" Cassi said. "You were in the hospital until three days ago?"

Jared nodded. "I lost more blood than the doctors thought, then I made it worse by going to look for you."

"You looked for me?"

"Yes, as soon as they bandaged me. Only by the time I got to the airport, you were gone, and I was bleeding again."

"I'm sorry. I didn't know," Cassi said, biting her lip and looking away from him. "I thought you would hate me for what I did to you and Laranda."

Jared's hand turned Cassi's face gently toward him. "It isn't your fault," he said. "It was an accident. I love you, and that will never change. Not ever."

"What about Laranda?" Cassi held her breath as she waited for the answer. For all she knew, Laranda was dead and Cassi was Jared's second choice. But, no! She had to have more faith in Jared, especially if she was going to marry him.

"She's all right. Well, she's out of critical condition, anyway. The doctors think she'll be paralyzed from the waist down. She's not getting much sympathy, though, because she brought it on herself. As for our friendship, it's broken beyond repair. And that's all she ever was to me: a friend. I never loved her at all compared to the feelings I have for you. You are my life and my future."

Relief flooded Cassi's body. He loved her, Cassi! Laranda belonged to the past. She let him kiss her again, feeling his passion and her own, and wishing they were already married.

She reluctantly pulled away. "You mean to tell me you got out of the hospital, packed up your things, and drove across America all by yourself, just to be with me?" she asked.

He shrugged. "I didn't see any point in hanging on to New York when my life was with you."

Cassi shook her head. No wonder he looked so tired! But at least they were together, and she could take care of him now.

"You know, this whole experience with Laranda and her smuggling really hurt," Jared said in a voice so low that Cassi had to lean her head closer to hear the words. "But I wouldn't change it for anything. Because of it I found you, and even Carl is finally accepting the gospel."

"He is?"

Jared grinned. "He married Maria the day after he flew to Mexico. They're still there, waiting for her visa to come through. When I told him I loved you, he said to tell you that he *and* Maria will be baptized on our wedding day. He thought that might make you accept my proposal faster."

Cassi laughed. She could almost picture the aura-sensitive Carl in his wheelchair, dressed in white. "So he married Maria. Well, good for him!"

What Jared had said was true. There had been great pain and risk in their adventure, but with their faith, everything had worked out. Except—

"We'll have to have a playroom hooked onto the gallery," she said. "That way our kids can be near us while we work. And we'll have to hire someone to manage the gallery when we go on buying trips, and a guard so you don't have to carry a gun, and—"

"Only if you'll promise to let me teach you how to cook," Jared said, rubbing his stomach. "We can start right now."

"What? With you so tired? I'm sure I have some frozen dinners I can pop in the microwave. There's no use in my learning; we'll have seven kids, and you can teach *them* how to cook."

"And vacuum?"

"That, too. Then they'll work while we go jogging every day."

Jared groaned, but his expression was happy. His hand stroked Cassi's unruly hair and slid down her back to tighten around her waist. Their lips met once more, and Cassi knew it would be a little while longer before they brought in the rest of the collection from the porch that evening. For, as exceptional as "Life" was, they were discovering for themselves how wonderful their lives could be.

About the Author

Rachel Ann Nunes (pronounced *noon-esh*) is a homemaker, student, and Church worker who lists writing as one of her favorite pursuits. *Love to the Highest Bidder* is her fourth novel to be published by Covenant; her first three novels in the *Ariana* series have been very popular in the LDS market.

In addition to writing and family activities, Rachel enjoys reading, camping, volleyball, softball, and traveling to or reading about foreign countries. She served an LDS mission to Portugal.

Rachel and her husband, TJ, are the parents of four children. They live in American Fork, Utah, where Rachel teaches Relief Society in her ward.

Rachel enjoys hearing from her readers. You can write to her at P.O. Box 353, American Fork, UT 84003-0353, send e-mail to rachel@ranunes.com, or visit her web site at http://www.ranunes.com.